THE TURNER DIARIES

THE
TURNER
DIARIES

a novel by

Andrew Macdonald

Second Edition

BARRICADE BOOKS, INC.

Published by Barricade Books, Inc.
150 Fifth Avenue
New York, NY 10011

Printed in the United States of America.

Library of Congress Cataloging Card Number: 80-82692

First Printing

Introduction by the Publisher:

There are some people who are born to do unpopular things that need doing. I seem to be one of them.

When I announced that I would publish *The Turner Diaries* in a trade edition for sale through bookshops, the response was awesome. I was denounced from pulpits. I was attacked in a letter to retail book chains by Morris Dees and his Southern Poverty Law Center. This is an organization that has monitored neo-Nazi antigovernment groups for more than a decade.

I happen to admire and respect Mr. Dees. But when you have lived life for what sometimes seems to have been thousands of years, you come to understand that those you admire may not always be right.

•   •   •   •   •

I have fought censorship all of my adult life. To me, the most precious of all rights in this marvelous country called the United States of America is the freedom to think, write, and say whatever is on your mind, subject to the laws of libel. That freedom also extends to thoughts that are stupid, ignorant, or incendiary.

No one needs a First Amendment to write about how cute newborn babies are or to publish a recipe for strawberry shortcake. Nobody needs a First Amendment for innocuous ideas or popular points of view. That's point one.

Point two is that the majority—you and I—must always protect the right of the minority—even a minority of one—to express the most outrageous and offensive ideas. Only then is total freedom of expression guaranteed.

•   •   •   •   •

The Turner Diaries is a dreadful book. It is ignorant. Even its author boasts, "It offends almost everyone; Afro-

Americans, feminists, gays and lesbians, liberals, communists, Mexicans, democrats, the FBI, egalitarians, and Jews. Especially Jews: for it portrays them as incarnations of everything that is evil and destructive.

That quote is from the author. Now, this is from me. Let's clear away some of the smoke.

How do I feel about blacks? One of the two closest friends I've had in my life was black. I led a rebellion against Jim Crow while in the Air Corps in World War II. After the war, my wife and I had to slip out of Lynchburg, Virginia at 2 a.m. because rocks were being thrown through our windows and mobs were gathering. I'd had the temerity to give a talk in the auditorium of the local (black) high school, the Paul Laurence Dunbar School. And I'd said things that deeply offended and aroused white Southern manhood such as assuring the student population that "The Bible and biology agree that man is of one blood. . ."

The problems of crime, drugs, and poverty in black communities have spread crime to all neighborhoods. There's an ironic poetic justice to this. It's the natural outcome of the way we so-called whites have disenfranchised and exploited black people for a couple of centuries.

How do I feel about gays? I'm totally comfortable with my own sexual orientation which happens to be heterosexual. But I have no objection to others doing whatever makes them happy, provided they do it with consenting adults.

How do I feel about Jews? I'm an atheist. My father was an atheist. But my grandfather was Jewish. He ran a religious Jewish school in Vienna. Although I don't feel a particular identity with any religion, I'm perfectly comfortable saying "I'm a Jew" when confronting a bigot. (Nor do I have any qualms about punching his head off.)

The Turner Diaries is a bigoted book. For that reason alone, should it be suppressed? Should be kept out of the hands of Middle America? Is the disease that it contains so infectious that anyone reading it will catch a dose of bigotry and hatred?

I don't think so and I hope not. But that is the risk one takes in making this book widely available. We live in a dangerous world and in dangerous times. We live in a world where some leaders are tyrants and others are power-hungry hypocrites. We live in a world of unimaginable cruelty. We live in a world of corruption and selfishness.

But we live in a nation where we have the right to know. In our nation, at least, we have that precious, though often delicate treasure. And that's what makes our nation the place where many groups of oppressed people want to live.

When I was a young man, there was a great furor when a major book house published Adolf Hitler's *Mein Kampf*. Not only was this terrible document going to fall into the wrong hands, but Hitler was to be paid royalties on its sale!

Even in my teens, I had the instinct that, of course, this book should be published. Of course it should be available to all who want to read it. People should be able to judge for themselves Hitler's dangerously sick plans and ideas and how seriously we should take them.

I feel no less strongly about *The Turner Diaries*.

This book is full of hate. It reflects those who hate other humans simply because of their religion or the shade of their skin. The haters are invariably people who suffer a serious lack of self-esteem. Their insecurities crave the desperate need to feel superior to those they fear. And those they fear, they fear largely because they don't understand them.

According to the Federal Bureau of Investigation, *The Turner Diaries* provided Timothy McVeigh with the blueprint for the Oklahoma City bombing.

If for no other reason than that, it has become a historic document. But, alas, there are other reasons.

The author, a former university professor, started to write some fiction in 1975. He finished in 1978. What he wrote, expressed his view of what he believed the world would be like in decades to come. He'd written a book-length novel.

The Turner Diaries is that novel. Unlike hundreds of novels which are published and quickly drown in the sea of small sales each year, this one captured the imagination of gun fanatics and rednecks. It quickly became an underground bestseller.

More than 185,000 copies were sold, and, to the best of

my knowledge, not more than a dozen or two of these were sold through bookshops.

The Turner Diaries came to the attention of the Justice Department in 1985 when a band of antigovernment terrorists, calling themselves "The Order" and modeled on the group of the same name in the book, committed a series of murders and bank and armored car robberies in an attempt to start a violent revolution.

Even then, the book remained inaccessible to the general public.

The author wrote to me to say: "If *the Turner Diaries* had been available to the general public. . .the Oklahoma City bombing would not have come as such a surprise."

For a long time, I've known that groups like the militia and the Freeman are not merely beer-drinking gun-toting patriots whose only joy is to shoot rabbits and deer.

They are, for the most part, people who have failed in our society. They lack something emotionally or economically or psychologically. They hate the United States government and want it overthrown *now!* They hate and fear authority ranging from the president to the local judges and sheriffs and drug enforcement agents and even simple government clerks. They want to kill them all.

That perennial nut case, G. Gordon Liddy, let their tiger out of the cage when he advised these groups that government enforcement officials may be wearing bullet-proof vests so it was best to aim for their heads.

These people are dangerous. Many of them could be considered certifiably insane.

We don't need censors to protect us. We're an intelligent people. Most of us have the good sense to know what to believe and what to reject. But we do have the right to know what the enemy is thinking.

This book will tell you that. In ways it may infuriate you. In ways it may make you want to throw up.

Should we know what inspires these people and shapes their values?

"Yes!" I say, and "Yes" again.

Finally, I'd like to commend the American Booksellers

Foundation for Free Expression. Its president, Oren J. Teicher responded to Morris Dees when the latter attacked me for planning to publish this book.

Teicher said in part: "As outrageous as the content of *The Turner Dairies* may be, we believe that even offensive and objectionable material is protected by the First Amendment. In fact, as you certainly understand, we do not need a First Amendment to protect the popular and non-controversial; it is the unpopular and controversial that requires our vigilance."

Teicher added: "People from all sides of the political debate. . . seem to want to interfere with others having access to ideas with which they disagree. In the spirit of free expression. . . I'd suggest a far more appropriate course of action would be to expose and debate those ideas in a concerted effort to make certain that the truth emerges."

My sentiments exactly!

Sincerely,

Lyle Stuart

Foreword

There exists such an extensive body of literature on the Great Revolution, including the memoirs of virtually every one of its leading figures who survived into the New Era, that yet another book dealing with the events and circumstances of that time of cataclysmic upheaval and rebirth may seem superfluous. *The Turner Diaries*, however, provides an insight into the background of the Great Revolution which is uniquely valuable for two reasons:

1) It is a fairly detailed and continuous record of a portion of the struggle during the years immediately before the culmination of the Revolution, written as it happened, on a day-to-day basis. Thus, it is free of the distortion which often afflicts hindsight. Although the diaries of other participants in that mighty conflict are extant, none which has yet been published provides as complete and detailed a record.

2) It is written from the viewpoint of a rank-and-file member of the Organization, and, although it consequently suffers from myopia occasionally, it is a totally frank document. Unlike the accounts recorded by some of the leaders of the Revolution, its author did not have one eye on his place in history as he wrote. As we read the pages which follow, we get a better understanding than from any other source, probably, of the true thoughts and feelings of the men and women whose struggle and sacrifice saved our race in its time of greatest peril and brought about the New Era.

Earl Turner, who wrote these diaries, was born in 43 BNE in Los Angeles, which was the name of a vast metropolitan area on the west coast of the North American continent in the Old Era, encompassing the present communities of Eckartsville and Wesselton as well as a great deal of the surrounding countryside. He grew up in the Los Angeles area and was trained as an electrical engineer.

After his education he settled near the city of Washington, which was then the capital of the United States. He was employed there by an electronics research firm.

He first became active in the Organization in 12 BNE. When this record begins, in 8 BNE (1991 according to the old chronology), Turner was 35 years old and had no mate.

These diaries span barely two years in Earl Turner's life, yet they give us an intimate acquaintance with one of those whose name is inscribed in the Record of Martyrs. For that reason alone his words should have a special significance for all of us, who in our school days were given the task of memorizing the names of all the Martyrs in that sacred Record handed down to us by our ancestors.

Turner's diaries consist, in their manuscript form, of five large, cloth-bound ledgers, completely filled, and a few pages at the beginning of a sixth. There are many loose inserts and notes between the ledger pages, apparently written by Turner on those days when he was away from his base and later interpolated into his permanent record.

The ledgers were discovered last year along with a wealth of other historically important material by the same team from the Historical Institute, led by Professor Charles Anderson, which earlier uncovered the Eastern Command Center of the Revolution in its excavations near the Washington ruins. It is fitting that they now be made available to the general public during this, the 100th anniversary year of the Great Revolution.

A.M.

New Baltimore
April 100

September 16, 1991. Today it finally began! After all these years of talking — and nothing but talking — we have finally taken our first action. We are at war with the System, and it is no longer a war of words.

I cannot sleep, so I will try writing down some of the thoughts which are flying through my head.

It is not safe to talk here. The walls are quite thin, and the neighbors might wonder at a late-night conference. Besides, George and Katherine are already asleep. Only Henry and I are still awake, and he's just staring at the ceiling.

I am really uptight. I am so jittery I can barely sit still. And I'm exhausted. I've been up since 5:30 this morning, when George phoned to warn that the arrests had begun, and it's after midnight now. I've been keyed up and on the move all day.

But at the same time I'm exhilarated. We have finally acted! How long we will be able to continue defying the System, no one knows. Maybe it will all end tomorrow, but we must not think about that. Now that we have begun, we must continue with the plan we have been developing so carefully ever since the Gun Raids two years ago.

What a blow *that* was to us! And how it shamed us! All that brave talk by patriots, "The government will never take *my* guns away," and then nothing but meek submission when it happened.

On the other hand, maybe we should be heartened by the fact that there were still so many of us who had guns then, nearly 18 months after the Cohen Act had outlawed all private ownership of firearms in the United States. It was only because so many of us defied the law and hid our weapons instead of turning them in that the government wasn't able to act more harshly against us after the Gun Raids.

I'll never forget that terrible day: November 9, 1989. They knocked on my door at five in the morning. I was completely unsuspecting as I got up to see who it was.

I opened the door, and four Negroes came pushing into the apartment before I could stop them. One was carrying a baseball bat, and two had long kitchen knives thrust into their belts. The one with the bat shoved me back into a corner and stood guard over me with his bat raised in a threatening position while the other three began ransacking my apartment.

My first thought was that they were robbers. Robberies of this sort had become all too common since the Cohen Act, with groups of Blacks forcing their way into White homes to rob and rape, knowing that even if their victims had guns they probably would not dare use them.

Then the one who was guarding me flashed some kind of card and informed me that he and his accomplices were "special deputies" for the Northern Virginia Human Relations Council. They were searching for firearms, he said.

I couldn't believe it. It just couldn't be happening. Then I saw that they were wearing strips of green cloth tied around their left arms. As they dumped the contents of drawers on the floor and pulled luggage from the closet, they were ignoring things that robbers wouldn't have passed up: my brand-new electric razor, a valuable gold pocket watch, a milk bottle full of dimes. They *were* looking for firearms!

Right after the Cohen Act was passed, all of us in the Organization had cached our guns and ammunition where they weren't likely to be found. Those in my unit had carefully greased our weapons, sealed them in an oil drum, and spent all of one tedious weekend burying the drum in an eight-foot-deep pit 200 miles away in the woods of western Pennsylvania.

But I had kept one gun out of the cache. I had hidden my .357 magnum revolver and 50 rounds of ammunition inside the door frame between the kitchen and the living room. By pulling out two loosened nails and removing one board from the door frame I could get to my revolver in about two minutes flat if I ever needed it. I had timed myself.

But a police search would never uncover it. And these inexperienced Blacks couldn't find it in a million years.

After the three who were conducting the search had looked in all the obvious places, they began slitting open my mattress and the sofa cushions. I protested vigorously at this and briefly considered trying to put up a fight.

About that time there was a commotion out in the hallway. Another group of searchers had found a rifle hidden under a bed in the apartment of the young couple down the hall. They had both been handcuffed and were being forcibly escorted toward the stairs. Both were clad only in their underwear, and the young woman was complaining loudly about the fact that her baby was being left alone in the apartment.

Another man walked into my apartment. He was a Caucasian, though with an unusually dark complexion. He also wore a green armband, and he carried an attache case and a clipboard.

2

The Blacks greeted him deferentially and reported the negative result of their search: "No guns here, Mr. Tepper."

Tepper ran his finger down the list of names and apartment numbers on his clipboard until he came to mine. He frowned. "This is a bad one," he said. "He has a racist record. Been cited by the Council twice. And he owned eight firearms which were never turned in."

Tepper opened his attache case and took out a small, black object about the size of a pack of cigarettes which was attached by a long cord to an electronic instrument in the case. He began moving the black object in long sweeps back and forth over the walls, while the attache case emitted a dull, rumbling noise. The rumble rose in pitch as the gadget approached the light switch, but Tepper convinced himself that the change was caused by the metal junction box and conduit buried in the wall. He continued his methodical sweep.

As he swept over the left side of the kitchen door frame the rumble jumped to a piercing shriek. Tepper grunted excitedly, and one of the Negroes went out and came back a few seconds later with a sledge hammer and a pry bar. It took the Negro substantially less than two minutes after that to find my gun.

I was handcuffed without further ado and led outside. Altogether, four of us were arrested in my apartment building. In addition to the couple down the hall, there was an elderly man from the fourth floor. They hadn't found a firearm in his apartment, but they had found four shotgun shells on his closet shelf. Ammunition was also illegal.

Mr Tepper and some of his "deputies" had more searches to carry out, but three large Blacks with baseball bats and knives were left to guard us in front of the apartment building.

The four of us were forced to sit on the cold sidewalk, in various states of undress, for more than an hour until a police van finally came for us.

As other residents of the apartment building left for work, they eyed us curiously. We were all shivering, and the young woman from down the hall was weeping uncontrollably.

One man stopped to ask what it was all about. One of our guards brusquely explained that we were all under arrest for possessing illegal weapons. The man stared at us and shook his head disapprovingly.

Then the Black pointed to me and said: "And that one's a racist." Still shaking his head, the man moved on.

Herb Jones, who used to belong to the Organization and was one of the most outspoken of the "they'll-never-get-my-gun" people before the Cohen Act, walked by quickly with his eyes averted. His apartment had been searched too, but Herb was clean. He had been practically the first man in town to turn his guns over to the police after the passage of the Cohen Act made him liable to ten years imprisonment in a Federal penitentiary if he kept them.

That was the penalty the four of us on the sidewalk were facing. It didn't work out that way, though. The reason it didn't is that the raids which were carried out all over the country that day netted a lot more fish than the System had counted on: more than 800,000 persons were arrested.

At first the news media tried hard to work up enough public sentiment against us so that the arrests would stick. The fact that there weren't enough jail cells in the country to hold us all could be remedied by herding us into barbed-wire enclosures outdoors until new prison facilities could be readied, the newspapers suggested. In freezing weather!

I still remember the *Washington Post* headline the next day: "Fascist-Racist Conspiracy Smashed, Illegal Weapons Seized." But not even the brainwashed American public could fully accept the idea that nearly a million of their fellow citizens had been engaged in a secret, armed conspiracy.

As more and more details of the raids leaked out, public restlessness grew. One of the details which bothered people was that the raiders had, for the most part, exempted Black neighborhoods from the searches. The explanation given at first for this was that since "racists" were the ones primarily suspected of harboring firearms, there was relatively little need to search Black homes.

The peculiar logic of this explanation broke down when it turned out that a number of persons who could hardly be considered either "racists" or "fascists" had been caught up in the raids. Among them were two prominent liberal newspaper columnists who had earlier been in the forefront of the antigun crusade, four Negro Congressmen (they lived in White neighborhoods), and an embarrassingly large number of government officials.

The list of persons to be raided, it turned out, had been compiled primarily from firearms sales records which all gun dealers had been required to keep. If a person had turned a gun in to the police after the Cohen Act was passed, his name was marked off the list. If he hadn't it stayed on, and he was raided on November 9 — unless he lived in a Black neighborhood.

In addition, certain categories of people were raided whether they had ever purchased a firearm from a dealer or not. All the members of the Organization were raided.

The government's list of suspects was so large that a number of "responsible" civilian groups were deputized to assist in the raids. I guess the planners in the System thought that most of the people on their list had either sold their guns privately before the Cohen Act, or had disposed of them in some other way. Probably they were expecting only about a quarter as many people to be arrested as actually were.

Anyway, the whole thing soon became so embarrassing and so unwieldy that most of the arrestees were turned loose again within a week. The group I was with — some 600 of us — was held for three days in a high school gymnasium in Alexandria before being released. During those three days we were fed only four times, and we got virtually no sleep.

But the police did get mug shots, fingerprints, and personal data from everyone. When we were released we were told that we were still technically under arrest and could expect to be picked up again for prosecution at any time.

The media kept yelling for prosecutions for awhile, but the issue was gradually allowed to die. Actually, the System had bungled the affair rather badly.

For a few days we were all more frightened and glad to be free than anything else. A lot of people in the Organization dropped out right then and there. They didn't want to take any more chances.

Others stayed in but used the Gun Raids as an excuse for inactivity. Now that the patriotic element in the population had been disarmed, they argued, we were all at the mercy of the System and had to be much more careful. They wanted us to cease all public recruiting activities and "go underground."

As it turned out, what they really had in mind was for the Organization to restrict itself henceforth to "safe" activities, such activities to consist principally in complaining — better yet, whispering — to one another about how bad things were.

The more militant members, on the other hand, were for digging up our weapons caches and unleashing a program of terror against the System immediately, carrying out executions of Federal judges, newspaper editors, legislators, and other System figures. The time was ripe for such action, they felt, because in the wake of the Gun Raids we could win public sympathy for such a campaign against tyranny.

5

It is hard to say now whether the militants were right. Personally, I think they were wrong — although I counted myself as one of them at the time. We could certainly have killed a number of the creatures responsible for America's ills, but I believe we would have lost in the long run.

For one thing, the Organization just wasn't well disciplined enough for waging terror against the System. There were too many cowards and blabbermouths among us. Informers, fools, weaklings, and irresponsible jerks would have been our undoing.

For a second thing, I am sure now that we were overoptimistic in our judgment of the mood of the public. What we mistook as general resentment against the System's abrogation of civil rights during the Gun Raids was more a passing wave of uneasiness resulting from all the commotion involved in the mass arrests.

As soon as the public had been reassured by the media that *they* were in no danger, that the government was cracking down only on the "racists, fascists, and other anti-social elements" who had kept illegal weapons, most relaxed again and went back to their TV and funny papers.

As we began to realize this, we were more discouraged than ever. We had based all our plans — in fact, the whole rationale of the Organization — on the assumption that Americans were inherently opposed to tyranny, and that when the System became oppressive enough they could be led to overthrow it. We had badly underestimated the degree to which materialism had corrupted our fellow citizens, as well as the extent to which their feelings could be manipulated by the mass media.

As long as the government is able to keep the economy somehow gasping and wheezing along, the people can be conditioned to accept any outrage. Despite the continuing inflation and the gradually declining standard of living, most Americans are still able to keep their bellies full today, and we must simply face the fact that that's the only thing which counts with most of them.

Discouraged and uncertain as we were, though, we began laying new plans for the future. First, we decided to maintain our program of public recruiting. In fact, we intensified it and deliberately made our propaganda as provocative as possible. The purpose was not only to attract new members with a militant disposition, but at the same time to purge the Organization of the fainthearts and hobbyists — the "talkers."

We also tightened up on discipline. Anyone who missed a scheduled meeting twice in a row was expelled. Anyone who failed to carry out a work assignment was expelled. Anyone who violated our rule against loose talk about Organizational matters was expelled.

We had made up our minds to have an Organization that would be *ready* the next time the System provided an opportunity to strike. The shame of our failure to act, indeed, our inability to act, in 1989 tormented us and drove us without mercy. It was probably the single most important factor in steeling our wills to whip the Organization into fighting trim, despite all obstacles.

Another thing that helped — at least, with me — was the constant threat of rearrest and prosecution. Even if I had wanted to give it all up and join the TV-and-funnies crowd, I couldn't. I could make no plans for a "normal," civilian future, never knowing when I might be prosecuted under the Cohen Act. (The Constitutional guarantee of a speedy trial, of course, has been "reinterpreted" by the courts until it means no more than our Constitutional guarantee of the right to keep and bear arms.)

So I, and I know this also applies to George and Katherine and Henry, threw myself without reservation into work for the Organization and made only plans for the future of the Organization. My private life had ceased to matter.

Whether the Organization actually *is* ready, I guess we'll find out soon enough. So far, so good, though. Our plan for avoiding another mass roundup, like 1989, seems to have worked.

Early last year we began putting a number of new members, unknown to the political police, into police agencies and various quasi-official organizations, such as the human relations councils. They served as our early-warning network and otherwise kept us generally informed of the System's plans against us.

We were surprised at the ease with which we were able to set up and operate this network. We never would have gotten away with it back in the days of J. Edgar Hoover.

It is ironic that while the Organization has always warned the public against the dangers of racial integration of our police, this has now turned out to be a blessing in disguise for us. The "equal opportunity" boys have really done a wonderful wrecking job on the FBI and other investigative agencies, and their efficiency is way down as a result. Still, we'd better not get over-confident or careless.

Omigod! It's 4:00 AM. Got to get some sleep!

II

September 18, 1991: These last two days have really been a comedy of errors, and today the comedy nearly became a

7

tragedy. When the others were finally able to wake me up yesterday, we put our heads together to figure what to do. The first thing, we all agreed, was to arm ourselves and then to find a better hideout.

Our unit — that is, the four of us — leased this apartment under a false name nearly six months ago, just to have it available when we needed it. (We just beat the new law which requires a landlord to furnish the police with the social security number of every new tenant, just like when a person opens a bank account.) Because we've stayed away from the apartment until now, I'm sure the political police haven't connected any of us with this address.

But it's too small for all of us to live here for any length of time, and it doesn't offer enough privacy from the neighbors. We were too anxious to save money when we picked this place.

Money is our main problem now. We thought to stock this place with food, medicine, tools, spare clothing, maps — even a bicycle — but we forgot about cash. Two days ago, when the word came that they were starting the arrests again, we had no chance to withdraw money from the bank; it was too early in the morning. Now our accounts are surely frozen.

So we have only the cash that was in our pockets at the time: a little over $70 altogether (*Note to the reader:* The "dollar" was the basic monetary unit in the United States in the Old Era. In 1991, two dollars would buy a half-kilo loaf of bread or about a quarter of a kilo of sugar.)

And no transportation except for the bicycle. According to plan, we had all abandoned our cars, since the police would be looking for them. Even if we had kept a car, we would have a problem trying to get fuel for it. Since our gasoline ration cards are magnetically coded with our social security numbers, when we stuck them into the computer at a filling station they would show blocked quotas — and instantaneously tell the Feds monitoring the central computer where we were.

Yesterday George, who is our contact with Unit 9, took the bicycle and pedaled over to talk to them about the situation. They're a little better off than we are, but not much. The six of them have about $400, but they're crowded into a hole in the wall which is even less satisfactory than ours, according to George.

They do have four automobiles and a fair-sized store of fuel, though. Carl Smith, who is with them, made some very convincing counterfeit license plates for everyone with a car in his unit. We should have done the same, but it's too late now.

They offered George one car and $50 cash, which he gratefully accepted. They didn't want to let go of any of their gasoline, though, other than the tankful in the car they gave us.

That still left us with no money to rent another place, nor enough gas to make the round trip to our weapons cache in Pennsylvania and back. We didn't even have enough money to buy a week's groceries when our food stock ran out, and that would be in about another four days.

The network will be established in ten days, but until then we are on our own. Furthermore, when our unit joins the network it is expected to have already solved its supply problems and be ready to go into action in concert with the other units.

If we had more money we could solve all our problems, including the fuel problem. Gasoline is always available on the black market, of course — at $10 a gallon, nearly twice what it costs at a filling station.

We stewed over our situation until this afternoon. Then, desperate not to waste any more time, we finally decided to go out and *take* some money. Henry and I were stuck with the chore, since we couldn't afford for George to get arrested. He's the only one who knows the network code.

We had Katherine do a pretty good makeup job on us first. She's into amateur theater and has the equipment and know-how to really change a person's appearance.

My inclination was just to walk into the first liquor store we came to, knock the manager on the head with a brick, and scoop up the money from the cash register.

Henry wouldn't go along with that, though. He said we couldn't use means which contradicted our ends. If we begin preying on the public to support ourselves, we will be viewed as a gang of common criminals, regardless of how lofty our aims are. Worse, we will eventually begin to think of ourselves the same way.

Henry looks at everything in terms of our ideology. If something doesn't fit, he'll have nothing to do with it.

In a way this may seem impractical, but I think maybe he's right. Only by making our beliefs into a living faith which guides us from day to day can we maintain the moral strength to overcome the obstacles and hardships which lie ahead.

Anyway, he convinced me that if we are going to rob liquor stores we have to do it in a socially conscious way. If we are going to cave in people's heads with bricks, they must be people who deserve it.

9

By comparing the liquor store listings in the Yellow Pages of the telephone directory with a list of supporting members of the Northern Virginia Human Relations Council which had been filched for us by the girl we sent over there to do volunteer work for them, we finally settled on Berman's Liquors and Wines, Saul I. Berman, proprietor.

There were no bricks handy, so we equipped ourselves with blackjacks consisting of good-sized bars of Ivory soap inside long, strong ski socks. Henry also tucked a sheath knife into his belt.

We parked about a block and a half from Berman's Liquors, around the corner. When we went in there were no customers in the store. A Black was at the cash register, tending the store.

Henry asked him for a bottle of vodka on a high shelf behind the counter. When he turned around I let him have it at the base of the skull with my "Ivory special." He dropped silently to the floor and remained motionless.

Henry calmly emptied the cash register and a cigar box under the counter which held the larger bills. We walked out and headed for the car. We had gotten a little over $800. It had been surprisingly easy.

Three stores down Henry suddenly stopped and pointed out the sign on the door: "Berman's Deli." Without a moment's hesitation he pushed open the door and walked in. Spurred on by a sudden, reckless impulse I followed him instead of trying to stop him.

Berman himself was behind the counter, at the back. Henry lured him out by asking the price of an item near the front of the store which Berman couldn't see clearly from behind the counter.

As he passed me, I let him have it in the back of the head as hard as I could. I felt the bar of soap shatter from the force of the blow.

Berman went down yelling at the top of his lungs. Then he started crawling rapidly toward the back of the store, screaming loudly enough to wake the dead. I was completely unnerved by the racket and stood frozen.

Not Henry though. He leaped onto Berman's back, seized him by the hair, and cut his throat from ear to ear in one, swift motion.

The silence lasted about one second. Then a fat, grotesque-looking woman of about 60 — probably Berman's wife — came charging out of the back room waving a meat cleaver and emitting an ear-piercing shriek.

10

Henry let fly at her with a large jar of kosher pickles and scored a direct hit. She went down in a spray of pickles and broken glass.

Henry then cleaned out the cash register, looked for another cigar box under the counter, found it, and scooped the bills out.

I snapped out of my trance and followed Henry out the front door as the fat woman started shrieking again. Henry had to hold me by the arm to keep me from running down the sidewalk.

It didn't take us but about 15 seconds to walk back to the car, but it seemed more like 15 minutes. I was terrified. It was more than an hour before I had stopped shaking and gotten enough of a grip on myself to talk without stuttering. Some terrorist!

Altogether we got $1426 — enough to buy groceries for the four of us for more than two months. But one thing was decided then and there: Henry will have to be the one to rob any more liquor stores. I don't have the nerves for it — although I had thought I was doing all right until Berman started yelling.

September 19: Looking back over what I've written, it's hard to believe these things have really happened. Until the Gun Raids two years ago, my life was about as normal as anyone's can be in these times.

Even after I was arrested and lost my position at the laboratory, I was still able to live pretty much like everyone else by doing consulting work and special jobs for a couple of the electronics firms in this area. The only thing out of the ordinary about my lifestyle was my work for the Organization.

Now everything is chaotic and uncertain. When I think about the future I become depressed. It's impossible to know what will happen, but it's certain that I'll never be able to go back to the quiet, orderly kind of life I had before.

Looks like what I'm writing is the beginning of a diary. Perhaps it will help me to write down what's happened and what my thoughts are each day. Maybe it will add some focus to things, some order, and make it easier for me to keep a grip on myself and become reconciled to this new way of life.

It's funny how all the excitement I felt the first night here is gone. All I feel now is apprehension. Maybe the change of scenery tomorrow will improve my outlook. Henry and I will be driving to Pennsylvania for our guns, while George and Katherine try to find us a more suitable place to live.

Today we made the preparations for our trip. Originally, the plan called for us to use public transportation to the little town of Bellefonte and then hike the last six miles into the woods to our cache. Now that we have a car, however, we'll use that instead.

We figured we only need about five gallons of gasoline, in addition to that already in the tank, to make the round trip. To be on the safe side, we bought two five-gallon cans of gas from the taxi-fleet operator in Alexandria who always bootlegs some of his allotment.

As rationing has increased during the last few years, so has petty corruption of every sort. I guess a lot of the large-scale graft in the government which Watergate revealed a few years back has finally filtered down to the man in the street. When people began realizing that the big-shot politicians were crooked, they were more inclined to try to cheat the System a little themselves. All the new rationing red tape has just exacerbated the tendency — as has the growing percentage of non-Whites in every level of the bureaucracy.

The Organization has been one of the main critics of this corruption, but I can now see that it gives us an important advantage. If everybody obeyed the law and did everything by the book, it would be nearly impossible for an underground group to exist.

Not only would we not be able to buy gasoline, but a thousand other bureaucratic obstacles with which the System increasingly hems the lives of our fellow citizens would be insurmountable for us. As it is, a bribe to a local official here or a few dollars under the counter to a clerk or secretary there will allow us to get around many of the government regulations which would otherwise trip us up.

The closer public morality in America approaches that of a banana republic, the easier it will be for us to operate. Of course, with everyone having his hand out for a bribe, we'll need plenty of money.

Looking at it philosophically, one can't avoid the conclusion that it is corruption, not tyranny, which leads to the overthrow of governments. A strong and vigorous government, no matter how oppressive, usually need not fear revolution. But a corrupt, inefficient, decadent government — even a benevolent one — is always ripe for revolution. The System we are fighting is both corrupt and oppressive, and we should thank God for the corruption.

The silence about us in the newspapers is worrisome. The Berman thing the other day wasn't connected to us, of course, and it was given only a paragraph in today's *Post*. Robberies of that sort — even where there is killing involved — are so common these days that they merit no more attention than a traffic accident

12

But the fact that the government launched a massive roundup of known Organization members last Wednesday and that nearly all of us, more than 2,000 persons, have managed to slip through their fingers and drop out of sight — why isn't *that* in the papers? The news media are collaborating closely with the political police, of course, but what is their strategy against us?

There was one small Associated Press article on a back page of yesterday's paper mentioning the arrest of nine "racists" in Chicago and four in Los Angeles on Wednesday. The article said that all 13 who were arrested were members of the same organization — evidently ours — but no further details were given. Curious!

Are they keeping quiet about the failure of the roundup so as not to embarrass the government? That's not like them.

Probably, they're a little paranoid about the ease with which we evaded the roundup. They may have fears that some substantial portion of the public is in sympathy with us and is aiding us, and they don't want to say anything that will give encouragement to our sympathizers.

We must be careful that this false appearance of "business as usual" doesn't mislead us into relaxing our vigilance. We can be sure that the political police are in a crash program to find us. It will be a relief when the network is established and we can once again receive regular reports from our informants as to just what the rascals are up to.

Meanwhile, our security rests primarily in our changed appearances and identities. We've all changed our hair styles and either dyed or bleached our hair. I've begun wearing new glasses with heavy frames instead of my old frameless ones, and Katherine has switched from her contact lenses to glasses. Henry has undergone the most radical transformation, by shaving off his beard and mustache. And we all have pretty convincing fake driver's licenses, although they won't stand up if they are ever checked against state records.

Whenever any of us has to do something like the robberies last week, Katherine can do a quick-change job and temporarily give him a third identity. For that she has wigs and plastic gimmicks which fit into the nostrils and inside the mouth and change the whole structure of a person's face — and even his voice. They're not comfortable, but they can be tolerated for a couple of hours at a time, just as I can do without my glasses for a while if necessary.

Tomorrow will be a long, hard day.

III

September 21, 1991. Every muscle in my body aches. Yesterday we spent 10 hours hiking, digging, and carrying loads of weapons through the woods. This evening we moved all our supplies from the old apartment to our new hideout.

It was a little before noon yesterday when we reached the turnoff near Bellefonte and left the highway. We drove as close to our cache as we could, but the old mining road we had used three years earlier was blocked and impassable more than a mile short of the point where we intended to park. The bank above the road had collapsed, and it would have taken a bulldozer to clear the way. (*Note to the reader*: Throughout his diaries Turner used so-called "English units" of measurement, which were still in common use in North America during the last years of the Old Era. For the reader not familiar with these units, a "mile" was 1.6 kilometers, a "gallon" was 3.8 liters, a "foot" was .30 meter, a "yard" was .91 meter, an "inch" was 2.5 centimeters, and a "pound" was the weight of .45 kilogram — approximately.)

The consequence was that we had nearly a two-mile hike each way instead of less than half a mile. And it took three round trips to get everything to the car. We brought shovels, a rope, and a couple of large canvas mail sacks (courtesy of the U.S. Postal Service), but, as it turned out, these tools were woefully inadequate for the task.

Hiking from the car to the cache with our shovels on our shoulders was actually refreshing, after the long drive up from Washington. The day was pleasantly cool, the autumn woods were beautiful, and the old dirt road, though heavily overgrown, provided easy walking most of the way.

Even digging down to the top of the oil drum (actually a 50-gallon chemical drum with a removable lid) in which we had sealed our weapons wasn't too bad. The ground was fairly soft, and it took us less than an hour to excavate a five-foot-deep pit and tie our rope to the handles which had been welded to the lid of the drum.

Then our trouble began. The two of us tugged on the rope as hard as we could, but the drum wouldn't budge an inch. It was as if it had been set in concrete.

Although the full drum weighed nearly 400 pounds, two of us had been able to lower it into the pit without undue difficulty three years ago. At that time, of course, there had been several inches of clearance all around it. Now the earth had settled and was packed tightly against the metal.

We gave up trying to get the drum out of the hole and decided to open it where it was. To do that we had to dig for nearly another hour, enlarging the hole and clearing a few inches all around the top of the drum so we could get our hands on the locking band which secured the lid. Even so, I had to go into the hole headfirst, with Henry holding my legs.

Although the outside of the drum had been painted with asphalt to prevent corrosion, the locking lever itself was thoroughly rusted, and I broke the only screwdriver we had trying to pry it loose. Finally, after much pounding, I was able to pry the lever out from the drum with the end of a shovel. With the locking band loosened, however, the lid remained as tightly in place as ever, apparently stuck to the drum by the asphalt coating we had applied.

Working upside down in the narrow hole was difficult and exhausting. We had no tool satisfactory for wedging under the lip of the lid and prying it up. Finally, almost in desperation, I once again tied the rope to one of the handles on the lid. Henry and I gave a hard tug, and the lid popped off!

Then it was just a matter of my going headfirst into the hole again, supporting myself with one arm on the edge of the drum, and passing the carefully wrapped bundles of weapons up past my body so that Henry could reach them. Some of the larger bundles — and that included six sealed tins of ammunition — were both too heavy and too bulky for this method and had to be hauled up by rope.

Needless to say, by the time we had the drum empty I was completely pooped. My arms ached, my legs were unsteady, and my clothing was drenched with perspiration. But we still had to carry more than 300 pounds of munitions half a mile through dense woods, uphill to the road, and then more than a mile back to the car.

With proper pack frames to distribute the loads on our backs we might have carried everything out in one trip. It could have been done easily in two trips. But with only the awkward mail sacks, which we had to carry in our arms, it took three excruciatingly painful trips.

We had to stop every hundred yards or so and put our loads down for a minute, and the last two trips were made in total darkness. Anticipating a daylight operation, we hadn't even brought a flashlight. If we don't do a better job of planning our operations in the future, we have some rough times ahead!

On the way back to Washington we stopped at a small roadside cafe near Hagerstown for sandwiches and coffee. There were about a dozen people in the place, and the 11 o'clock news was just beginning on the TV set behind the counter when we walked in. It was a news broadcast I'll never forget.

The big story of the day was what the Organization had been up to in Chicago. The System, it seems, had killed one of our people, and in turn we had killed three of theirs and then engaged in a spectacular — and successful — gunfight with the authorities. Nearly the whole newscast was occupied in recounting these events.

We already knew from the papers that nine of our members had been arrested in Chicago last week, and apparently they had had a rough time in the Cook County Jail, where one of them had died. It was impossible to be sure exactly what had happened from what the TV announcer said, but if the System had behaved true to form the authorities had stuck our people individually into cells full of Blacks and then shut their eyes and ears to what ensued.

That has long been the System's extra-legal way of punishing our people when they can't pin anything on them that will "stick" in the courts. It's a more ghastly and dreadful punishment than anything which ever took place in a medieval torture chamber or in the cellars of the KGB. And they can get away with it because the news media usually won't even admit that it happens. After all, if you're trying to convince the public that the races are really equal, how can you admit that it's worse to be locked in a cell full of Black criminals than in a cell full of White ones?

Anyway, the day after our man — the newscaster said his name was Carl Hodges, someone I've not heard of before — was killed, the Chicago Organization fulfilled a promise they'd made more than a year ago, in the event one of our people was ever seriously hurt in a Chicago jail. They ambushed the Cook County sheriff outside his home and blew his head off with a shotgun. They left a note pinned to his body which read: "This is for Carl Hodges."

That was last Saturday night. On Sunday the System was up in arms. The sheriff of Cook County had been a political bigwig, a front-rank *shabbos goy*, and they were really raising hell.

Although they broadcast the news only to the Chicago area on Sunday, they trotted out several pillars of the community there to denounce the assassination and the Organization in special TV appearances. One of the spokesmen was a "responsible conservative," and another was the head of the Chicago Jewish

16

community. All of them described the Organization as a "gang of racist bigots" and called on "all right-thinking Chicagoans" to cooperate with the political police in apprehending the "racists" who had killed the sheriff.

Well, early this morning the responsible conservative lost both his legs and suffered severe internal injuries when a bomb wired to the ignition of his car exploded. The Jewish spokesman was even less fortunate. Someone walked up to him while he was waiting for an elevator in the lobby of his office building, pulled a hatchet from under his coat, cleaved the good Jew's head from crown to shoulder blades, then disappeared in the rush-hour crowd. The Organization immediately claimed responsibility for both acts.

After that, it really hit the fan. The governor of Illinois ordered National Guard troops into Chicago to help local police and FBI agents hunt for Organization members. Thousands of persons were being stopped on Chicago streets today and asked to prove their identity. The System's paranoia is really showing.

This afternoon three men were cornered in a small apartment building in Cicero. The whole block was surrounded by troops, while the trapped men shot it out with the police. TV crews were all over the place, anxious not to miss the kill.

One of the men in the apartment apparently had a sniper's rifle, because two Black cops more than a block away were picked off before it was realized that Blacks were being singled out as targets and uniformed White cops were not being shot at. This White immunity apparently was not extended to the plainclothes political police, however, because an FBI agent was killed by a burst of submachinegun fire from the apartment when he momentarily exposed himself to hurl a teargas grenade through a window.

We watched breathlessly as this action was shown on the TV screen, but the real climax came for us when the apartment was stormed and found empty. A quick room-by-room search of the building also failed to turn up the gunmen.

Disappointment at this outcome was evident in the TV newsman's voice, but a man sitting at the other end of the counter from us whistled and clapped when it was announced that the "racists" had apparently slipped away. The waitress smiled at this, and it seemed clear to us that, while there certainly was no unanimous approval for the Organization's actions in Chicago, neither was there unanimous disapproval.

Almost as if the System anticipated this reaction to the afternoon's events, the news scene switched to Washington, where the attorney general of the United States had called a special news conference. The attorney general announced to the nation that the Federal government was throwing all its police agencies into the effort to root out the Organization. He described us as "depraved, racist criminals" who were motivated solely by hatred and who wanted to "undo all the progress toward true equality" which had been made by the System in recent years.

All citizens were warned to be alert and to assist the government in breaking up the "racist conspiracy." Anyone observing any suspicious action, especially on the part of a stranger, was to report it immediately to the nearest FBI office or Human Relations Council.

And then he said something very indiscreet, which really betrayed how worried the System is. He stated that any citizen found to be concealing information about us or offering us any comfort or assistance "would be dealt with severely." Those were his very words — the sort of thing one might expect to hear in the Soviet Union, but which would ring harshly on most American ears, despite the best propaganda efforts of the media to justify it.

All the risks taken by our people in Chicago were more than rewarded by provoking the attorney general into such a psychological blunder. This incident also proves the value of keeping the System off balance with surprise attacks. If the System had kept its cool and thought more carefully about a response to our Chicago actions, it not only would have avoided a blunder which will bring us hundreds of new recruits, but it would probably have figured a way to win much wider public support for its fight against us.

The news program concluded with an announcement that an hour-long "special" on the "racist conspiracy" would be broadcast Tuesday night (i.e., tonight). We've just finished watching that "special," and it was a real hatchet job, full of errors and outright invention and not very convincing, we all felt. But one thing is certain: the media blackout is over. Chicago has given the Organization instant celebrity status, and we must certainly be the number-one topic of conversation everywhere in the nation.

As last night's TV news ended, Henry and I choked down the last of our meal and stumbled outside. I was filled with emotions: excitement, elation over the success of our people in Chicago, nervousness about being one of the targets of a nationwide

18

manhunt, and chagrin that none of our units in the Washington area had shown the initiative of our Chicago units.

I was itching to do something, and the first thing that occurred to me was to try to make some sort of contact with the fellow in the cafe who had seemed sympathetic to us. I wanted to take some leaflets from our car and put one under the windshield wiper of every vehicle in the parking lot.

Henry, who always keeps a cool head, emphatically vetoed the idea. As we sat in the car he explained that it was sheer folly to risk calling any attention whatever to ourselves until we had completed our present mission of safely delivering our load of weapons to our unit. Furthermore, he reminded me, it would be a breach of Organization discipline for a member of an underground unit to engage in any direct recruiting activity, however minimal. That function has been relegated to the "legal" units.

The underground units consist of members who are known to the authorities and have been marked for arrest. Their function is to destroy the System through direct action.

The "legal" units consist of members not presently known to the System. (Indeed, it would be impossible to prove that most of them are members. In this we have taken a page from the communists' book.) Their role is to provide us with intelligence, funding, legal defense, and other support.

Whenever an "illegal" spots a potential recruit, he is supposed to turn the information over to a "legal," who will approach the prospect and sound him out. The "legals" are also supposed to handle all the low-risk propaganda activity, such as leafleting. Strictly speaking, we should not even have had any Organization leaflets with us.

We waited until the man who had applauded the escape of our members in Chicago came out and got in a pickup truck. We drove by him and noted his license number as we pulled out of the lot. When the network is established, the information will go to the proper person for a follow-up.

When we arrived back at the apartment, George and Katherine were as excited as Henry and I. They had also seen the TV newscast. Despite the exertions of the day, I could no more sleep than they, and we all piled back in the car, George and Katherine sharing the back seat with part of our greasy cargo, and went to an all-night drive-in. We could stay in the car and talk safely there without arousing suspicion, and that's what we did — until the early-morning hours.

One thing we decided was that we would move immediately to new quarters George and Katherine located yesterday. The old apartment just wasn't satisfactory. The walls were so thin that we had to whisper to one another to avoid being overheard by our neighbors. And I'm sure that our irregular hours had already caused the neighbors to speculate on just what we do for a living. With the System warning everyone to report suspicious-looking strangers, it had become downright dangerous to us to remain in a place with so little privacy.

The new place is much better in every way except the rent. We have a whole building to ourselves. It is actually a cement-block commercial building which once housed a small machine shop in a single, garage-like room downstairs, with offices and a storeroom upstairs.

The place has been condemned, because it lies on the right-of-way for a new access road to the highway which has been in the planning stages for the last four years. Like all government projects these days, this one is also bogged down — probably permanently. Although hundreds of thousands of men are being paid to build new highways, none are actually being built. In the last five years most of the roads in the country have deteriorated badly, and, although one always sees repair crews standing around, nothing ever seems to get fixed.

The government hasn't even gotten around to actually purchasing the land it has condemned for the new highway, leaving the property owners holding the bag. Legally, the owner of this building isn't supposed to rent it, but he evidently has an arrangement with someone in city hall. The advantage for us is that there is no official record of the occupancy of the building — no social security numbers for the police, no county building inspectors or fire marshals coming around to check. George just has to take $600 — in cash — to the owner once a month.

George thinks the owner, a wrinkled old Armenian with a heavy accent, is convinced we intend to use the place for manufacturing illegal drugs or storing stolen goods and doesn't want to know the details. I suppose that's good, because it means he won't be snooping around.

The place really looks like hell on the outside. It's surrounded on three sides by a sagging, rusty chain-link fence. The grounds are littered with discarded water heaters, stripped-down engine blocks, and rusting junk of every description. The concrete parking area in front is broken and black with old crankcase oil.

There is a huge sign across the front of the building which has come loose at one end. It says: "Welding and Machining, J.T.

Smith & Sons.'' Half the window panes on the ground floor are missing, but all the ground-floor windows are boarded up on the inside anyway.

The neighborhood is a thoroughly grubby light-manufacturing area. Next door to us is a small trucking company garage and warehouse. Trucks are coming and going at all hours of the night, which means the cops will not have their suspicions aroused if they see us driving in this area at odd hours.

So, having decided to make the move, we did it today. Since there was no electricity, water, or gas in the new place, it was my job to solve the heating, lighting, and plumbing problems while the others moved our things.

Restoring the water was easy, as soon as I had located the water meter and gotten the lid off. After turning the water on I dragged some heavy junk over the meter lid so no one from the water company would be likely to find it, in case anyone ever came looking.

The electric problem was a good deal more difficult. There were still lines up from the building to a power pole, but the current had been shut off at the meter, which was on an outside wall. I had to carefully knock a hole through the wall behind the meter, from the inside, and then wire jumpers across the terminals. That took me the better part of the day.

The rest of my day was occupied in carefully covering all the chinks in the boards over the downstairs windows and in tacking heavy cardboard over the upstairs windows, so no ray of light can be seen from the building at night.

We still have no heat and no kitchen facilities beyond the hotplate we brought over from the other place. But at least the john works now, and our living quarters are tolerably clean, if rather bare. We can continue sleeping on the floor in our sleeping bags for a while, and we'll buy a couple of electric heaters and some other amenities in the next few days.

IV

September 30, 1991. There's been so much work in the last week that I've had no time to write. Our plan for setting up the network was simple and straightforward, but actually doing it has required a terrific effort, at least on my part. The difficulties I've had to overcome have emphasized for me once again the fact that even the best-laid plans can be dangerously misleading unless they have built into them a large amount of flexibility to allow for unforeseen problems.

Basically, the network linking all the Organization's units together depends on two modes of communication: human couriers and highly specialized radio transmissions. I'm responsible not only for our own unit's radio receiving equipment but also for the overall maintenance and supervision of the receivers of the eleven other units in the Washington area and the transmitters of Washington Field Command and Unit 9. What really messed up my week was the last-minute decision at WFC to equip Unit 2 with a transmitter too. I had to do the equipping.

The way the network is set up, all communications requiring consultation or lengthy briefing or situation reports are done orally, face-to-face. Now that the telephone company maintains a computerized record of all local calls as well as long-distance calls, and with the political police monitoring so many conversations, telephones are ruled out for our use except in unusual emergencies.

On the other hand, messages of a standard nature, which can be easily and briefly coded, are usually transmitted by radio. The Organization put a great deal of thought into developing a "dictionary" of nearly 800 different, standardized messages, each of which can be specified by a three-digit number.

Thus, at a particular time, the number "2006" might specify the message: "The operation scheduled by Unit 6 is to be postponed until further notice." One person in each unit has memorized the entire message dictionary and is responsible for knowing what the current number coding of the dictionary is at all times. In our unit that person is George.

Actually, it's not as hard as it sounds. The message dictionary is arranged in a very orderly way, and once one has memorized its basic structure it's not too difficult to memorize the whole thing. The number-coding of the messages is randomly shifted every few days, but that doesn't mean that George has to learn the dictionary all over again; he just needs to know the new numerical designation of a single message, and he can then work out the designations for all the others in his head.

Using this coding system allows us to maintain radio contact with good security, using extremely simple and portable equipment. Because our radio transmissions never exceed a second in duration and occur very infrequently, the political police are not likely to get a directional fix on any transmitter or to be able to decode any intercepted message.

Our receivers are even simpler than our transmitters and are a sort of cross between a transistorized pocket broadcast receiver and a pocket calculator. They remain "on" all the time, and if a numerical pulse with the right tone-coding is broadcast by any of our transmitters in the area they will pick it up and display and hold a numerical readout, whether they are being monitored at the moment or not.

My major contribution to the Organization so far has been the development of this communications equipment — and, in fact, the actual manufacture of a good bit of it.

The first series of messages broadcast by Washington Field Command to all units in this area was on Sunday. It gave instructions for each unit to send its contact man to a numerically specified location to receive a briefing and deliver a unit situation report.

When George returned from Sunday's briefing he relayed the news to the rest of us. The gist of it was that, although there has been no trouble in the Washington area yet, WFC is worried by the reports which it has received from our informants with the political police.

The System is going all-out to get us. Hundreds of persons who are suspected to have sympathies for the Organization or some remote affiliation with us have been arrested and interrogated. Among these are several of our "legals," but apparently the authorities haven't been able to pin anything definite on any of them yet and the interrogations haven't produced any real clues. Still, the System's reaction to last week's events in Chicago has been more widespread and more energetic than expected.

One thing on which they are working is a computerized, universal, internal passport system. Every person 12 years or more of age will be issued a passport and will be required, under threat of severe penalties, to carry it at all times. Not only can a person be stopped on the street by any police agent and asked to show his passport, but they have worked out a plan to make the passports necessary for many everyday operations, such as purchasing an airline, bus, or train ticket, registering in a motel or hotel, and receiving any medical service in a hospital or clinic.

All ticket counters, motels, physician's offices, and the like will be equipped with computer terminals linked by telephone lines to a huge, national data bank and computer center. A customer's magnetically coded passport number will routinely be fed into the computer whenever he buys a ticket, pays a bill, or registers for a service. If there is any irregularity, a warning light will go on in

23

the nearest police precinct station, showing the location of the offending computer terminal — and the unfortuante customer.

They've been developing this internal passport system for several years now and have everything worked out in detail. The only reason it hasn't been put into operation has been squawks from civil-liberties groups, who see it as another big step toward a police state — which, of course, it is. But now the System is sure it can override the resistance of the libertarians by using us as an excuse. Anything is permitted in the fight against "racism"!

It will take at least three months to install the necessary equipment and get the system operational, but they are going ahead with it as fast as they can, figuring to announce it as a *fait accompli* with full backing from the news media. Later, the system will gradually be expanded, with computer terminals eventually required in every retail establishment. No person will be able to eat a meal in a restaurant, pick up his laundry, or buy groceries without having his passport number magnetically read by a computer terminal beside the cash register.

When things get to that point the System will really have a pretty tight grip on the citizenry. With the power of modern computers at their disposal, the political police will be able to pinpoint any person at any time and know just where he's been and what he's done. We'll have to do some hard thinking to get around this passport system.

From what our informants have told us so far, it won't be a simple matter of just forging passports and making up phony numbers. If the central computer spots a phony number, a signal will automatically be sent to the nearest police station. The same thing will happen if John Jones, who lives in Spokane and is using his passport to buy groceries there, suddenly seems to be buying groceries in Dallas too. Or even if, when the computer has Bill Smith safely located in a bowling alley on Main Street, he simultaneously shows up at a dry-cleaning establishment on the other side of town.

All this is an awesome prospect for us — something which has been technically feasible for quite a while but which, until recently, we never would have dreamed the System would actually attempt.

One piece of news George brought back from his briefing was a summons for me to make an immediate visit to Unit 2 to solve a technical problem they had. Ordinarily, neither George nor I would have known Unit 2's base location, and if it became necessary to meet someone from that unit the meeting would have taken place elsewhere. This problem required my going to their hideout, however, and George repeated to me the directions he had been given.

They are up in Maryland, more than 30 miles from us, and, since I had to take all my tools with me anyway, I took the car.

They have a nice place, a large farmhouse and several outbuildings on about 40 acres of meadow and woodland. There are eight members in their unit, somewhat more than in most, but apparently not one of them knows a volt from an ampere or which end of a screwdriver is which. That is unusual, because some care was supposed to have been taken when forming our units to distribute valuable skills sensibly.

Unit 2 is reasonably close to two other units, but all three are inconveniently far from the other nine Washington-area units — and especially from Unit 9, which was the only unit with a transmitter for contacting WFC. Because of this, WFC had decided to give Unit 2 a transmitter, but they hadn't been able to make it work.

The reason for their difficulty became obvious as soon as they ushered me into their kitchen, where their transmitter, an automobile storage battery, and some odds and ends of wire were spread out on a table. Despite the explicit instructions which I had prepared to go with each transmitter, and despite the plainly visible markings beside the terminals on the transmitter case, they had managed to connect the battery to the transmitter with the wrong polarity.

I sighed and got a couple of their fellows to help me bring in my equipment from the car. First I checked their battery and found it to be almost completely discharged. I told them to put the battery on the charger while I checked out the transmitter. Charger? What charger, they wanted to know? They didn't have one!

Because of the uncertainty of the availability of electrical power from the lines these days, all our communications equipment is operated from storage batteries which are trickle-charged from the lines. This way we are not subject to the power blackouts and brownouts which have become a weekly, if not daily, phenomenon in recent years.

Just as with most other public facilities in this country, the higher the price of electricity has zoomed, the less dependable it has become. In August of this year, for example, residential electrical service in the Washington area was out completely for an average total of four days, and the voltage was reduced by more than 15 per cent for an average total of 14 days.

The government keeps holding hearings and conducting investigations and issuing reports about the problem, but it just keeps getting worse. None of the politicians are willing to face the real issues involved here, one of which is the disastrous effect Washington's Israel-dominated foreign policy during the last two decades has had on America's supply of foreign oil.

I showed them how to hook up the battery to their truck for an emergency charge and then began looking into their transmitter to see what damage had been done. A charger for their battery would have to be found later.

The most critical part of the transmitter, the coding unit which generates the digital signal from a pocket-calculator keyboard, seemed to be OK. It was protected by a diode from damage due to a polarity error. In the transmitter itself, however, three transistors had been blown.

I was pretty sure WFC had at least one more spare transmitter in stock, but in order to find out I would have to get a message to them. That meant sending a courier over to Unit 9 to transmit a query and then arranging to have someone from WFC deliver the transmitter to us. I hesitated to bother WFC, in view of our policy of restricting radio transmissions from field units to messages of some urgency.

Since Unit 2 needed a battery charger anyway, I decided to obtain the replacement transistors from a commercial supply house at the same time I picked up a charger, and install them myself. Locating the parts I needed turned out to be easier said than done, however, and it was after six in the evening when I finally got back to the farmhouse.

The fuel gauge in the car was reading "empty" when I pulled into their driveway. Being afraid to risk using my gasoline ration card at a filling station and not knowing where to find black-market gasoline around there, I had to ask the people in Unit 2 to give me a few gallons of fuel to return home. Well, sir, not only did they have a grand total of about one gallon in their truck, but they didn't know where any black-market gas was to be had either.

I wondered how such an inept and unresourceful group of people were going to survive as an underground unit. It seems that they were all people that the Organization decided would not be suited for guerrilla activities and had lumped together in one unit. Four of them are writers from the Organization's publications department, and they are carrying on their work at the farm, turning out copy for propaganda pamphlets and leaflets. The other four are acting only in a supporting role, keeping the place supplied with food and other needs.

Since nobody in Unit 2 really needs automotive transportation, they hadn't worried much about fuel. Finally, one of them volunteered to go out later that night and siphon some gasoline from a vehicle at a neighboring farm. It was about that time that we had another power failure in the area, so I couldn't use my soldering iron. I called it quits for the day.

It took me all of the next day and well into last night to finally get their transmitter working properly, because of several difficulties I hadn't anticipated. When the job was finally done, around midnight, I suggested that the transmitter be installed in a better location than the kitchen, preferably in the attic, or at least on the second floor of the house.

We found a suitable location and carried everything upstairs. In the process I managed to drop the storage battery on my left foot. At first I was sure I had broken my foot. I couldn't walk at all on it.

The result was that I spent another night in the farmhouse. Despite their shortcomings, everyone in Unit 2 was really very kind to me, and they were properly appreciative of my efforts on their behalf.

As had been promised, stolen fuel was provided for my return trip. Furthermore, they insisted on loading up the car with a great quantity of canned food for me to take back, of which they seemed to have an unlimited supply. I asked where they got it all, but the only reply I received was a smile and an assurance that they could get plenty more when they needed it. Perhaps they are more resourceful than I thought at first.

It was 10 o'clock this morning when I got back to our building. George and Henry were both out, but Katherine greeted me as she opened the garage door for me to drive in. She asked if I had eaten breakfast yet.

I told her I had eaten with Unit 2 and wasn't hungry, but that I was concerned about the condition of my foot, which was throbbing painfully and had swelled to nearly twice its normal size. She assisted me as I hobbled up the stairs to the living quarters, and then she brought me a large basin of cold water to soak my foot in.

The cold water relieved the throbbing almost immediately, and I leaned back gratefully on the pillows which Katherine propped behind me on the couch. I explained how I had hurt my foot, and we exchanged other news on the events of the last two days.

The three of them had spent all of yesterday putting up shelves, making minor repairs, and finishing the cleaning and painting which has kept us all busy for more than a week. With the odds

27

and ends of furniture we picked up earlier for the place, it is really beginning to look livable. Quite an improvement from the bare, cold, and dirty machine shop it was when we moved in.

Last night, Katherine informed me, George was summoned by radio to another meeting with a man from WFC. Then, early this morning, he and Henry left together, telling her only that they would be gone all day.

I must have dozed off for a few minutes, and when I awakened I was alone and my footbath was no longer cold. My foot felt much better, though, and the swelling had subsided noticeably. I decided to take a shower.

The shower is a makeshift, cold-water-only arrangement which Henry and I installed in a large closet last week. We did the plumbing and put in a light, and Katherine covered the walls and floor with a self-adhesive vinyl for waterproofing. The closet opens off the room which George, Henry, and I use for sleeping. Of the other two rooms over the shop, Katherine uses the smaller one for a bedroom, and the other is a common room which also serves as a kitchen and eating area.

I undressed, got a towel, and opened the door to the shower. And there was Katherine, wet, naked, and lovely, standing under the bare light bulb and drying herself. She looked at me without surprise and said nothing.

I stood there for a moment and then, instead of apologizing and closing the door again, I impulsively held out my arms to Katherine. Hesitantly, she stepped toward me. Nature took her course.

We lay in bed for a long while afterward and talked. It was the first time I have really talked to Katherine, alone. She is an affectionate, sensitive, and very feminine girl beneath the cool, professional exterior she has always maintained in her work for the Organization.

Four years ago, before the Gun Raids, she was a Congressman's secretary. She lived in a Washington apartment with another girl who also worked on Capitol Hill. One evening when Katherine came home from work she found her apartment mate's body lying in a pool of blood on the floor. She had been raped and killed by a Negro intruder.

That's why Katherine bought a pistol and kept it even after the Cohen Act made gun ownership illegal. Then, along with nearly a million others, she was swept up in the Gun Raids of 1989. Although she had never had any previous contact with the Organization, she met George in the detention center they were both held in after being arrested.

28

Katherine had been apolitical. If anyone had asked her, during the time she was working for the government or, before that, when she was a college student, she would have probably said she was a "liberal." But she was liberal only in the mindless, automatic way that most people are. Without really thinking about it or trying to analyze it, she superficially accepted the unnatural ideology peddled by the mass media and the government. She had none of the bigotry, none of the guilt and self-hatred that it takes to make a really committed, full-time liberal.

After the police released them, George gave her some books on race and history and some Organization publications to read. For the first time in her life she began thinking seriously about the important racial, social, and political issues at the root of the day's problems.

She learned the truth about the System's "equality" hoax. She gained an understanding of the unique historical role of the Jews as the ferment of decomposition of races and civilizations. Most important, she began acquiring a sense of racial identity, overcoming a lifetime of brainwashing aimed at reducing her to an isolated human atom in a cosmopolitan chaos.

She had lost her Congressional job as a consequence of her arrest, and, about two months later, she went to work for the Organization as a typist in our publications department. She is smart and a hard worker, and she was soon advanced to proofreader and then to copy editor. She wrote a few articles of her own for Organization publications, mostly exploring women's roles in the movement and in the larger society, and just last month she was named editor of a new Organization quarterly directed specifically toward women.

Her editorial career has now been shelved, of course, at least temporarily, and her most useful contribution to our present effort is her remarkable skill at makeup and disguise, something she developed in amateur-theater work as a student.

Although her initial contact was with George, Katherine has never been emotionally or romantically involved with him. When they first met, George was still married. Later, after George's wife, who never approved of his work for the Organization, had left him and Katherine had joined the Organization, they were both too busy in different departments for much contact. George, in fact, whose work as a fund raiser and roving organizer kept him on the road, wasn't really around Washington much.

It is only a coincidence that George and Katherine were assigned to this unit together, but George pretty obviously feels a

29

proprietary interest in her. Although Katherine never did or said anything to support my assumption, until this morning I had taken it for granted from George's behavior toward her that there was at least a tentative relationship between them.

Since George is nominally our unit leader, I have heretofore kept my natural attraction toward Katherine under control. Now I'm afraid that the situation has become a bit awkward. If George is unable to adjust graciously to it, things will be strained and may only by resolved by some personnel transfers between our unit and others in the area.

For the time being, however, there are other problems to worry about — big ones! When George and Henry finally got back this evening, we found out what they'd been doing all day: casing the FBI's national headquarters downtown. Our unit has been assigned the task of blowing it up!

The initial order came all the way down from Revolutionary Command, and a man was sent from the Eastern Command Center to the WFC briefing George attended Sunday to look over the local unit leaders and pick one for this assignment.

Apparently Revolutionary Command has decided to take the offensive against the political police before they arrest too many more of our "legals" or finish setting up their computerized passport system.

George was given the word after he was summoned by WFC for a second briefing yesterday. A man from Unit 8 was also at yesterday's briefing. Unit 8 will be assisting us.

The plan, roughly, is this: Unit 8 will secure a large quantity of explosives — between five and ten tons. Our unit will hijack a truck making a legitimate delivery to the FBI headquarters, rendezvous at a location where Unit 8 will be waiting with the explosives, and switch loads. We will then drive into the FBI building's freight-receiving area, set the fuse, and leave the truck.

While Unit 8 is solving the problem of the explosives, we have to work out all the other details of the assignment, including a determination of the FBI's freight-delivery schedules and procedures. We have been given a ten-day deadline.

My job will be the design and construction of the mechanism of the bomb itself.

V

October 3, 1991. I've been breaking up my work on the FBI project with some handyman activity around our building. Last night I finished our perimeter-alarm system, and today I did some rough and very dirty work on our emergency escape tunnel.

Along both sides and the back of the building I buried a row of pressure-sensitive pads, which are wired to a light and an alarm buzzer inside. The pads are the sort which are often installed under doormats inside stores to signal the arrival of a customer. They consist of two-foot-long metal strips sealed inside a flexible plastic sheet, and they are waterproof. Covered with an inch of soil they are undetectable, but they will signal us if anyone steps on the ground above them.

This method could not be used in front of our building, because nearly all the ground there is covered by the concrete driveway and parking area. After considering and rejecting an ultrasonic detector for the front, I settled on a photoelectric beam between two steel fence posts on either side of the concrete area.

In order to keep the light source and photocell unnoticeable, it was necessary to place them inside the fence post on one side, with a very small and inconspicuous reflector mounted on the other. I had to drill several holes in one post, and quite a bit of tinkering was necessary to make everything work properly.

Katherine was a big help with this, carefully adjusting the reflector while I lined up the light and photocell. It was also at her suggestion that I changed the alarm system inside the building, so that it not only warns us at the instant an intruder steps on one of the pressure-sensitive pads or interrupts the light beam, but it also turns on an electric clock in the garage. This way we will know whether someone has been around while we were all out of the building — and we will know when.

In cleaning out a filthy collection of empty oil cans, greasy rags, and miscellaneous trash from the service pit which had been used for changing oil and working underneath automobiles in the garage, we discovered that the service pit opens directly into a storm sewer through a steel grating in the concrete floor.

Prying up the grating, we found that it is possible to crawl into the storm sewer, which is a concrete pipe four feet in diameter. The pipe runs about 400 yards to a large, open drainage ditch. Along the way there are about a dozen smaller pipes emptying into the main conduit, apparently from street drains. The open end of the sewer is protected by a grating of half-inch reinforcing rods set into the concrete.

Today I took a hacksaw, scuttled down to the end of the sewer, and sawed through all but two of the steel rods. This left the grating firmly in place but made it possible, with a great deal of effort, to bend it aside far enough to crawl out.

I did so and took a brief look around. The side of the ditch is heavily overgrown, providing good concealment from the nearby road. And from the road it is not possible to see our building or any part of the street on which it fronts, because of intervening structures. When I reentered the sewer, I grunted and strained until I had bent the grating back in place again.

Unfortunately, the people who ran the garage and machine shop before we moved in must have been dumping all their waste oil into the storm sewer for years, because there's about four inches of thick, black sludge along the bottom of the sewer pipe near the opening from the service pit. When I crawled out into the shop again I was covered with the stuff.

Henry and George were both out, and Katherine made me strip and hosed me down in the service pit before she would even let me go upstairs to take a shower. She declared the shoes and clothes I had been wearing a total loss and threw them out.

Every time I take an ice-cold shower I bitterly regret that Henry and I didn't take the time to add hot water to our make-shift shower stall.

October 6. Today I completed the detonating mechanism for the bomb we'll use against the FBI building. The trigger mechanism itself was quite easy, but I was held up on the booster until yesterday, because I didn't know what sort of explosives we would be using.

The people in Unit 8 had planned to raid a supply shed in one of the areas where the Washington subway system is being extended, but they didn't have any luck at all until yesterday — and then not much. They were only able to steal two cases of blasting gelatin, and one case wasn't even full. Less than 100 pounds.

But that solved my problem, at least. The blasting gelatin is sensitive enough to be initiated by one of my homemade lead azide detonators, and 100 pounds of it will be more than sufficient to detonate the main charge, when and if Unit 8 finds more explosives, regardless of what they are or how they are packaged.

I packed about four pounds of the blasting gelatin into an empty applesauce can, primed it, placed the batteries and timing mechanism in the top of the can, and wired them to a small toggle switch on the end of a 20-foot extension cord. When we load the truck with explosives, the can will go in back, on top of the two cases of blasting gelatin. We'll have to poke small holes in the walls of the trailer and the cab to run the extension cord and the switch into the cab.

Either George or Henry — probably Henry — will drive the truck into the freight-receiving area inside the FBI building. Before he gets out of the cab he will flip the switch, starting the timer. Ten minutes later the explosives will go off. If we're lucky, that will be the end of the FBI building — and the government's new three-billion-dollar computer complex for their internal-passport system.

Six or seven years ago, when they first started releasing "trial balloons" to see what the public reaction to the new passport system would be, it was said that its main purpose would be to detect illegal aliens, so they could be deported.

Although some citizens were properly suspicious of the whole scheme, most swallowed the government's explanation of why the passports were needed. Thus, many labor union members, who saw illegal aliens as a threat to their jobs during a time of high unemployment, thought it was a fine idea, while liberals generally opposed it because it sounded "racist" — illegal aliens being virtually all non-White. Later, when the government granted automatic citizenship to everyone who had managed to sneak across the Mexican border and remain in the country for two years, the liberal opposition evaporated — except for a hard core of libertarians who were still suspicious.

All in all, it has been depressingly easy for the System to deceive and manipulate the American people — whether the relatively naive "conservatives" or the spoiled and pseudo-sophisticated "liberals." Even the libertarians, inherently hostile to all government, will be intimidated into going along when Big Brother announces that the new passport system is necessary to find and root out "racists" — namely, us.

If the freedom of the American people were the only thing at stake, the existence of the Organization would hardly be justified. Americans have lost their right to be free. Slavery is the just and proper state for a people who have grown as soft, self-indulgent, careless, credulous, and befuddled as we have.

Indeed, we are already slaves. We have allowed a diabolically clever, alien minority to put chains on our souls and our minds. These spiritual chains are a truer mark of slavery than the iron chains which are yet to come.

Why didn't we rebel 35 years ago, when they took our schools away from us and began converting them into racially mixed jungles? Why didn't we throw them all out of the country 50

33

years ago, instead of letting them use us as cannon fodder in their war to subjugate Europe?

More to the point, why didn't we rise up three years ago, when they started taking our guns away? Why didn't we rise up in righteous fury and drag these arrogant aliens into the streets and cut their throats then? Why didn't we roast them over bonfires at every streetcorner in America? Why didn't we make a final end to this obnoxious and eternally pushy clan, this pestilence from the sewers of the East, instead of meekly allowing ourselves to be disarmed?

The answer is easy. We *would* have rebelled if all that has been imposed on us in the last 50 years had been attempted at once. But because the chains that bind us were forged imperceptibly, link by link, we submitted.

The adding of any single, new link to the chain was never enough for us to make a big fuss about. It always seemed easier — and safer — to go along. And the further we went, the easier it was to go just one step further.

One thing the historians will have to decide — if any men of our race survive to write a history of this era — is the relative importance of deliberation and inadvertence in converting us from a society of free men to a herd of human cattle.

That is, can we justly blame what has happened to us entirely on deliberate subversion, carried out through the insidious propaganda of the controlled mass media, the schools, the churches, and the government? Or must we place a large share of the blame on inadvertent decadence — on the spiritually debilitating life style into which the Western people have allowed themselves to slip in the twentieth century?

Probably the two things are intertwined, and it will be difficult to blame either cause separately. Brainwashing has made decadence more acceptable to us, and decadence has made us less resistant to brainwashing. In any event, we are too close to the trees now to see the outline of the forest very clearly.

But one thing which is quite clear is that much more than our freedom is at stake. If the Organization fails in its task now, *everything* will be lost — our history, our heritage, all the blood and sacrifices and upward striving of countless thousands of years. The Enemy we are fighting fully intends to destroy the racial basis of our existence.

No excuse for our failure will have any meaning, for there will be only a swarming horde of indifferent, mulatto zombies to hear it. There will be no White men to remember us — either to blame us for our weakness or to forgive us for our folly.

34

If we fail, God's great Experiment will come to an end, and this planet will once again, as it did millions of years ago, move through the ether devoid of higher man.

October 11. Tomorrow is the day! Despite the failure of Unit 8 to find as much explosives as we want, we are going ahead with the FBI operation.

The final decision on this came late this afternoon in a conference at Unit 8's headquarters. Henry and I were both there, as well as a staff officer from Revolutionary Command — an indication of the urgency with which the Organization's leadership views this operation.

Ordinarily Revolutionary Command personnel do not become involved with unit actions on an operational level. We receive operational orders from and report to Washington Field Command, with representatives from the Eastern Command Center participating occasionally in conferences when matters of special importance must be decided. Only twice previously have I attended meetings with anyone from Revolutionary Command, both times to make basic decisions concerning the Organization's communications equipment, which I was designing. And that, of course, was before we went underground.

So the presence of Major Williams (a pseudonym, I believe) at our meeting this afternoon made a strong impression on all of us. I was asked to attend because I am responsible for the proper functioning of the bomb. Henry was there because he will be delivering it.

And the reason for the meeting was Unit 8's failure to obtain what I and Ed Sanders estimate to be the minimum quantity of explosives needed to do a thorough job. Ed is Unit 8's ordnance expert — and, interestingly enough, a former special agent of the FBI who is familiar with the structure and layout of the FBI building.

As carefully as we could, we calculated that we should have at least 10,000 pounds of TNT or an equivalent explosive to destroy a substantial portion of the building and wreck the new computer center in the sub-basement. To be on the safe side, we asked for 20,000 pounds. Instead, what we have is a little under 5,000 pounds, and nearly all of that is ammonium nitrate fertilizer, which is much less effective than TNT for our purpose.

After the initial two cases of blasting gelatin, Unit 8 was able to pick up 400 pounds of dynamite from another subway construction shed. We have given up hope of assembling the necessary quantity of explosives in this way, however. Although

35

large quantities of explosives are used each day on the subway, it is stored in small batches and access is very difficult. Two of Unit 8's people had a close call when they swiped the dynamite.

Last Thursday, with our deadline for completing the job upon us, three men from Unit 8 made a night raid on a farm-supply warehouse near Fredericksburg, about 50 miles south of here. They found no explosives, as such, but did find some ammonium nitrate, which they cleaned out: forty-four 100-lb. bags of the stuff.

Sensitized with oil and tightly confined, it makes an effective blasting agent, where the aim is simply to move a quantity of dirt or rock. But our original plan for the bomb called for it to be essentially unconfined and to be able to punch through two levels of reinforced-concrete flooring while producing an open-air blast wave powerful enough to blow the facade off a massive and strongly constructed building.

Finally, two days ago, Unit 8 set about doing what it should have done at the beginning. The same three fellows who had gotten the ammonium nitrate headed up into Maryland with their truck to rob a military arsenal. I gather from what Ed Sanders says that we have a legal on the inside there who will be able to help.

But, as of this afternoon, there has been no word from them, and Revolutionary Command isn't willing to wait any longer. The pros and cons of going ahead with what we have now are these:

The System is hurting us badly by continuing to arrest our legals, upon whom the Organization is largely dependent for its financing. If the supply of funds from our legals is cut off, our underground units will be forced to turn to robbery on a large scale in order to support themselves.

Thus, Revolutionary Command feels it is essential to strike the System immediately with a blow which will not only interrupt the FBI roundup of our legals, at least temporarily, but will also raise morale throughout the Organization by embarrassing the System and demonstrating our ability to act. From what Williams said, I gather that these two goals have become even more pressing than the original objective of knocking out the computer bank.

On the other hand, if we strike a blow which does not do some real damage to the System's secret police we may not only fail to achieve these new goals but, by forewarning the enemy of our intentions and tactics, also make it much more difficult to hit the computers later. This was the viewpoint expressed by Henry, whose great gift is his ability to always keep a cool head and not be distracted from future goals by immediate difficulties. But he is also a good soldier and is completely willing to carry through with his part of tomorrow's action, despite his feeling that we should hold off until we are certain that we can do a thorough job.

I believe the people in Revolutionary Command also understand the danger in hasty, premature action. But they must take into consideration many factors which we cannot. Williams is clearly convinced that it is imperative to throw a monkey wrench into the FBI's gears immediately, otherwise they will flatten us like a steamroller. Thus, most of our discussion this afternoon centered on the narrow question of just how much damage we can do with our present quantity of explosives.

If, in accord with our original plan, we drive a truck into the main freight entrance of the FBI building and blow it up in the freight-receiving area, the explosion will take place in a large, central courtyard, surrounded on all sides by heavy masonry and open to the sky above. Ed and I both agree that with the present quantity of explosives we will not be able to do any really serious structural damage under those conditions.

We can wreak havoc in all the offices with windows opening on the courtyard, but we cannot hope to blow away the inner facade of the building or to punch through to the sub-basement where the computers are. Several hundred people will be killed, but the machine will probably keep running.

Sanders pleaded for another day or two for his unit to find more explosives, but his case was weakened by their failure to find what was needed in the last 12 days. With nearly a hundred of our legals being arrested every day, we can't take a chance on waiting even another two days, Williams said, unless we can be certain that those two days will bring us what we need.

What we finally decided is to attempt to get our bomb directly into the first-level basement, which also has a freight entrance on 10th Street, next to the main freight entrance. If we detonate our bomb in the basement underneath the courtyard, the confinement will make it substantially more effective. It will almost certainly collapse the basement floor into the sub-basement, burying the computers. Furthermore it will destroy most, if not all, the communications and power equipment for the building, since those are on the basement levels. The big unknown is whether it will do enough structural damage to the building to make it uninhabitable for an extended period. Without a detailed blueprint of the building and a team of architects and civil engineers we simply can't answer that question.

The drawback to going for the basement is that relatively few freight deliveries are made there, and the entrance is usually closed. Henry is willing to crash the truck right through the door, if necessary.

So be it. Tomorrow night we'll know a lot more than we do today.

VI

October 13, 1991. At 9:15 yesterday morning our bomb went off in the FBI's national headquarters building. Our worries about the relatively small size of the bomb were unfounded; the damage is immense. We have certainly disrupted a major portion of the FBI's headquarters operations for at least the next several weeks, and it looks like we have also achieved our goal of wrecking their new computer complex.

My day's work started a little before five o'clock yesterday, when I began helping Ed Sanders mix heating oil with the ammonium nitrate fertilizer in Unit 8's garage. We stood the 100-pound bags on end one by one and poked a small hole in the top with a screwdriver, just big enough to insert the end of a funnel. While I held the bag and funnel, Ed poured in a gallon of oil.

Then we slapped a big square of adhesive tape over the hole, and I turned the bag end over end to mix the contents while Ed refilled his oil can from the feeder line to their oil furnace. It took us nearly three hours to do all 44 sacks, and the work really wore me out.

Meanwhile, George and Henry were out stealing a truck. With only two-and-a-half tons of explosives we didn't need a big tractor-trailer rig, so we had decided to grab a delivery truck belonging to an office-supply firm. They just followed the truck they wanted in our car until it stopped to make a delivery. When the driver — a Negro — opened the back of the truck and stepped inside, Henry hopped in after him and dispatched him swiftly and silently with his knife.

Then George followed in the car while Henry drove the truck to the garage. They backed in just as Ed and I were finishing our work. They are certain that no one on the street noticed a thing.

It took us another half hour to unload about a ton of mimeograph paper and miscellaneous office supplies from the truck and then to carefully pack our cases of dynamite and bags of sensitized fertilizer in place. Finally, I ran the cable and switch from the detonator through a chink from the cargo area into the cab of the truck. We left the driver's body in the back of the truck.

George and I headed for the FBI building in the car, with Henry following in the truck. We intended to park near the 10th Street freight entrances and watch until the freight door to the basement level was opened for another truck, while Henry waited with "our" truck two blocks away. We would then give him a signal via walkie-talkie.

As we drove by the building, however, we saw that the basement entrance was open and no one was in sight. We signalled Henry and kept going for another seven or eight blocks, until we found a good spot to park. Then we began walking back slowly, keeping an eye on our watches.

We were still two blocks away when the pavement shuddered violently under our feet. An instant later the blast wave hit us — a deafening "ka-whoomp," followed by an enormous roaring, crashing sound, accentuated by the higher-pitched noise of shattering glass all around us.

The plate glass windows in the store beside us and dozens of others that we could see along the street were blown to splinters. A glittering and deadly rain of glass shards continued to fall into the street from the upper stories of nearby buildings for a few seconds, as a jet-black column of smoke shot straight up into the sky ahead of us.

We ran the final two blocks and were dismayed to see what, at first glance, appeared to be an entirely intact FBI headquarters — except, of course, that most of the windows were missing. We headed for the 10th Street freight entrances we had driven past a few minutes earlier. Dense, choking smoke was pouring from the ramp leading to the basement, and it was out of the question to attempt to enter there.

Dozens of people were scurrying around the freight entrance to the central courtyard, some going in and some coming out. Many were bleeding profusely from cuts, and all had expressions of shock or dazed disbelief on their faces. George and I took deep breaths and hurried through the entrance. No one challenged us or even gave us a second glance.

The scene in the courtyard was one of utter devastation. The whole Pennsylvania Avenue wing of the building, as we could then see, had collapsed, partly into the courtyard in the center of the building and partly into Pennsylvania Avenue. A huge, gaping hole yawned in the courtyard pavement just beyond the rubble of collapsed masonry, and it was from this hole that most of the column of black smoke was ascending.

Overturned trucks and automobiles, smashed office furniture, and building rubble were strewn wildly about — and so were the bodies of a shockingly large number of victims. Over everything hung the pall of black smoke, burning our eyes and lungs and reducing the bright morning to semi-darkness.

We took a few steps into the courtyard in order to better evaluate the damage we had caused. We had to wade through a waist-deep sea of paper, which had spilled out of a huge jumble of file cabinets to our right, perhaps a thousand of them. It looked like they had slid *en masse* into the courtyard from one of the upper stories of the collapsed wing, and now there was a tangled heap of smashed and burst cabinets 20 feet high and 80 to 100 feet long interspersed with their disgorged contents, which had spread out beyond the heap until most of the courtyard was covered with paper.

As we gaped with a mixture of horror and elation at the devastation, Henry's head suddenly appeared a few feet away. He was climbing out of a crevice in the mountain of smashed file cabinets. We were both startled to see him, as he was supposed to have left the area as soon as he parked the truck and then waited for us to pick him up at the rendezvous point.

He quickly explained that everything had gone so smoothly in the basement that he had decided to wait in the area for the blast. He had flipped the switch to the detonator timer as he drove the truck down the ramp into the building, so that there could be no chance of any difficulties which might arise causing him to change his mind. But no difficulties arose. He received no challenge, only a casual wave from a Black guard, as he pulled into the basement. Two other trucks were unloading at a freight platform, but Henry drove on past them, stopping his truck as nearly under the center of the Pennsylvania Avenue wing of the building as he could judge.

He had a hoked-up set of delivery documents to hand to anyone who questioned him, but no one did. He walked past the inattentive Black guard, back up the ramp, and out onto the street.

He waited by a public phone booth a block away until one minute before the explosion was due, then placed a call to the newsroom of the *Washington Post*. His brief message was: "Three weeks ago you and yours killed Carl Hodges in Chicago. We are now settling the score with your pals in the political police. Soon we'll settle the score with you and all other traitors. White America shall live!''

That should rattle their cage enough to provoke a few good headlines and editorials!

Henry had beat us back to the FBI building by less than a minute, but he had put that minute to good use. He pointed to a few curls of lighter, grayish smoke which were beginning to rise from the tangle of smashed file cabinets from which he had just emerged, and then he flashed a quick grin as he dropped his cigarette lighter back into his pocket. Henry is a one-man army.

As we turned to leave, I heard a moan and looked down to see a girl, about 20 years old, half under a steel door and other debris. Her pretty face was smudged and scraped, and she seemed to be only half conscious. I lifted the door off her and saw that one leg was crumpled under her, badly broken, and blood was spurting from a deep gash in her thigh.

I quickly removed the cloth belt from her dress and used it to make a tourniquet. The flow of blood slowed somewhat, but not enough. I then tore off a portion of her dress and folded it into a compress, which I held against the cut in her leg while George removed his shoelaces and used them to tie the compress in place. As gently as we could George and I picked her up to carry her out to the sidewalk. She moaned loudly as her broken leg straightened.

The girl seemed to have no serious injuries other than her leg, and she will probably pull through all right. Not so for many others, though. When I stooped to stop the girl's bleeding I became aware for the first time of the moans and screams of dozens of other injured persons in the courtyard. Not twenty feet away another woman lay motionless, her face covered with blood and a gaping wound in the side of her head — a horrible sight which I can still see vividly every time I close my eyes.

According to the latest estimate released, approximately 700 persons were killed in the blast or subsequently died in the wreckage. That includes an estimated 150 persons who were in the sub-basement at the time of the explosion and whose bodies have not been recovered.

It may be more than two weeks before enough rubble has been cleared away to allow full access to that level of the building, according to the TV news reporter. That report and others we've heard yesterday and today make it virtually certain that the new computer banks in the sub-basement have either been totally destroyed or very badly damaged.

All day yesterday and most of today we watched the TV coverage of rescue crews bringing the dead and injured out of the building. It is a heavy burden of responsibility for us to bear, since most of the victims of our bomb were only pawns who were no more committed to the sick philosophy or the racially destructive goals of the System than we are.

But there is no way we can destroy the System without hurting many thousands of innocent people — no way. It is a cancer too deeply rooted in our flesh. And if we don't destroy the System before it destroys us — if we don't cut this cancer out of our living flesh — our whole race will die.

We have gone over this before, and we are all completely convinced that what we did is justified, but it is still very hard to see our own people suffering so intensely because of our acts. It is because Americans have for so many years been unwilling to make unpleasant decisions that we are forced to make decisions now which are stern indeed.

And is that not a key to the whole problem? The corruption of our people by the Jewish-liberal-democratic-equalitarian plague which afflicts us is more clearly manifested in our soft-mindedness, our unwillingness to recognize the harder realities of life, than in anything else.

Liberalism is an essentially feminine, submissive world view. Perhaps a better adjective than feminine is infantile. It is the world view of men who do not have the moral toughness, the spiritual strength to stand up and do single combat with life, who cannot adjust to the reality that the world is not a huge, pink-and-blue, padded nursery in which the lions lie down with the lambs and everyone lives happily ever after.

Nor should spiritually healthy men of our race even *want* the world to be like that, if it could be so. That is an alien, essentially Oriental approach to life, the world view of slaves rather than of free men of the West.

But it has permeated our whole society. Even those who do not consciously accept the liberal doctrines have been corrupted by them. Decade after decade the race problem in America has become worse. But the majority of those who wanted a solution, who wanted to preserve a White America, were never able to screw up the courage to look the obvious solutions in the face.

All the liberals and the Jews had to do was begin screeching about "inhumanity" or "injustice" or "genocide," and most of our people who had been beating around the edges of a solution took to their heels like frightened rabbits. Because there was never a way to solve the race problem which would be "fair for

42

everybody," or which everyone concerned could be politely persuaded into accepting without any fuss or unpleasantness, they kept trying to evade it, hoping that it would go away by itself. And the same has been true of the Jewish problem and the immigration problem and the overpopulation problem and the eugenics problem and a thousand related problems.

Yes, the inability to face reality and make difficult decisions, that is the salient symptom of the liberal disease. Always trying to avoid a minor unpleasantness now, so that a major unpleasantness becomes unavoidable later, always evading any responsibility to the future — that is the way the liberal mind works.

Nevertheless, every time the TV camera focuses on the pitiful, mutilated corpse of some poor girl — or even an FBI agent — being pulled from the wreckage, my stomach becomes tied in knots and I cannot breathe. It is a terrible, terrible task we have before us.

And it is already clear that the controlled media intend to convince the public that what we are doing is terrible. They are deliberately emphasizing the suffering we have caused by interspersing gory closeups of the victims with tearful interviews with their relatives.

Interviewers are asking leading questions like, "What kind of inhuman beasts do you think could have done something like this to your daughter?" They have clearly made the decision to portray the bombing of the FBI building as the atrocity of the century.

And, indeed, it is an act of unprecedented magnitude. All the bombings, arsons, and assassinations carried out by the Left in this country have been rather small-time in comparison.

But what a difference in the attitude of the news media! I remember a long string of Marxist acts of terror 20 years ago, during the Vietnam war. A number of government buildings were burned or dynamited, and several innocent bystanders were killed, but the press always portrayed such things as idealistic acts of "protest."

There was a gang of armed, revolutionary Negroes who called themselves "Black Panthers." Every time they had a shootout with the police, the press and TV people had their tearful interviews with the families of the Black gang members who got killed — not with the cops' widows. And when a Negress who belonged to the Communist Party helped plan a courtroom shootout and even supplied the shotgun with which a judge was murdered, the press formed a cheering section at her trial and tried to make a folk hero out of her.

43

Well, as Henry warned the *Washington Post* yesterday, we will soon begin settling that score. One day we will have a truly American press in this country, but a lot of editors' throats will have to be cut first.

October 16. I'm back with my old friends in Unit 2. These words are being written by lantern light in the place they fixed up in the loft of their barn for Katherine and me. A bit chilly and primitive, but at least we have complete privacy. This is the first time we've had a whole night together by ourselves.

Actually we didn't come here for a romp in the hay but to pick up a load of munitions. The fellows from Unit 8 who were sent up here last week to find explosives for the FBI job were at least partly successful: they didn't get much in the way of bulk explosives, and they were too late with what they did get, and they nearly got themselves killed — but they did acquire quite a grab bag of miscellaneous ordnance for the Organization.

They didn't tell me all the details, but they were able to get a 2½-ton truck into the Aberdeen Proving Ground, about 25 miles from here, load it with munitions, and get it out again — with the help of one of our people on the inside. Unfortunately, they were surprised in the act of raiding a storage bunker and had to shoot their way out. In the process one of them was very seriously wounded.

They managed to elude their pursuers and get as far as Unit 2's farm outside Baltimore, and they have been in hiding here ever since. The man who was shot nearly died from shock and loss of blood, but no major organs were damaged and it now looks as if he'll pull through, although he's still too weak to be moved.

The other two have been keeping themselves busy working on their truck, which is parked right beneath us. They've repainted it and made a couple of other changes, so it won't be recognizable when they eventually head back toward Washington in it.

They won't be taking the bulk of their munitions back with them, however. Most of it will be stored here and used to supply units throughout the area. Washington Field Command is letting our unit have first pick of this material.

There's quite an assortment. Probably most valuable are 30 cases of fragmentation grenades — that's 750 hand grenades! We'll take two cases back with us.

Then there are about 100 land mines of various types and sizes — handy for making boobytraps. We'll pick out two or three of those.

And there are fuzes and boosters galore. Cases of fuzes for bombs, mines, grenades, et cetera. And eight spools of detonating cord. And a case of thermite grenades. And lots of other odds and ends.

And there's even a 500-lb., general-purpose bomb. They made such a racket trying to get that onto the truck that a guard heard them. But we'll take it back with us. It's filled with about 250 pounds of tritonal, a mixture of TNT and aluminum powder, and we can melt it out of the bomb casing and use it for smaller bombs.

Katherine and I are both very happy we could make this trip together, but the circumstances are troubling. George first asked Henry and me to go, but Katherine objected. She complained that she had not yet been given a chance to participate in the activities of our unit and, in fact, had hardly been outside our two hideouts during the last month. She had no intention, she said, of being nothing but a cook and housekeeper for the rest of us.

We were all under a bit of tension following the big bombing, and Katherine came across a bit shrill — almost like a women's libber. (*Note to the reader:* "Women's lib" was a form of mass psychosis which broke out during the last three decades of the Old Era. Women affected by it denied their femininity and insisted that they were "people," not "women." This aberration was promoted and encouraged by the System as a means of dividing our race against itself.) George hotly protested that she was not being discriminated against, that her makeup-and-disguise abilities had been particularly valuable to our unit, and that he assigned tasks solely on the basis of how he thought we could function most effectively.

I tried to smooth things over by suggesting that perhaps it would be better for a man and a woman to be driving a carload of contraband than two men. The police have been stopping lots of cars at random in the Washington area for searches in the last few days.

Henry agreed with my suggestion, and George reluctantly went along with it. I am afraid, however, that he suspects that at least part of the reason for Katherine's outburst is that she preferred to be with me rather than to be left alone for a whole day with him.

We have not flaunted our relationship, but it is not likely that either Henry or George has failed to guess by now that Katherine and I are lovers. That creates a rather awkward situation for all of us. Completely aside from the fact that George and Henry are both healthy males and Katherine is the only female among us is the problem of Organizational discipline.

The Organization has made allowances for married couples, where both man and wife are members of a unit, in that husbands have veto power over any orders given to their wives. But, with that exception, women are subject to the same discipline as men, and, despite the informality which prevails in nearly all units, any infraction of Organizational discipline is an extremely serious matter.

Katherine and I have talked about this, and, just as we are unwilling to regard our growing relationship as purely sexual, bearing no obligations, neither are we inclined to formalize it yet. For one thing, we still have a lot to learn about each other. For another, we each have an overriding commitment to the Organization and to our unit, and we must not lightly do anything which might infringe upon that commitment.

Nevertheless, we'll have to resolve things one way or another pretty soon.

VII

October 23, 1991. This morning is my first chance to write since Katherine and I picked up the munitions in Maryland last week. Our unit has carried out three missions in the last six days.

Altogether, the Organization is held responsible for more than 200 separate incidents in different parts of the country, according to news reports. We are really into the thick of a guerrilla war now.

Last Monday night, Henry, George, and I raided the *Washington Post*. It was a quick thing, requiring little preparation, although we did argue for a few minutes ahead of time about the way it should be done.

Henry was for going after personnel, but we ended up wrecking one of their presses instead. Henry's idea was that the three of us should force our way into the newsroom and editorial offices on the sixth floor of the *Washington Post* building and kill as many people as we could with fragmentation grenades and machine guns. If we struck just before their 7:30 PM deadline, we would catch nearly everyone in.

George overruled that maneuver as being too risky to be carried out without detailed planning. Hundreds of people work in the *Washington Post* building, and the sounds of grenades and shooting on the sixth floor would probably bring a lot of them swarming into the stairwells and lobby. If we tried to come down on the elevators, someone could pull the main switch on us, and we'd be trapped.

46

On the other hand, the *Post*'s pressroom is visible through a big plate-glass window from the lobby. So I rigged up a makeshift bomb by taping a hand grenade to a small anti-tank mine. The whole thing weighed about six pounds and was quite awkward, but it could be thrown about 50 feet like an oversized grenade.

We parked in an alley about 100 yards from the main entrance of the *Post*. As soon as George had disarmed the guard, Henry blasted a huge hole in the pressroom window with his sawed-off shotgun. Then I pulled the pin on the grenade-mine contraption I had rigged and heaved it into the rollers of the nearest press, which was just being plated up for the night's run.

We ducked behind the masonry parapet while the bomb exploded, and then Henry and I hurriedly threw half-a-dozen thermite grenades into the pressroom. We were all back in the alley before anyone had even come out onto the sidewalk, and so no one saw our car. Katherine, of course, had done her usual magic with our faces.

The next morning the *Post* appeared on the streets about an hour later than usual, and home subscribers missed their papers altogether, since the early editions had been skipped, but the *Post* was otherwise apparently none the worse for wear. We had substantially damaged only one press with our bomb and smoked things up a bit with our incendiary grenades, one of which set a barrel of ink afire, but the *Post* had lost virtually none of its capacity for spreading its lies and venom as a result of our efforts.

We were quite chagrined by this outcome. It became clear to us that we had foolishly taken a risk far out of proportion to any advantage which could have been reasonably expected.

We have resolved that, in the future, we will undertake no mission on our own initiative until we have carefully evaluated its objective and convinced ourselves that it is worth the risk. We cannot afford to strike the System simply for the sake of striking, or we will become like an army of gnats trying to bite an elephant to death. Each blow must be carefully calculated for its effect.

Henry's idea of attacking the *Post*'s newsroom and editorial offices seems much better in retrospect. We should have held off for a few days in order to work out a sound plan which would have really crippled the *Post*, instead of rushing into our half-assed raid on its presses. All we really succeeded in doing was putting the *Post* on guard and making any future raids much more hazardous.

We did redeem ourselves a bit the morning after the raid, however. Surmising that the editorial staff had spent most of the night in their offices writing new copy about the events of the evening and would, therefore, be at home sleeping late, we decided to pay one of them a visit.

After looking over the newspaper, we settled on the editorial-page editor, who had written a particularly vicious editorial against us. His words dripped with Talmudic hatred. Racists like us, he said, deserve no consideration from the police or any decent citizen. We should be shot down on sight like mad dogs. Quite a contrast with his usual solicitude for Black rapists and murderers and his tirades against "police brutality" and "overreaction"!

Since his editorial was an incitement to murder, it seemed to us only appropriate that he be given a taste of his own remedy.

Henry and I rode a bus downtown and then waved down a taxi with a Black driver. By the time we pulled up in the editor's driveway in Silver Spring, the Black was in the trunk — dead.

I waited in the taxi while Henry rang the bell and told the woman who answered that he was delivering a package from the *Post* and needed a signed receipt. When the sleepy-eyed editor appeared at the door in his bathrobe a few moments later, Henry literally blew him in half with two blasts from the sawed-off shotgun he had been carrying under his jacket.

On Wednesday all four of us (Katherine drove the car) completely destroyed the Washington area's most powerful TV transmitter. That one was hairy, and there were moments when I didn't think we were going to get away.

It is still not clear what effect all our activity is having on the general public. For the most part they are just going about their affairs as they always have.

There have been effects, though. The National Guards of a dozen states have been called up to reinforce local police forces, and there are now large, around-the-clock guard details stationed outside every government building in Washington, the major media offices in a number of cities, and the homes of hundreds of government officials.

Within a week, I suspect, every Congressman, every Federal judge, and every Federal bureaucrat from the assistant-secretary level on up will have been assigned a permanent bodyguard detail. All the sandbags, machine guns, and khaki uniforms that one is beginning to see everywhere in Washington cannot help but raise the consciousness of the public — although I'm sure the situation is much less dramatic out in Iowa than it is here.

Our biggest difficulty is that the public sees us and everything we do only through the media. We are able to make ourselves enough of a nuisance that the media can't afford to ignore or belittle us, and so they are using the opposite tactic of deluging the public with distortions, half-truths, and lies about us. For the last two weeks they've been giving us a non-stop roasting, trying to convince everyone that we are the incarnation of evil, a threat to everything decent, noble, and worthwhile.

They have unleashed the full power of the mass media on us; not just the usual biased-news treatment, but long "background" articles in the Sunday supplements, complete with faked photographs of Organization meetings and activities, discussions by "experts" on TV panel shows — everything! Some of the stories they've invented about us are really incredible, but I'm afraid the American public is just gullible enough to believe them.

What's happening now is reminiscent of the media campaign against Hitler and the Germans back in the 1940's: stories about Hitler flying into rages and chewing carpets, phony German plans for the invasion of America, babies being skinned alive to make lampshades and then boiled down into soap, girls kidnapped and sent to Nazi "stud farms." The Jews convinced the American people that those stories were true, and the result was World War II, with millions of the best of our race butchered — by us — and all of eastern and central Europe turned into a huge, communist prison camp.

Now it looks very much like the System has again made the deliberate decision to build up a state of war hysteria in the public by representing us as an even bigger threat than we really are. We are the new Germans, and the country is being wound up psychologically to lick us.

Thus, the System is cooperating more fully than we could have imagined in arousing the public's consciousness of our struggle. What is unnerving about it is my strong suspicion that the top echelons in the System aren't really that worried about our threat to them and are cynically using us as an excuse for carrying through certain programs of their own, such as the internal-passport program.

Our unit was assigned the general task — right after the FBI bombing — of combating the media in this area by direct action, just as other units were assigned other arms of the System as targets. But it is clear that we can't win by direct action alone; there are too many of them and too few of us. We must convince a substantial portion of the American people that what we are doing is both necessary and proper.

The latter is a propaganda task, and so far we haven't been very successful. Units 2 and 6 are primarily responsible for propaganda in the Washington area, and I understand that Unit 6's people have strewn out tons of leaflets in the streets; Henry picked up one from a sidewalk downtown yesterday. I'm afraid that leaflets alone can't make much headway against the System's mass media, though

Our most spectacular propaganda effort here occurred last Wednesday, and it ended in a major tragedy. The same day our unit blew up the TV station, three men from Unit 6 seized a radio station and began broadcasting a call for the public to join the Organization's fight to smash the System.

They had pre-recorded their message on tape, and they booby-trapped the doors to the station, after locking all the station employees in a supply closet. They intended to make their getaway while the tape was being broadcast, hoping that the police would think they were still inside and would lay siege to the place with tear gas — thus giving them half an hour or more of air time.

But the police arrived sooner than expected and stormed the station almost immediately, trapping our men inside. Two were shot to death in the ensuing fight, and the third is not expected to live. The Organization's message was on the air for less than 10 minutes.

Those were the first casualties we've suffered here, but they just about wiped out Unit 6. Their survivors, two women and a man, have moved into our place temporarily. With one of their members in the hands of the police, they had to abandon their own headquarters immediately, of course.

With it we lost one of the Organization's two printing presses in the Washington area, although we were able to clear out most of their printing supplies and lighter equipment. And we gained their pickup truck, which will really be handy if they stay here.

October 28. Last night I had to do the most unpleasant thing that I have been called to do since joining the Organization four years ago. I participated in the execution of a mutineer.

Harry Powell was Unit 5's leader. Last week, when Washington Field Command gave his unit the assignment of assassinating two of the most obnoxious and outspoken advocates of racial mixing in this area — a priest and a rabbi, coauthors of a widely publicized petition to Congress requesting special tax advantages for racially mixed married couples — Powell refused the assignment. He sent a message back to WFC saying that he was opposed to the further use of violence and that his unit would not participate in any acts of terrorism.

He was immediately placed under arrest, and yesterday one representative from each unit under WFC — including Unit 5 — was summoned to judge him. Unit 10 was not able to send anyone, and so 11 members — eight men and three women — met with an officer from WFC in the basement storeroom of a gift shop owned by one of our "legals." I was Unit 1's representative.

The officer from WFC stated the case against Powell very briefly. The Unit 5 representative then confirmed the facts: Powell had not only refused to obey the assassination order, but he had instructed the members of his unit not to obey either. Fortunately, they had not allowed themselves to be subverted by him.

Powell was then given an opportunity to speak in his behalf. He did so for more than two hours, interrupted occasionally by a question from one of us. What he said really shook me, but it made our decision easier for all of us, I am sure.

Harry Powell was, in essence, a "responsible conservative." The fact that he was not only a member of the Organization but had become a unit leader reflects more on the Organization than it does on him. His basic complaint was that all our acts of terror against the System were only making things worse by "provoking" the System into taking more and more repressive measures.

Well, of *course*, we all understood that! Or, at least, I *thought* we all understood it. Apparently Powell didn't. That is, he didn't understand that one of the major purposes of political terror, always and everywhere, is to force the authorities to take reprisals and to become more repressive, thus alienating a portion of the population and generating sympathy for the terrorists. And the other purpose is to create unrest by destroying the population's sense of security and their belief in the invincibility of the government.

As Powell continued talking, it became clearer and clearer that he was a conservative, not a revolutionary. He talked as if the whole purpose of the Organization were to force the System to institute certain reforms, rather than to destroy the System, root and branch, and build something radically and fundamentally different in its place.

He was opposed to the System because it taxed his business too heavily. (He had owned a hardware store before we were forced underground.) He was opposed to the System's permissiveness with Blacks, because crime and rioting were bad for business. He was opposed to the System's confiscation of firearms, because he felt he needed a gun for personal security. His were the motivations of a libertarian, the sort of self-centered individual who sees the basic evil in government as a limitation on free enterprise.

Someone asked him whether he had forgotten what the Organization has repeated over and over, namely, that our struggle is to secure the future of our race, and that the issue of individual freedom is subordinate to that one, overwhelming purpose. His retort was that the Organization's violent tactics are benefiting neither our race nor individual freedom.

This answer proved again that he didn't really understand what we are trying to do. His initial approval of the use of force against the System was based on the naive assumption that, by God, we'll show those bastards! When the System, instead of backing down, began tightening the screws even faster, he decided that our policy of terrorism is counter-productive.

He simply could not accept the fact that the path to our goal cannot be a retracing of our course to some earlier stage in our history, but must instead be an overcoming of the present and a forging ahead into the future — with us choosing the direction instead of the System. Until we have torn the rudder out of its grasp and thrown the System overboard, the ship of state will go careening on its hazardous way. There will be no stopping, no going back. Since we are already among rocks and shoals, we are bound to get scraped up pretty badly before we find any clear sailing.

Maybe he was right that our tactics are wrong; the reaction of the people will eventually answer that question. But his whole attitude, his whole orientation was wrong. As I listened to Powell I was reminded of the late-19th century writer, Brooks Adams, and his division of the human race into two classes: spiritual man and economic man. Powell was the epitome of economic man.

Ideologies, ultimate purposes, the fundamental contradiction between the System's world view and ours — all these things had no meaning for him. He regarded the Organization's philosophy as just so much ideological flypaper designed to catch recruits for us. He saw our struggle against the System as a contest for power and nothing more. If we could not whip them, then we should try to force them to compromise with us.

I wondered how many others in the Organization thought the way Powell did, and I shuddered. We have been forced to grow too quickly. There has not been sufficient time to develop in all our people the essentially religious attitude toward our purpose and our doctrines which would have prevented the Powell incident by screening him out early.

As it was, we had no real choice in deciding Powell's fate. There was not only his disobedience to consider, but also the fact that he had revealed himself to be fundamentally unreliable. To have one of us — and a unit leader, at that — talking openly to other members about trying to find a way to compromise with the System, with the war just beginning . . . . There was only one way to deal with such a situation.

The eight male members present drew straws, and three of us, including me, ended up on the execution squad. When Powell realized that he was going to be killed, he tried to make a break. We tied his hands and feet, and then we had to gag him when he began shouting. We drove him to a wooded area off the highway about 10 miles south of Washington, shot him, and buried him.

I got back a little after midnight, but I still haven't been able to get to sleep. I am very, very depressed.

VIII

November 4, 1991. Soup and bread again tonight, and not much of that. Our money is almost gone, and there still hasn't been anything from WFC. If our pay doesn't come through in the next couple of days, we'll have to resort to armed robbery again — an unpleasant prospect.

Unit 2 still has what seems to be an unlimited supply of food, and we'd already be in a much worse way if they hadn't given us that carload of canned goods a month ago — especially since we now have seven mouths to feed. But it is just too dangerous to drive up to Maryland for our food supply. The chances are too great of running into a police roadblock.

That is the most noticeable — and to the public it must be by far the most irritating — consequence to date of our terror campaign. Travel by private automobile has become — at least, in the Washington area — a nightmare, with enormous traffic jams everywhere caused by the police checks. In the last few days this police activity has increased significantly, and it looks as if it will remain a regular feature of life for the foreseeable future.

So far, however, they haven't been stopping pedestrians, bicyclists, or buses. We can still get around, although less conveniently than before.

Oops, there go the lights again. This is the second time this evening we've had to break out the candles. Until this year, the worst power shortages have occurred in the summer, but it's November now and we're still stuck with the "temporary" 15 per cent voltage reduction they imposed in July. Even this perpetual "brownout" isn't saving us from an increasing number of involuntary blackouts.

It's obvious that somebody's profiting from the power shortage, though. When Katherine was lucky enough to find some candles at one of the grocery stores last week, she had to pay $1.50 apiece for them. The price of kerosene and gasoline lanterns has gone out of sight, but the hardware stores never have any of them in stock anyway. When I next have some free time, I'll see what I can improvise in that direction.

We have been maintaining the pressure against the System during the past week with a lot of one-man, low-risk activities. There have been approximately 40 grenade attacks against Federal buildings and media facilities in Washington, for example, and our unit is responsible for 11 of them.

Since it is now virtually impossible to enter any Federal building except a post office without a complete body-search, we have had to be ingenious. On one occasion Henry simply pulled the pin on a fragmentation grenade and then slipped it down between two cartons on a big pallet of freight waiting outside the freight door of the *Washington Post*, wedging it so that the safety lever was held in place by the cartons. He didn't wait around, but news reports later confirmed that there was an explosion inside the *Post* building which killed one employee and seriously wounded three others.

Most often, however, we have used grenade-throwers improvised from shotguns. They give us a maximum range of more than 150 yards, but the grenade always explodes sooner than that unless the delay element is modified. All one needs to use them effectively is a place of concealment within about 100 yards of the target.

We have fired from the back seat of a moving auto, from the restroom window of an adjacent building, and — at night — from a patch of shrubbery in a small park across the street from the target building. With luck one can hit a window and get an explosion inside an office or a corridor. But even when the grenade bounces off an outside wall the explosion shatters windows, and the shrapnel keeps people jumping.

If we keep it up long enough we can probably force the government to shutter all the windows in Federal buildings, which will certainly help raise the consciousness of Federal workers. But it is clear that we can't maintain this kind of activity indefinitely. We lost one of our best activists yesterday — Roger Greene, from Unit 8 — and we are bound to lose more as time passes. The System must inevitably win any sort of war of attrition, considering the numerical advantage they have over us.

We have talked this problem over among ourselves many times, and we always come back to the same stumbling block: a revolutionary attitude is virtually non-existent in America, outside the Organization, and all our activities to date don't seem to have changed this fact. The masses of people certainly aren't in love with the System — in fact, their grumbling has increased steadily over the past six or seven years as living conditions have deteriorated — but they are still far too comfortable and complacent to entertain the idea of revolt.

On top of this is the enormous disadvantage we suffer from having the System controlling the image of us which reaches the public. We receive a continuous feedback from our "legals" on what the public is thinking, and most people have accepted without hesitation the System's portrayal of us as "gangsters" and "murderers."

Without some sort of empathy between us and the general public we can never find enough new recruits to make up for our losses. And with the System controlling virtually every channel of communication with the public, it's hard to see how we're going to develop that empathy. Our leaflets and the occasional seizure of a broadcasting station for a few minutes just can't make much headway against the non-stop torrent of brainwashing the System uses for keeping the people in line.

The lights have just come on again — now that I'm ready to hit the sack. Sometimes I think the System's own weaknesses will bring about its downfall just as quickly without our help as with it. The incessant power failures are only one crack among thousands in this crumbling edifice we are trying so desperately to pull down.

November 8. The last few days have seen a major change in our domestic affairs. The population in our shop increased to eight last Thursday, and now it's down to four again: myself, Katherine, and Bill and Carol Hanrahan, formerly of Unit 6.

Henry and George have teamed up with Edna Carlson, who also came to us after Unit 6's disaster, and with Dick Wheeler, the only survivor of a police raid on Unit 11's hideout Thursday. The four of them have moved to a new location, in the District.

The new arrangement has us better divided along functional lines than before — as well as solving the personal problem which had been worrying Katherine and me. We here in the shop are now essentially a technical-services unit, while the four who left are a sabotage-and-assassination unit.

Bill Hanrahan is a machinist, a mechanic, and a printer. Until two months ago he and Carol operated a printing shop in Alexandria. His wife doesn't share his mechanical genius, but she is a reasonably competent printer. As soon as we get another press set up here, her job will be to produce many of the leaflets and other propaganda materials which the Organization clandestinely distributes in this area.

I will continue to be responsible for the Organization's communications equipment and for specialized ordnance. Bill will assist me with the latter and will also be our gunsmith and armory-keeper.

Katherine will have a chance to exercise her editorial skills again, to a limited extent, in that she will have the responsibility for tranforming the typewritten propaganda we receive from WFC into camera-ready headlines and text for Carol. She will be able to use her own discretion in making condensations, deletions, and other changes necessary for copy-fitting.

Bill and I finished our first special-ordnance job together yesterday. We modified a 4.2 inch mortar to handle 81 mm projectiles. The modification was necessary because we have so far been unable to pick up an 81 mm mortar for the projectiles which we grabbed in the raid on Aberdeen Proving Ground last month. One of our gun-buff members, however, had a serviceable 4.2 inch mortar which he had kept hidden away since the late 1940's.

The Organization is planning a very important mission in the next day or two, in which the mortar will be used, and Bill and I were under pressure to finish the job on time. Our main difficulty was in finding a piece of steel tube of the right I.D. to weld inside the 4.2 inch tube, since we have no lathe or other machine tools at this time. Once we found a supplier for the tube the rest was fairly easy, and we are proud of the result — although it weighs more than three times as much as an 81 mm mortar should.

Today we did a job which was simple enough in theory but which gave us more trouble in practice than we had anticipated: melting the explosive filler out of a 500-lb bomb casing. With a great deal of straining and swearing — and with several good burns from the boiling water we managed to splash all over ourselves — we got most of the tritonal explosive from the bomb into a variety of empty grapefruit-juice cans, peanut-butter jars, and other containers. The work took all day and exhausted everyone's patience, but now we have the makings for enough medium-sized bombs to last us for months.

I think that I will find Bill Hanrahan a congenial comrade-in-arms for carrying out our unit's new duties for the Organization. (We are now designated Unit 6, and I am in charge.) Certainly the new living arrangement here is more congenial for Katherine and me, now that we are sharing our building with another married couple instead of with two bachelors.

I just wrote "another married couple," but, of course, that was a slip of the pen, since Katherine and I are not formally married. In the last two months — and particularly in the last two or three weeks — however, we have experienced so much together and become so dependent on one another for companionship that a bond at least as strong as that of marriage has developed between us.

In the past, whenever one of us had an Organizational assignment to carry out, we usually contrived to work together on it. Now such collaboration will not require any contrivance.

It is interesting that the Organization, which has imposed on all of us a life which is unnatural in many respects, has led to a more natural relationship between the sexes inside the Organization than exists outside. Although unmarried female members are theoretically "equal" to male members, in that they are subject to the same discipline, our women are actually cherished and protected to a much larger degree than women in the general society are.

Consider rape, for example, which has become such an omnipresent pestilence these days. It had already been increasing at a rate of 20 to 25 per cent per year since the early 1970's until last year, when the Supreme Court ruled that all laws making rape a crime are unconstitutional, because they presume a legal difference between the sexes. Rape, the judges ruled, can only be prosecuted under the statutes covering non-sexual assaults.

In other words, rape has been reduced to the status of a punch in the nose. In cases where no physical injury can be proved, it is now virtually impossible to obtain a prosecution or even an arrest. The result of this judicial mischief has been that the incidence of rape has zoomed to the point that the legal statisticians have recently estimated that one out of every two American women can expect to be raped at least once in her lifetime. In many of our big cities, of course, the statistics are much worse.

The women's-lib groups have greeted this development with dismay. It isn't exactly what they had in mind when they bagan agitating for "equality" two decades ago. At least, there's dismay among the rank and file of such groups; I have a suspicion that their leaders, most of whom are Jewesses, had this outcome in mind from the beginning.

Black civil rights spokesmen, on the other hand, have had only praise for the Supreme Court's decision. Rape laws, they said, are "racist," because a disproportionately large number of Blacks have been charged under them.

Nowadays gangs of Black thugs hang around parking lots and school playgrounds and roam the corridors of office buildings and apartment complexes, looking for any attractive, unescorted White girl and knowing that punishment, either from the disarmed citizenry or the handcuffed police, is extremely unlikely. Gang rapes in school classrooms have become an especially popular new sport.

Some particularly liberal women may find that this situation provides a certain amount of satisfaction for their masochism, a way of atoning for their feelings of racial "guilt." But for normal White women it is a daily nightmare.

One of the sickest aspects of the whole thing is that many young Whites, instead of opposing this new threat to their race, have apparently decided to join it. White rapists have become more common, and there have even been instances of integrated rape-gangs recently.

Nor have the girls remained entirely passive. Sexual debauchery of every sort on the part of young White men and women — and even children in their pre-teens — has reached a level which would have been unimaginable only two or three years ago. The queers, the fetishists, the mixed-race couples, the sadists, and the exhibitionists — urged on by the mass media — are parading their perversions in public, and the public is joining them.

Just last week, when Katherine and I went into the District to pick up the salaries for our unit — which finally came through, when we were down nearly to our last can of soup — there was a nasty little incident. While we were waiting at a bus stop for a homeward-bound bus I decided to run into a drugstore a few feet away to buy a newspaper. I was gone for no more than 20 seconds, but when I came back a greasy-looking youth — approximately White, but with the "Afro" hair style popular among young degenerates — was taunting Katherine with obscenities while dancing and weaving around her like a boxer.

(*Note to the reader:* "Afro" refers to the Negro or African race, which, until its sudden disappearance during the Great Revolution, exerted an increasingly degenerative influence on the culture and life styles of the inhabitants of North America.)

I grabbed him by the shoulder, spun him around, and hit him in the face as hard as I could. As he went down I had the deep, primitive satisfaction of seeing four or five of his teeth come washing out of his shattered mouth on a copious flow of dark-red blood.

I reached into my pocket for my pistol, fully intending to kill him on the spot, but Katherine seized my arm, and caution returned. Instead of shooting him, I straddled him and directed three kicks at his groin with all my strength. He jerked convulsively and emitted a short, choking scream with the first kick, and then he lay still.

Passersby averted their eyes and hurried on. Across the street two Blacks gawked and hooted. Katherine and I hurried around the corner. We walked about six blocks, then doubled back and caught the bus at another stop.

Katherine told me later that the youth had run up to her as soon as I had entered the drugstore. He had put his arm around her, propositioned her, and started pawing her breasts. She is fairly strong and agile, and she was able to jerk away from him, but he blocked her from following me into the drugstore.

As a rule Katherine carries a pistol, but the day was unseasonably warm, unsuited for a coat, and she wore clothes which left no room for concealing a firearm. Since she was with me she hadn't even bothered to carry one of the tear-gas cannisters which have become essential articles of dress for women these days.

In that regard it is interesting to note that the same people who agitated so hysterically for gun confiscation before the Cohen Act are now calling for tear gas to be outlawed too. There have even been cases recently where women who used their tear gas to fend off would-be rapists have been charged with armed assault! The world has become so crazy that nothing really comes as a surprise any more.

In contrast to the situation outside, rape inside the Organization is almost unthinkable. But there is no doubt at all in my mind that if a genuine case of forcible rape did occur, the perpetrator would be rewarded with eight grams of lead within a matter of hours.

When we got back to the shop, Henry and another man were waiting for us. Henry wanted me to give him a final rundown on the sight settings for the mortar we had modified. When they left, they took the mortar with them. I still don't know what they will use it for.

Katherine and I are both very fond of Henry, and we will miss his presence in our new unit. He is the kind of person on whom the success of the Organization will ultimately depend.

Katherine had already taught Henry most of her tricks of makeup and disguise, and when he left with the mortar she gave him the greater part of her supply of wigs, beards, plastic gizmoes, and cosmetics.

IX

November 9, 1991. What a day! At two o'clock this afternoon an extraordinary session of the Congress convened to hear an address by the President. He was to ask for special legislation which would allow the government to stamp out "racism" and combat terrorism more effectively.

One thing he intended to ask the Congress for, according to the press, was the long-expected internal-passport law. Despite our destruction last month of the computer to be used with this passport program, the government is obviously pressing ahead with it.

The Capitol had been surrounded by somewhere between 3,000 and 5,000 secret policemen and armed, uniformed soldiers. Jeeps with mounted machine guns were everywhere. There were even two tanks and several APC's.

Members of the press and Congressional staffers had to pass through three separate rings of barricades and barbed wire, at each of which they were thoroughly searched for weapons, in order to approach the Capitol. Helicopters whirred overhead. No band of guerrillas bent on sabotage or assassination could have gotten within two blocks of the place, even in a suicide dash.

In fact, the government obviously overdid the security arrangements just to heighten the sense of urgency of the occasion. The spectacle of all the troops and guns around the Capitol left no doubt in the minds of the TV viewers, I am sure, that there is an emergency situation in the country which calls for the strongest possible measures from the government.

Then, as the TV cameras were preparing to switch from the crowded scene outside the Capitol to the speaker's podium in the House chamber, where the President would be speaking, a mortar round — although no one realized that's what it was —

exploded about 200 yards northwest of the building. TV watchers heard the explosion but couldn't see anything except an indistinct puff of gray smoke floating above the Capitol.

For the next few seconds there was general confusion. Soldiers with gas masks on were scurrying in one direction, while grim-faced secret policemen with drawn pistols were running in the other direction. The TV commentator announced breathlessly that someone had set off a bomb in one of the Capitol parking lots.

He babbled on for a little less than a minute, speculating as to who had done it, how they had managed to get the bomb past the security forces, how many persons had been hurt by the blast, and so on. Then the second round landed.

This one went off with a bang and a flash about 50 yards in front of the TV camera. It made almost a direct hit on a squad of soldiers manning a machine gun behind a heap of sandbags in the Capitol's east parking lot.

"It's our mortar!" I shouted. It must have also dawned simultaneously on every man with military experience watching the scene that a mortar was responsible for the two explosions.

Mortars are marvelous little weapons, especially for guerrilla warfare. They drop their deadly rounds silently and almost vertically onto their target. They can be fired from total cover, and persons in the target area cannot tell from which direction the projectiles are coming.

In this case I guessed immediately that our people were firing from a secluded, densely wooded area on the west bank of the Potomac, just over two miles from the Capitol. Henry and I had checked the area out some time ago for just such a purpose, because every important Federal building in Washington is within 81 mm-mortar range of it.

About 45 seconds after the second round the third one landed on the roof of the south wing of the Capitol and exploded inside the building. They had the range now, and the projectiles began raining down at four-to-five second intervals. Practically everyone, including most of the TV crews, had scrambled for cover, but one intrepid cameraman remained at his post.

We saw beautiful blossoms of flame and steel sprouting everywhere, dancing across the asphalt, thundering in the midst of splintered masonry and burning vehicles, erupting now inside and now outside the Capitol, wreaking their bloody toll in the ranks of tyranny and treason.

It was all over in about three minutes, but while it lasted it was the most magnificent spectacle I have ever seen. What an impression it must have made on the general public watching it on TV!

And there was more excitement today, both in California and New York. The Los Angeles City Council was convened for the sake of watching a telecast of the President's address to Congress before voting on several "anti-racist" ordinances of their own. Just about the time the fireworks started here, four of our men, using phony police identification, walked into the council meeting there and began throwing grenades. Eight council members were killed outright, and our men made a clean getaway.

An hour earlier, in New York, the Organization used a bazooka to shoot down an airliner which had just taken off for Tel Aviv with a load of vacationing dignitaries, mostly Jews. There were no survivors. (*Note to the reader:* A "bazooka" was a portable launcher for small rockets, used primarily as an infantry weapon against armored vehicles during World War II, 60-54 BNE, and already obsolete by 8 BNE. Tel Aviv was the largest city in Palestine during the period of Jewish occupation of that unfortunate country in the Old Era. The ruins of the city are still too radioactive for human habitation.)

All in all, it has been a busy day for the Organization! I am greatly invigorated by these demonstrations of our capability for launching multiple, simultaneous strikes against the System, and I am sure that the same is true of all our comrades.

Despite all the noise and smoke and wreckage caused by our attack on the Capitol, only 61 persons were killed, we learned from later news reports. Among these are two Congressmen, one sub-cabinet official, and four or five senior Congressional staffers. But the real value of all our attacks today lies in the psychological impact, not in the immediate casualties.

For one thing, our efforts against the System gained immeasurably in credibility. More important, though, is what we taught the politicians and the bureaucrats. They learned this afternoon that not one of them is beyond our reach. They can huddle behind barbed wire and tanks in the city, or they can hide behind the concrete walls and alarm systems of their country estates, but we can still find them and kill them. All the armed guards and bulletproof limousines in America cannot guarantee their safety. That is a lesson they will not forget.

Now they are all raging at us and solemnly promising the public that they will stamp us out, but after they have had a chance to think about it some of them will be ready to consider "buying insurance." The great weakness of the System is its utter moral corruption. They have us vastly outmanned and outgunned, but not one of their leaders is motivated by anything other than self-interest. They are ready to betray the System the instant they can see an advantage in doing so.

For now, we mustn't let them know that they are all inevitably headed for the gallows. Let them think they can make a deal with us and save their necks when the System falls. Only the Jews are under no illusions in this regard.

As for the public, it's a little early yet to know what the spectrum of their reactions to today's exploits will be. Most of them, of course, will believe just what they're told to believe. Basically, they want to be left alone with their beer and their television sets. Their mentality is a reflection of the movie-fan magazines and the TV sitcoms with which the System keeps them saturated. (*Note to the reader:* The word "sitcom" apparently refers to a type of television program popular during the last years of the Old Era.)

Nevertheless, we must carefully monitor the public's feelings toward the System and toward us. Although the great majority of them will continue to support the System as long as their refrigerators are kept full, it is from the public that we must draw our recruits in order to make up for our losses.

Our present inability to recruit is a source of great worry to everyone. Rumor has it that there has not been a single new recruit in the Washington area in the last two months. During that time we've lost approximately 15 per cent of our strength. I hope conditions aren't as bad elsewhere.

Of all the segments of the population from which we had hoped to draw new members, the "conservatives" and "right wingers" have been the biggest disappointment. They are the world's worst conspiracy-mongers — and also the world's greatest cowards. In fact, their cowardice is exceeded only by their stupidity.

The current conspiracy theory being circulated among conservatives is that the Organization is actually in the pay of the System. We are hired provocateurs whose job is to raise enough hell to justify the repressive counterrevolutionary and anti-racist measures the System is taking. If we would just stop rocking the boat, things would be easier on everyone. Whether they believe that theory or not, it gives them an excuse for not joining us.

At the other extreme, the knee-jerk liberals have forgotten all about their "radical chic" enthusiasm of a few years ago, now that we are the radicals. They take their ideological cues from the "smart" magazines and columnists, and the "in" thing at the moment is to be solidly pro-System. In their own way, the liberals, despite their pretensions to sophistication, are as mindless and as easily manipulated as the conservatives.

The Christians are a mixed bag. Some of them are among our most devoted and courageous members. Their hatred of the System is based on — in addition to the reasons the rest of us have — their recognition of the System's role in undermining and perverting Christendom.

But all the ones who are still affiliated with major churches are against us. The Jewish takeover of the Christian churches and corruption of the ministry are now virtually complete. The pulpit prostitutes preach the System's party line to their flocks every Sunday, and they collect their 30 pieces of silver in the form of government "study" grants, "brotherhood" awards, fees for speaking engagements, and a good press.

The libertarians are another group which is divided. About half of them support the System and half are against it. They are *all* against us, however. The ones who are against the System just happen to see the System as a bigger threat than the Organization. As our credibility grows, more and more libertarians will support the System. There is probably no way we can use this group.

No, there is not much hope for making inroads into any of these various ideological segments of the population. If we are able to find new recruits, it will be among those who are presently uncommitted.

The System's brainwashing has not bent everyone's mind out of shape. There are still millions and millions of good people out there who neither believe the System's propaganda nor have allowed themselves to be seduced to the animal-like level of existence of so many who live solely for the sake of gratifying their senses. How can we motivate these people to join us?

Life is uglier and uglier these days, more and more Jewish. But it is still moderately comfortable, and comfort is the great corrupter, the great maker of cowards. It seems that, for the time being, we have already caught all the real revolutionaries in America in our net. Now we must learn how to make some more, and quickly.

November 14. We had a visit from Henry today, and I learned some of the details of Monday's mortar attack on the Capitol. It had involved only three of our people: Henry and the man who helped him carry the mortar parts and the projectiles to their pre-selected firing spot in the woods and get everything set up, and a girl with a small transmitter in a park a few blocks from the Capitol who served as a spotter. She radioed range corrections to Henry's helper, while Henry dropped the projectiles into the tube. The range settings I had calculated had been almost perfect.

They used up all the 81 mm ammunition which was stolen from Aberdeen last month, and Henry wanted to know whether I could improvise some more. I explained to him the difficulty of the task.

Bombs we can make — fairly sophisticated ones, too. But mortar projectiles are something else. They are far too complex for our present capabilities. Anything I might be able to improvise would be a very crude approximation to the real thing, with nowhere near the accuracy. We will just have to raid another armory, with all the risks that entails, before we can use our mortar again.

Another thing I talked to Henry about is the rash of relatively minor bombings which have occurred in the last two or three days. There have been a hundred or more of them all around the country, including four in Washington, and they have puzzled me in several respects, mainly the choice of targets — banks, department stores, corporation offices — but also their apparent amateurishness. For every bomb which exploded, it seems that the police discovered at least one which fizzled.

Henry confirmed my suspicions: the bombings — at least, those in this area — are not the work of the Organization. That is interesting. We seem to have unintentionally galvanized some of the latent anarchists — or God knows what — who have been lurking in the woodwork.

The media, of course, have been attributing everything to us — which is embarrassing, in view of the amateurishness — but perhaps the phenomenon itself is not a bad development. At least, the secret police will have a lot more to keep them busy, and that will take some of the pressure off us.

The growth of nihilism, which the System has encouraged for so long, may now be paying off for us instead of for the System. Today I had a rather interesting experience myself in this regard.

I had to go into Georgetown to take care of a minor communications problem for Unit 4. Georgetown, once the most stylish area of Washington, has succumbed in the last five years to the same plague which has turned the rest of the nation's capital into an asphalt jungle. Most of the high-priced shops have given way to "gay" bars, massage parlors, porn stalls, liquor stores, and similar capitalist ventures. Garbage litters the sidewalks, and Blacks, who used to be pretty scarce there, are swarming all over.

But there are still many Whites living in Georgetown — after a fashion. The once-fashionable townhouses have their windows boarded up now, but many are occupied by colonies of squatters, mostly young dropouts and runaways.

They lead a marginal, brutal existence, begging for handouts in the streets, rummaging through trash bins for leftovers, occasionally stealing. Some of the girls engage in casual prostitution. Virtually all of them — or so I thought until today — keep themselves in a permanently drugged condition. Since the System stopped enforcing the drug laws last year, heroin has been about as cheap and easy to get as cigarettes.

The cops generally leave them alone, although some of the stories about what goes on among these kids are horrifying. Inside their strongholds, the boarded-up buildings in which they cook and eat and sleep and make love and give birth and pump dope into their veins and die, they seem to have reverted to a pre-civilized life style. Kooky religious cults, involving lots of incense and incantations, flourish among them. Various brands of Satan-worship, reminiscent of the ancient Semitic cults, are especially prevalent. Ritual torture and ritual murder are rumored to take place, as well as ritual cannibalism, ritual sex orgies, and other non-Western practices.

I had finished my chore for Unit 4 — which, having some of our more Bohemian members, blends more unobtrusively into the Georgetown scene than any of our other units could — and was headed back to the bus stop when I came across an all-too-familiar incident. Two young thugs — they looked like Puerto Ricans or Mexicans — were struggling on the sidewalk with a redheaded girl, trying to pull her into a doorway.

A prudent citizen would have passed by without interfering, but I stopped, watched for a moment, and then started toward the struggling trio. The two swarthy males were distracted just enough by my approach to give the girl a chance to break free. They glared at me and shouted a few obscenities, but they did not try to catch the girl, who quickly put a hundred feet or so between herself and her would-be abductors.

I turned and went on my way. The girl walked slowly, allowing me to catch up to her. "Thanks," she said, flashing me a warm smile. She was really quite pretty, but very shabbily dressed and no older than 17 — obviously one of Georgetown's "street people."

66

I chatted with her as we walked along. One of the first pieces of information I elicited from her was that she had not eaten in two days and was very hungry. We stopped at a sidewalk diner, and I bought her a hamburger and a milkshake. After that she was still hungry, so I bought another hamburger and some french fries for her.

While she ate we talked, and I learned several interesting things. One was that life among the dropouts is more diversified than I had thought. There are colonies which are on drugs and colonies which strictly abstain from drugs, colonies which are racially mixed and all-White colonies, sexually balanced colonies and all-male "wolf packs." The groups are also divided along religious-cult lines.

Elsa — that is her name — said she has never been on drugs. She left the group she was living with two days ago, after a domestic dispute, and was in the process of being dragged into the lair of a "wolf pack" when I happened by.

She also gave me some good leads as to who is responsible for the recent bombings which puzzled Henry and me. It seems to be general knowledge among her friends that several of the Georgetown colonies are "into that sort of thing — you know, trashing the pigs."

Elsa herself seems to be completely apolitical and not concerned one way or another about the bombings. I didn't want to pry too much and make her think I was a cop, so I didn't push her for more information on the subject.

Under the circumstances I really couldn't afford to bring Elsa back to our headquarters with me — but I still had to fight the temptation. I slipped her a five-dollar bill when we parted, and she assured me she would find a place for herself in one of the groups without difficulty. Probably she would go back to the group she had left. She gave me their address, so I could look her up.

Thinking it over this evening, it seems to me that we may be overlooking some potentially useful allies among these young dropouts. Individually they are not very impressive, to be sure, but it may very well be that we can make use of them in a collective way. It bears further consideration.

X

November 16, 1991. The response of the System to last week's mortar attack is taking shape. For one thing it's more difficult to move around in public now. Police and troops have greatly stepped up their spot checks, and they're stopping everyone, pedestrians as well as vehicles. There are announcements on the radio about once an hour warning people that they are subject to summary arrest if they are unable to establish their identity when stopped.

The Organization has already been able to furnish some of us with forged driver's licenses and other false identification, but it will be some time before everyone in the Washington area has been taken care of. Yesterday Carol had a close call. She had gone to a supermarket to buy the week's groceries for our unit, and a police patrol arrived while she was in the checkout line. They stationed men at each exit and required everyone leaving the store to show them satisfactory identification.

Just as Carol was ready to leave, there was a commotion at one exit. The police had been questioning a man who apparently ws carrying no identification, and he became belligerent. When the cops tried to put handcuffs on him he slugged one of them and tried to run.

They tackled him before he had gone more than a few feet, but the cops stationed at the other exits all ran over to help. Carol was able to slip out a temporarily unguarded exit with her groceries.

All this identity-checking has diverted the police from their regular duties, and the Blacks and other criminal elements are really taking advantage of it. Some Army personnel are also participating in the identity-checking and other police operations, but their main duty is still guarding government buildings and media facilities.

The most interesting development is that the Human Relations Councils have also been given emergency police powers, and they are "deputizing" large numbers of Blacks from the welfare rolls, the way they did for the Gun Raids. In the District and in Alexandria some of these deputized Blacks are already swaggering around and stopping Whites on the streets.

There are rumors that they are demanding bribes from those they stop, threatening them with arrest if they don't pay. And they have been hauling some White women into their "field headquarters" for "questioning." There they are stripped, gang-raped, and beaten — all in the name of the law!

The news media aren't breathing a word about these outrages, of course, but the word is still getting around. People are angry and frightened, but they don't know what to do. Without arms, there is little they *can* do. They are completely at the mercy of the System.

It's hard to figure why the System is deliberately stirring things up by deputizing Blacks again, after the enormous amount of resentment that caused two years ago. We've talked it over among ourselves in the unit, and our opinions are divided. Everyone but me seems to think that the events of last Monday panicked the System and caused them to overreact again.

Maybe, but I don't think so. They've had two months now to become used to the idea of a guerrilla war between them and us. And it's been nearly five weeks since we really bloodied their noses for the first time by blowing up the FBI building.

They know that our underground strength nationwide couldn't be more than 2,000 — and they must also know that they are wearing us down. I think they are unleashing the Blacks on the Whites strictly as a preventive measure. By terrifying the White population they will make it more difficult for us to recruit, thus speeding our demise.

Bill argues, to the contrary, that the White reaction to the renewed activities of the Human Relations Councils and their gangs of "deputies" will make recruiting easier for us. To a certain extent that was true in 1989, but White Americans have become so acclimatized to the growing openness of the System's tyranny in the last two years that I believe the latest move will serve more to intimidate than to arouse them. We'll see.

Meanwhile, there's a mountain of work waiting for me. Washington Field Command has requested that I furnish them with 30 new transmitters and 100 new receivers before the end of the year. I don't know how I can do it, but I'd better get started.

November 27. Until today, I've been working my tail off, day and night, trying to get the communications equipment built that WFC wants. Three days ago — Tuesday — I rounded up the last of the components needed and set up an assembly line here in the shop, pressing Carol and Katherine into service. By having them perform some of the simpler operations in the assembly process, I may be able to meet my deadline after all.

Yesterday, however, I received a summons from WFC which kept me away from the shop from early this morning until 10 o'clock tonight. One of the purposes of the summons was a "loyalty check."

I didn't know that before I reached the address I had been given, however. It was the little gift shop in which Harry Powell's trial took place.

A guard ushered me into a small office off the basement storeroom. Two men were waiting for me there. One was the

Major Williams from Revolutionary Command whom I met earlier. The other was a Dr. Clark — one of our legals — and, as I soon learned, a clinical psychologist.

Williams explained to me that the Organization has developed a testing process for new underground recruits. Its function is to determine the recruit's true motivations and attitudes and to screen out those sent to us as infiltrators by the secret police, as well as those deemed unfit for other reasons.

In addition to new recruits, however, a number of veteran members of the Organization are also being tested: namely, those whose duties have given them access to information which would be of special value to the secret police. My detailed knowledge of our communications system alone would put me in that category, and my work has also brought me into contact with an unusually large number of our members in other units.

We originally planned that no member in an underground unit would know the identity being used by — or the unit location of — any member outside his own unit. In practice, though, we have badly compromised that plan. The way things have developed in the last two months, there are now several of us in the Washington area who could betray — either voluntarily or through torture — a large number of other members.

We exercised great care in the recruiting and evaluation of new members after the Gun Raids, of course, but nothing like what I was subjected to this morning. There were injections of some drug — at least two, but I was in a fog after the first one and can't be sure how many more there were — and half-a-dozen electrodes were attached to various parts of my body. A bright, pulsing light filled my eyes, and I lost all contact with my surroundings, except through the voices of my interrogators.

The next thing I remember is yawning and stretching as I woke up on a cot in the basement nearly three hours later, although I was told that the interrogation itself lasted less than half an hour. I felt refreshed, with no apparent aftereffects of whatever drug I was given.

The guard came over to me as I stood up. I could hear muffled voices from the closed office; someone else was being interrogated. And I saw another man sleeping on a cot a few feet from mine. I suspect he had recently gone through the same process I had.

I was led into another basement room, a tiny cubicle containing only a chair and a small, metal table — actually, a typewriter stand. On the table was a black, plastic binder, perhaps two inches thick, of the sort in which typewritten reports are bound.

70

The guard told me that I was to read everything in the binder very carefully, and that Major Williams would then talk to me again. He pulled the door closed as he went out.

I had barely sat down when a girl brought me a plate of sandwiches and a mug of hot coffee. I thanked the girl, and, as I was hungry, I began sipping the coffee and munching a sandwich while I casually read the first page of the material in the binder.

When I finished the last page some four hours later I noticed that the sandwiches — including an uneaten portion of the one I had started — were still on the plate. The mug was nearly full of thoroughly cold coffee. It was as if I had just returned to earth — to the room — after a thousand-year voyage through space.

What I had read — it amounted to a book of about 400 typed pages — had lifted me out of this world, out of my day-to-day existence as an underground fighter for the Organization, and it had taken me to the top of a high mountain from which I could see the whole world, with all its nations and tribes and races, spread out before me. And I could see the ages spread out before me too, from the steaming, primordial swamps of a hundred million years ago to the unlimited possibilities which the centuries and the millennia ahead hold for us.

The book placed our present struggle — the Organization and its goals and what is at stake — in a much larger context than I have ever really considered before. That is, I had thought about many of the things in the book before, but I had never put them all together into a single, coherent pattern. I had never seen the whole picture so clearly. (*Note to the reader:* It is obvious that Turner is referring to the Book. We know from other evidence that it was written approximately ten years before the Record of Martyrs, in which it is mentioned — i.e., probably sometime in 9 BNE, or 1990 according to the old chronology. Turner mentions "typed pages," but it is not clear whether he means reproductions of typewritten pages or the originals themselves. If the latter is the case, then we may have here the only extant reference to the original copy of the Book! Several reproductions of the original typescript in binders fitting Turner's description have survived and are preserved in the Archives, but archeologists still have found no trace of the original.)

For the first time I understand the deepest meaning of what we are doing. I understand now why we *cannot* fail, no matter what we must do to win and no matter how many of us must perish in doing it. Everything that has been and everything that is yet to be depend on us. We are truly the instruments of God in the fulfillment of His Grand Design. These may seem like strange words to be coming from me, who has never been religious, but they are utterly sincere words.

I was still sitting there, thinking about what I had read, when Major Williams opened the door. He started to ask me to go with him, when he noticed that I hadn't finished my sandwiches. He brought another chair into the tiny room and invited me to finish eating while we talked.

I learned several very interesting things during our brief conversation. One is that, contrary to my earlier belief, the Organization *is* getting a steady trickle of new recruits. None of us had realized it, because WFC has been putting the new people into brand-new units. That's why the new communications equipment is needed.

Another thing I found out is that a significant fraction of the new recruits have been secret-police spies. Fortunately, the Organization's leadership foresaw this threat and devised a remedy in time. They realized that, once we went underground, the only way we could safely continue recruiting would be to screen new people in a foolproof way.

Here's the way it works: When our legals have someone who says he wants to join the Organization, he is turned over immediately to Dr. Clark. Dr. Clark's method of interrogation leaves no room for evasion or deceit. As Major Williams explained it, if the candidate flunks the test he never wakes up from his little nap afterward.

That way, the System can never find out why their spies are disappearing. So far, he said, we have caught more than 30 would-be infiltrators, including several women.

I shuddered to think what would have happened if my own interrogation had revealed me to be too unstable or lacking in loyalty to be trusted with what I know. And I felt a momentary flash of resentment that Dr. Clark, who is not even an underground member, should have held the decision of life or death for me in his hands.

The resentment quickly passed, however, when I considered that there is really no stigma to being a legal. The only reason Dr. Clark is not in the underground is that his name was not on the FBI's arrest list in September. Our legals play just as vital a role in our struggle as do those of us underground. They are vital to our propaganda and recruiting effort — our only close contact with the world outside the Organization — and they run even more of a risk of being found out and arrested than we do.

Major Williams must have sensed my thoughts, because he put his hand on my shoulder, smiled, and assured me that my test had gone very well. So well, in fact, that I was to be initiated into a select, inner structure within the Organization. Reading the book I had just finished was the first step in that initiation.

The next step took place about an hour later. Six of us were gathered in a loose semi-circle in the shop upstairs. It was after business hours, and the blinds were tightly drawn. The only light came from two large candles toward the back of the shop.

I was the next to the last to enter the room. At the top of the stairs the same girl who had brought my sandwiches stopped me and handed me a robe of some coarse, grey material with a hood attached — something like a monk's robe. After I had put on the robe she showed me where to stand and cautioned me to be silent.

Their features shadowed by their hoods, I could not make out the faces of any of my companions in that strange, little gathering. As the sixth participant reached the doorway at the top of the stairs, however, I turned and was startled to glimpse a tall, burly man in the uniform of a sergeant of the District of Columbia Metropolitan Police slipping into a robe.

Finally, from another door, at the back, Major Williams entered. He also wore one of the grey robes, but his hood was thrown back so that the two candles, one on either side, illuminated his face.

He spoke to us in a quiet voice, explaining that each of us who had been selected for membership in the Order had passed the test of the Word and the test of the Deed. That is, we have all proved ourselves, not only through a correct attitude toward the Cause, but also through our acts in the struggle for the realization of the Cause.

As members of the Order we are to be the bearers of the Faith. Only from our ranks will the future leaders of the Organization come. He told us many other things too, reiterating some of the ideas I had just read.

The Order, he explained, will remain secret, even within the Organization, until the successful completion of the first phase of our task: the destruction of the System. And he showed us the Sign by which we might recognize one another.

And then we swore the Oath — a mighty Oath, a moving Oath that shook me to my bones and raised the hair on the back of my neck.

As we filed out one by one, at intervals of about a minute, the girl at the door took our robes, and Major Williams placed a gold chain with a small pendant around each of our necks. He had already told us about these. Inside each pendant is a tiny, glass capsule. We are to wear them at all times, day and night.

Whenever danger is especially imminent and we might be captured, we are to remove the capsules from the pendants and carry them in our mouths. And if we are captured and can see no hope of immediate escape, we are to break the capsules with our teeth. Death will be painless and almost instantaneous.

Now our lives truly belong only to the Order. Today I was, in a sense, born again. I know now that I will never again be able to look at the world or the people around me or my own life in quite the same way I did before.

When I undressed for bed last night, Katherine immediately spotted my new pendant and asked about it, of course. She also wanted to know what I had been doing all day.

Fortunately, Katherine is the sort of girl with whom one can be completely truthful — a rare jewel, indeed. I explained to her the function of the pendant and told her that it is necessary because of a new task I am undertaking for the Organization — a task whose details I have obliged myself to tell no one, at least for the present. She was obviously curious, but she didn't press me further.

XI

November 28, 1991. A disturbing thing happened tonight which could have had fatal consequences for all of us. A carload of young junkies tried to break into the building here, evidently thinking it was deserted, and we had to dispose of all of them and their car. This is the first time something like this has happened, but the abandoned appearance of this place may invite more trouble of the same sort in the future.

We were all upstairs eating when the car pulled into our parking area and triggered our perimeter alarm. Bill and I went into the darkened garage downstairs and uncovered a peephole, so that we could see who was outside.

The car had cut off its lights, and one occupant had gotten out and was trying our door. He then began pulling loose the boards which were nailed over the glass in the door. Another youth got out and came over to help him. We couldn't see their features in the darkness, but we could hear them talking. They were obviously Negroes, and they obviously intended to get into the place, one way or another.

Bill tried to discourage them. In his best imitation-ghetto accent he shouted through the door: "Hey, man, dis place occupied. Move yo' ass on outa heah."

74

The two Blacks jumped back from the door, startled. They began whispering to one another, and two other figures from the car joined them. Then a dialogue began between Bill and one of the Blacks. It went about like this:

"We didn' know anybody was here, brother. We jes' lookin' for a place to shoot up."

"Well, now you knows. So, git!"

"Why you so hostile, brother? Let us in. We got some stuff and some chicks. You by yo'se'f?"

"No, I ain' by myse'f, an' I don' wan' no stuff. You jes' better move on, man." (*Note to the reader:* The dialect of the Negroes in America contained many special terms relating to drug usage, which was endemic among them up to the end. "Stuff" meant heroin, an opium derivative which was especially popular. To "shoot up" was to inject the heroin into a vein. Both the Negro's drug habits and much of his dialect spread to the White population of America during the period of government-enforced racial mixing in the last five decades of the Old Era.)

But Bill was unsuccessful in his attempt to discourage them. The second Black began a rhythmic pounding on the garage door, chanting over and over, "Open up, brother, open up." Someone in the car turned on a radio, and Negro music began blaring at a deafening volume.

Since the last thing we could afford was to attract the attention of the police or of someone at the trucking firm next door with a continuation of this noisy scene, Bill and I quickly made a plan. We armed both the girls with shotguns and posted them behind crates to one side of the shop area. I took a pistol, slipped out the rear door, and silently crept around the side of the building, so that I could cover the intruders from the outside. Then Bill announced, "Awright, awright. I open de do', man. You drive yo' car right in."

While Bill began raising the garage door, one of the Blacks went back to the car and started the engine. Bill stood to one side and kept his head lowered, so that when the car's lights hit him his white skin was not conspicuous. When everyone was inside, he began lowering the door again. The Blacks' car had not pulled in far enough for the door to close completely, however, and the driver ignored his command to move ahead another foot.

Then one of the Blacks on foot got a better look at Bill and immediately raised the alarm. "Dis ain' no brother," he cried.

Bill flipped on the shop lights, and the girls came out from their places of concealment as I slipped in under the partly closed door.

"Everyone out of the car and flat on the floor," Bill ordered, yanking open the door on the driver's side. "Come on, niggers, move!"

They looked at the four guns trained on them, and then they moved, although not without loud protest. Two of them, however, were not Negroes. When they were all stretched out on the concrete floor face down, all six of them, we saw that we had three Black males, one Black female — and two White sluts. I shook my head in disgust at the sight of the two White girls, neither of whom appeared to be over 18.

It didn't take long to decide what to do. We couldn't afford the noise of gunshots, so I took a heavy crowbar and Bill picked up a shovel. We started at opposite ends of the crew on the floor, while the girls kept them covered with their shotguns. We worked quickly but precisely, one blow on the back of the head sufficing for each of them.

Until the last two, that is. The blade of Bill's shovel glanced off the skull of one of the Black males and struck the shoulder of the White girl beside him, cutting into her flesh but not inflicting a lethal wound. Before I could bring my crowbar into play to finish her off, the little bitch was up like a shot.

I had pushed the garage door down as far as I could after coming in, but it still had not latched properly and had meanwhile crept up about six inches. She scooted through this narrow opening and headed for the street, with me about 10 yards behind her.

I froze with horror as I saw an arc of light swing along the dark pavement just in front of the running girl. A large truck was turning into the street from the parking lot next door. If the girl reached the street she would be illuminated by the truck's headlights, and the driver could not fail to see her.

Without hesitation I raised my pistol and fired, instantly dropping the girl in her tracks beside the weed-overgrown fence separating our parking area from that of the trucking firm. It was a very lucky shot, not only in its effect, but also in that the roar from the engine of the accelerating truck effectively masked the report. I crouched in the driveway, drenched in a cold sweat, until the truck had thundered off into the distance.

Bill and I loaded the six corpses into the back of the Blacks' car. He drove it off, with Carol following him in our vehicle, and left the grisly cargo parked outside a Black restaurant in downtown Alexandria. Let the police figure it out!

The work on the new communications equipment is coming along quite well. The girls put so many units together before

76

supper today — and the unfortunate events of the evening — that I couldn't keep up with the tuning and testing, which is my part of the work. If I had a better oscilloscope and a few other instruments, I could do more.

November 30. In thinking over Saturday's events, what surprises me is that I feel no remorse or regret for killing those two White whores. Six months ago I couldn't imagine myself calmly butchering a teen-aged White girl, no matter what she had done. But I have become much more realistic about life recently. I understand that the two girls were with the Blacks only because they had been infected with the disease of liberalism by the schools and the churches and the plastic pop-culture the System churns out for young people these days. Presumably, if they had been raised in a healthy society they would have had some racial pride.

But such considerations are irrelevant to the present phase of our struggle. Until we have in our hands the means for bringing about a general cure for the disease, we must deal with it by other means, just as one must ruthlessly weed out and dispose of diseased animals in any flock, unless one wants to lose the whole flock. This is no time for womanly hand-wringing.

This lesson was brought home forcefully to all of us by what we saw on the TV news this evening. The Human Relations Council in Chicago organized a huge "anti-racism" rally today. The purported excuse for the rally was to protest the machine-gunning of a carload of Black "deputies" Friday, in downtown Chicago in broad daylight, presumably by the Organization. Only three Blacks were killed in the incident, but the System seized on it in order to squelch the seething White resentment against the Human Relations Councils and their deputized Black goon squads. Apparently these Black "deputies" have perpetrated even more shocking outrages against defenseless Whites in Chicago than they have around here.

The Chicago rally, which was vigorously promoted by all the mass media in the Chicago area, involved nearly 200,000 demonstrators in its initial stage — more than half of them Whites. Hundreds of special buses, contributed by the city transit authorities, brought in people from all the suburbs for the occasion. Thousands of young Black thugs, wearing the armbands of the Chicago Human Relations Council, strutted arrogantly through the huge mob — "maintaining order."

The rally was addressed by all the usual political prostitutes and pulpit prostitutes, who issued pious calls for "brotherhood"

77

and "equality." Then the System trotted out one of their local Toms, who gave a rousing speech about stamping out "the evil of White racism" once and for all. (*Note to the reader:* A "Tom" was a Negro front man for the authorities or for Jewish interests. Experts at manipulating the masses of their own race, they were paid well for their services. Some "Toms" were even employed briefly by the Organization during the final stages of the Revolution, when it was desired to flush millions of Negroes out of certain urban areas into holding camps with a minimum loss of White lives.)

After that, the skilled agitators of the Human Relations Council worked various sections of the crowd up into a real brotherhood frenzy. These swarthy, kinky-haired little Jewboys with transistorized megaphones really knew their business. They had the mob screaming with real blood lust for any "White racist" who might be unfortunate enough to fall into their hands.

Chanting "Kill the racists" and other expressions of brotherly love, the mob began a march through downtown Chicago. Shoppers, workers, and businessmen on the sidewalks were ordered by the Black "deputies" to join the march. Anyone who refused was beaten without mercy.

Then gangs of Blacks began going into the stores and office buildings along the march route, using bullhorns to order everyone out into the street. Usually it was only necessary to kick one or two stubborn Whites into a senseless, bloody pulp before the rest of the occupants of a department store or building lobby got the idea and enthusiastically joined the demonstration.

As the crowd swelled, approaching a half-million persons toward the end, the Blacks with the armbands became more and more belligerent. Any White in the crowd who looked as if he wasn't chanting loudly enough was likely to be attacked.

And there were several particularly vicious incidents which the TV cameras gloatingly zoomed in on. Someone in the crowd started the rumor that a book store they were approaching sold "racist" books. Within a minute or two a group of several hundred demonstrators — mostly young Whites this time — had split off from the main crowd and converged on the book store. Windows were smashed, and teams of demonstrators inside the store began hurling armloads of books to others outside.

After an initial flurry of rage was dissipated by wildly tearing handsful of pages from the books and throwing them into the air, a bonfire was started on the sidewalk for the rest of the books. Then they dragged out a White salesclerk and began beating him. He fell to the pavement, and the mob surged over him, stomping

78

and kicking. The television screen showed a closeup of the scene. The faces of the White demonstrators were contorted with hatred — for their own race!

Another incident in which the TV viewers were treated to closeup coverage was the killing of a cat. A large, white alley cat was spotted by someone in the crowd, who started the cry, "Get the honky cat!" About a dozen demonstrators took off down an alley after the unfortunate cat. When they reappeared a few moments later, holding up the bloody carcass of the cat, an exultant cheer went up from those in the crowd near enough to see what had happened. Sheer insanity!

It is impossible to put into words how depressed we all are by the spectacle in Chicago. That, of course, was the aim of the organizers of the rally. They are expert psychologists, and they thoroughly understand the use of mass terror for intimidation. They know that millions of people who still oppose them inwardly will now be too frightened to open their mouths.

But how could our people — how could White Americans — be so spineless, so crawling, so eager to please their oppressors? How can we recruit a revolutionary army from such a rabble?

Is this really the same race that walked on the moon and was reaching for the stars 20 years ago? How low we have been brought!

It is frighteningly clear now that there is no way to win the struggle in which we are engaged without shedding torrents — veritable rivers — of blood.

The carload of carrion we left in Alexandria Saturday was mentioned briefly on the local news but not at all on the national news. The reason for the downplay, I suspect is not that sextuple killings have become too commonplace to be newsworthy, but that the authorities recognized the racial significance of the thing and decided not to encourage imitation.

XII

December 4, 1991. I went over to Georgetown today to talk to Elsa, the little redheaded "dropout" I met there a couple of weeks ago. The reason for my visit was to try to make a better evaluation of the potential of some of Elsa's friends for playing a role in our fight against the System.

Actually, some of them — or, at least, people in similar circumstances — already are involved in their own war against the System. In the last month there's been a bewildering proliferation of incidents in which the Organization has not been involved. These have included bombings, arson, kidnaping, violent public demonstrations, sabotage, death threats against prominent figures, even two widely publicized assassinations. Credit for the various incidents has been claimed by so many different groups — anarchists, tax rebels, "liberation fronts" of one stripe or another, half-a-dozen far-out religious cults — that no one can keep up with it all. Every nut with an ax to grind seems to have gotten into the act.

Most of these people are such careless amateurs that even our racially integrated FBI has been doing a fairly creditable job of rounding them up, but more seem to keep cropping up. The general atmosphere of revolutionary violence and governmental counter-violence that the Organization's activities have brought on is apparently responsible for encouraging most of them.

The most interesting aspect of all this is the proof it represents that the System's grip on the minds of the citizenry is less than total. Most Americans, of course, are still marching in mental lockstep with the high priests of the TV religion, but a growing minority have broken step and regard the System as an enemy. Unfortunately, their hostility is usually based on the wrong reasons, and it would be nearly impossible to coordinate their activities.

In fact, in the great majority of cases there is no reasoned basis at all for their activity. It is really just a massive venting of frustrations in the form of *vandalism* rather than political terrorism. They just want to smash something, to inflict some injury on the people they see as responsible for the unlivable world they are forced to live in. Vandalism on the massive scale we are seeing now is something with which the political police simply cannot continue to cope for very long. It is running them ragged.

Besides the political vandals and the loonies, two other segments of the population have been playing an important role in recent events: the Black separatists and the organized criminals. Until a few weeks ago everyone assumed that the System had finally bought off the last of the nationalist-minded Blacks back in the '70's. Apparently they've just been lying low and minding their own business, and now they see a chance to get a few licks in. Mostly they seem to have been blowing up the offices of Tom groups and shooting each other, but they organized a pretty good riot in New Orleans last week, in which there was a lot of window-breaking and looting. More power to them!

The Mafia, two or three of the big labor unions they own, and a couple of other organized-crime groups have been capitalizing on the disorder and the public apprehension by substantially stepping up their extortion activities. When they tell a businessman or a merchant that they'll bomb his place of business unless he coughs up a "protection" payment, they are more likely to be believed than they were a few months ago. And kidnaping has become a big business. The cops are too busy working on things the System is really worried about (namely, us) to bother the professional thugs, and they are having a field day.

Taking a strictly cold-blooded view, we must welcome even this upsurge in crime, since it helps to undermine the confidence of the public in the System. But the day must also come when we will take every one of these elements which the System's "bought" judges have coddled for so long and put them up against the wall without further ado — along with the judges.

I knocked at the address Elsa gave me — it is the basement entrance of what was once an elegant townhouse — and when I asked for Elsa I was invited in by an obviously pregnant young woman with a bawling infant in her arms. When my eyes adjusted to the dim light, I saw that the whole basement is being used as a communal living area. Blankets and sheets tied to the pipes which run along the low ceiling serve to crudely partition off half-a-dozen corners and niches as semi-private sleeping areas. In addition, there are several mattresses on the floor in the main portion of the basement. Other than a card table next to the laundry sink, where two young women were washing some cooking utensils, there is no furniture, not even a chair.

Against one wall there is an ancient, wood-burning stove, which gives off the only heat in the basement. As I learned later, running water is the only public utility which the little commune has at its disposal, and they obtain fuel for their stove by scavenging in the neighborhood or by sending a raiding party upstairs to break up doors, bannisters, window jambs, even floorboards. Another, larger commune occupies the upper portion of the house, beyond the heavily barricaded steel door at the head of the basement stairs, but they often indulge in wild drug parties, after which they are in no condition to repel fuel-raiders from downstairs.

The basement dwellers shun hard drugs and regard themselves as quite superior to the upstairs people. They nevertheless prefer the grubby basement for themselves, because it is easier to heat and easier to defend than upstairs, the only windows being a few tiny, dirt-streaked panes near the ceiling, far too small to admit any hostile intruder. In addition, it is cooler in the summer.

Seven or eight of them were sprawled on mattresses, watching some inane "game" program on a battery-powered television receiver and smoking marijuana cigarettes, when I entered. The whole place was permeated by the stink of stale beer, unwashed laundry, and marijuana smoke. (They don't regard marijuana as a drug.) Two small boys, about four years old, both stark naked, were rolling on the floor and fighting near the stove. A gray cat, perched comfortably on one of the idle heating pipes near the ceiling, stared down at me curiously.

The people on the mattresses, though, after a brief glance, paid no further attention to me. I could see that none of the faces illuminated by the TV screen was Elsa's. When the girl who had admitted me called out her name, however, one of the blanket-partitions in a far corner was suddenly thrust aside, and Elsa's head and bare shoulders became momentarily visible. She squealed with delight when she saw me, ducked back behind her blanket, and emerged a moment later in her "granny" dress. I was vaguely disturbed to catch a glimpse of another form on the mattress in the dim recess as Elsa parted the blanket and came out. A twinge of jealousy?

Elsa gave me a quick hug of genuine affection and then offered me a cup of steaming coffee, which she poured from a battered pot on the stove. I gratefully accepted the coffee, for the walk from the bus stop had thoroughly chilled me. We sat on an unoccupied mattress near the stove. The sound from the TV and the noise being made by the crying baby and the two scuffling boys allowed us to talk in relative privacy.

We talked of many things, for I didn't want to blurt out immediately the true reason for my visit. I learned a lot about Elsa and the people she is living with. Some of the things I learned saddened me, and some profoundly shocked me.

I was saddened by Elsa's story of herself. She is the only child of upper-middle-class parents. Her father is (or was — she hasn't been in touch with her family for more than a year) a speech writer for one of the most powerful Senators in Washington. Her mother is an attorney for a left-wing foundation whose principal activity is buying up houses in White, suburban neighborhoods and moving Black welfare families into them.

Until she was 15 Elsa had been very happy. Her family had lived in Connecticut until then, and Elsa had attended an exclusive, private school for girls. (Single-sex schools are illegal now, of course.) She spent the summers with her parents at their vacation home on the beach. Elsa's face glowed as she described the woods and trails around their summer home and the long walks she took by herself. She had her own little sailboat and often sailed to a tiny island offshore for private picnics and long, happy hours of lying in the sun and daydreaming.

Then the family moved to Washington, and her mother insisted that they take an apartment in a predominantly Black neighborhood near Capitol Hill, rather than living in a White suburb. Elsa was one of only four White students at the junior-high school to which they sent her.

Elsa had developed early. Her natural warmth and open, uninhibited nature combined with her outstanding physical charms to produce a girl who had been extraordinarily attractive sexually even at 15. The result was that the Black males, who also continually badgered the one other White girl at the school, gave Elsa no peace. The Black girls, seeing this, hated Elsa with special passion and tormented her in every way they could.

Elsa dared not go into the restroom or even let herself out of the sight of a teacher for a moment while she was at school. She soon found that the teachers offered no real protection, when a Black assistant principal cornered her in his office one day and tried to put his hand inside her dress.

Each day Elsa came home from school in tears and begged her parents to send her to another school. Her mother's response was to scream at her, slap her face, and call her a "racist." If the Black boys were bothering her, it was her fault, not theirs. And she should try harder to make friends with the Black girls.

Nor did her father offer her any comfort, even when she told him about the incident with the assistant principal. The whole issue embarrassed him, and he didn't want to hear about it. His liberalism was more passive than her mother's, but he was usually intimidated by his thoroughly "liberated" wife into going along on any matters that touched on race. Even when three young, Black thugs accosted him on his very doorstep, took his wallet and wristwatch, and then knocked him down and stomped on his eyeglasses, Elsa's mother wouldn't let him call the police and report the robbery. She regarded the very thought of filing a police complaint against Blacks as somewhat "fascist."

Elsa stood it for three months, and then she ran away from home. She was taken in by the little commune she is with now, and, having a basically cheerful disposition, she learned to be tolerably happy in her new situation.

Then, about a month ago, the trouble arose which led to my meeting her. A new girl, Mary Jane, had joined their group, and there was friction between Elsa and Mary Jane. The boy Elsa was sharing her mattress with at the time had apparently known Mary Jane earlier, before either had joined the group, and Mary Jane regarded Elsa as a usurper. Elsa in turn resented Mary Jane's none-too-subtle efforts to entice her boyfriend away. The result was a screaming, clawing, hairpulling fight between the two one day which Mary Jane, being the stronger, had won.

Elsa had wandered the streets for two days — that's when I met her — and then she had returned to the basement commune. Mary Jane, meanwhile, had gotten on the wrong side of another of the girls in the group, and Elsa pressed this advantage by issuing an ultimatum: either Mary Jane must go or she, Elsa, would leave permanently. Mary Jane had responded by threatening Elsa with a knife.

"So, what happened?" I asked.

"We sold her," was Elsa's simple reply.

"You *sold* her? What do you mean?" I exclaimed.

Elsa explained: "Mary Jane refused to leave after everyone sided with me, so we sold her to Kappy the Kike. He gave us the TV and two hundred dollars for her."

"Kappy the Kike," it turned out, is a Jew named Kaplan who makes his living in the White slave trade. He makes regular trips to Washington from New York for the purpose of buying runaway girls. His usual suppliers are the "wolf packs," from one of which I had rescued Elsa. These predatory groups snatch girls off the street, keep them for a week or so, and then, if their disappearance has caused no comment in the newspapers, sell them to Kaplan.

What happens to the girls after that no one can say with certainty, but it is thought that most are confined in certain exclusive clubs in New York where the wealthy go to satisfy strange and perverted appetites. Some, it is rumored, are eventually sold to a Satanist club and painfully dismembered in gruesome rituals. Anyway, someone in the commune had heard that Kaplan was in town and "buying," so when Mary Jane wouldn't leave they tied her up, located Kaplan, and made the sale.

I had thought I was unshockable, but I was horrified by Elsa's story of Mary Jane's fate. "How," I asked in a tone of outrage, "could you sell a White girl to a Jew?" Elsa was embarrassed by my obvious displeasure. She admitted that it was a terrible thing to have done and that she sometimes feels guilty when she thinks about Mary Jane, but it had seemed like a convenient solution to the commune's problem at the time. She offered the feeble excuse

84

that it happens all the time, that the authorities apparently know all about it and don't interfere, and so it is really more society's fault than anyone's.

I shook my head in disgust, but this turn of our conversation gave me a convenient opening to the topic in which I was mainly interested. "A civilization which tolerates the existence of Kaplan and his filthy business should be burned to the ground," I said. "We should make a bonfire of the whole thing and then start over fresh."

I had unconsciously raised my voice loud enough for my last comment to be heard by everyone in the basement. A shaggy individual got up from his mattress in front of the TV and sauntered over. "What can anyone do?" he asked, not really expecting an answer. "Kappy the Kike's been arrested at least a dozen times, but the cops always turn him loose. He's got political connections. Some of the big Jews in New York are his customers. And I've heard that two or three Congressmen go up there regularly to visit some of the clubs he supplies."

"Then someone should blow up the Congress," I answered.

"I guess that's already been tried," he laughed, apparently referring to the Organization's mortar attack.

"Well, if I had a bomb now I'd try it myself," I said. "Where can I get some dynamite?"

The fellow shrugged his shoulders and wandered back to the TV set. I then tried pumping Elsa for information. Which groups in Georgetown have been doing bombings? How can I get in touch with one of them?

Elsa tried to be helpful, but she just didn't know. It was a subject in which she had no particular interest. Finally, she called out to the man who had strolled over earlier: "Harry, aren't the people over on 29th Street, the ones who call themselves 'Fourth World Liberation Front,' into fighting the pigs?"

Harry was obviously not pleased by her question. He jumped to his feet, glared fiercely at the two of us, and then stomped out of the basement without answering, slamming the door behind him.

One of the women at the laundry sink turned around and reminded Elsa that it was her day to prepare the midday meal and that she hadn't even put the potatoes on the stove to boil yet. I squeezed Elsa's hand, wished her well, and made my exit.

I guess I botched things rather badly. It was incredibly naive of me to imagine that I could just walk into the "dropout" community and be politely directed to someone engaged in violent and illegal activity against the System. Obviously every undercover cop in Washington has been trying the same thing. Now the word must certainly be out everywhere that I'm a cop too. That blows any chance I may have had of making contact with anti-System militants in that particular milieu.

Of course, we could send someone else over to try to find the "Fourth World Liberation Front," whatever the hell it is. But I wonder now whether there's any point in that. My visit with Elsa has pretty well convinced me that, in the people who share her life-style, there's just not much potential for constructive collaboration with the Organization. They lack self-discipline and any real sense of purpose. They've given up. All they really want to do is lie around all day screwing and smoking pot. I almost believe that if the government would double their welfare allowances, even the bomb throwers would lose their militance.

Elsa is basically a good kid, and there must be a number of others whose instincts are mostly all right but who just couldn't cope with this nightmare world and so they dropped out. Although we both reject the world in its present condition and have both dropped out, in a sense, the difference between the people in the Organization and Elsa's friends is that we are capable of coping and they aren't. I cannot imagine myself or Henry or Katherine or anyone else in the Organization just sitting around watching TV and letting the world go by when so much needs to be done. It is a difference of human quality.

But there's more than one kind of quality that's important to us. Most Americans are still coping, some barely and some quite successfully. They haven't dropped out, because they lack a certain sensitivity — a sensitivity which I believe we in the Organization share with Elsa and the best of her friends — a sensitivity which allows us to smell the stink of this decaying society and which makes us gag. The copers out there, just like many of the non-copers, either can't smell the stink or it doesn't bother them. The Jews could lead them to any kind of pigsty at all, and as long as there was plenty of swill they would adapt to it. Evolution has made skilled survivors of them, but it has failed them in another respect.

How fragile a thing is man's civilization! How superficial it is to his basic nature! And upon how few of the teeming multitudes to whose lives it gives a pattern does it depend for its sustenance!

Without the presence of perhaps one or two per cent of the most capable individuals — the most aggressive, intelligent, and hardworking of our fellow citizens — I am convinced that neither this civilization nor any civilization could long sustain itself. It would gradually disintegrate, over centuries, perhaps, and the people would not have the will or the energy or the genius to patch up the cracks. Eventually, all would return to their natural, pre-civilized state — a state not too different from that of Georgetown's dropouts.

But even energy and will and genius are not enough, clearly. America still has enough over-achievers to keep the wheels turning. But these over-achievers seem not to have noticed that the machine their exertions keep running long ago ran off the road and is now hurtling headlong into an abyss. They are insensitive to the ugliness and unnaturalness, as well as to the ultimate danger, of the direction they have taken.

It is really only a minority of a minority which led our race out of the jungle and along the first few steps toward true civilization. We owe everything to those few of our ancestors who had both the sensitivity to *feel* what needed doing and the ability to do it. Without the sensitivity no amount of ability can lead to truly great achievement, and without the ability sensitivity leads only to daydreams and frustration. The Organization has selected from the great mass of humanity those of our present generation who posses this rare combination. Now we must do whatever is necessary to prevail.

XIII

March 21, 1993. Today a new beginning. Quite a coincidence that it's the first day of spring. For me it is like a return from the dead — 470 days of living death. To be back with Katherine, back with my other comrades, able to resume the struggle again after so much wasted time — the thought of these things fills me with an indescribable joy.

So much has happened since my last entry in this diary (how glad I am that Katherine was able to save it for me!) that it's difficult to decide how to condense it all here. Well, first things first.

It was about four o'clock in the morning, pitch dark, a Sunday. We were all sound asleep. The first thing I remember is Katherine shaking me by the shoulder, trying to wake me up. I could hear an insistent buzzing in the background, which, in my sleep-fogged condition, I assumed was our bedroom alarm clock.

"Surely, it's not time to get up yet," I mumbled.

"It's the warning buzzer downstairs," Katherine whispered urgently. "Somebody's outside the building."

That snapped me awake, but before I could even get my feet on the floor, there was a loud crash, as something trailing a stream of sparks came hurtling through the carefully boarded-up bedroom window. Almost immediately the room was filled with a choking cloud of gas, and I was gasping for breath in agony.

The next couple of minutes are a little hazy in my memory. Somehow we all got our gas masks on without turning on any lights. Bill and I raced downstairs, leaving Katherine and Carol to man the upstairs windows. Fortunately, no one had yet tried to enter the building, but as Bill and I reached the bottom of the stairs we could hear someone outside with a bullhorn ordering us to come out with our hands up.

I took a quick look through our peephole. The darkness outside had been turned bright as day by dozens of searchlights, all trained on our building. The glare kept me from seeing much of anything beyond the lights, but it was instantly clear that there were several hundred troops and policemen, with lots of equipment, out there.

It was obviously futile to attempt to shoot our way out, but we laid down a brief barrage anyway — half-a-dozen quick shots each — from the upstairs and downstairs windows, front and back, just to discourage the people outside from attempting to force a quick entry into the building. After that, we all stayed clear of the windows and doors, which were immediately riddled with a withering return fire, and concentrated on getting as much of our essential equipment out through our escape tunnel as we could. The cement-block walls of the garage offered protection from the small-arms fire being sprayed at us from every direction.

Bill, Katherine, and Carol relayed our gear down the long, dark tunnel, while I stayed in the shop and gathered together for them the things I thought we should try to save. In a frantic and exhausting three-quarters of an hour, they assembled a small mountain of armaments and communications equipment in the drainage ditch at the far end of the tunnel.

Although the three of them did most of the carrying, at least they were not in danger of being shot. I had bullets whistling around my ears the whole while, and I was stung at least a dozen times by splinters of concrete chipped from the walls by ricochets. I still don't understand how I avoided being killed. I even managed to fire a few rounds back through the door at our attackers every five minutes or so, just to keep them under cover.

Finally, we had gotten out all our small arms and ammunition, about half our bulk explosives and heavier weapons, and all the completed communications units. Bill's tools were saved, because

88

he has the tidy habit of keeping them all together in a tool box, but we abandoned most of my test equipment, because it was scattered all over the shop.

We huddled briefly in the grease pit and decided that Bill and the girls would steal a vehicle and load our things into it while I stayed in the shop and prepared a demolition charge that would cover the entrance of our escape tunnel. I would give them 30 minutes, then I would light the fuse and make my own exit.

Katherine broke away and ran quickly back upstairs, where she grabbed some of our personal items — including my diary — and then I shooed her back into the tunnel with the others for the last time.

The downstairs doors and the boards over the windows were about half shot away by this time, and so much light was coming into the shop from the searchlights that any movement was becoming extremely hazardous. Working with nervous haste, I assembled a 20-pound charge of tritonal in the grease pit, just above the tunnel entrance, and primed it.

Then I crawled along the floor, heading for the wall where approximately another 100 pounds of tritonal was stacked in small containers. I intended to run a length of primacord from that batch to the charge in the grease pit, so that the whole shop would go up in one blast, thoroughly covering everything in rubble. It would take the cops a couple of days to sift through the debris and discover that we had escaped.

But I never made it to the wall. Somehow — I still don't understand exactly what happened — the charge in the grease pit exploded prematurely. Perhaps a ricocheting bullet hit the primer. Or perhaps sparks from one of the tear gas grenades which were still being lobbed into the place ignited the fuse. In any event, the concussion knocked me cold — and very nearly killed me. I regained consciousness on an operating table in a hospital emergency room.

The next few days were extraordinarily painful ones. I wince at the memory. I was taken directly from the emergency room to an interrogation cell in the sub-basement of the FBI building, which was still only partially cleared of the rubble from our bombing seven weeks earlier.

Although I was still disoriented and in extreme pain from my wounds, I was handled very roughly. My wrists were tightly handcuffed behind me, and I was kicked and punched whenever I stumbled or failed to respond fast enough to an order. Forced to stand in the center of the cell while half-a-dozen FBI agents shouted questions at me from all sides, I could hardly do more than mumble incoherently, even if I had wanted to cooperate with them.

Even in my agony, however, I felt a surge of elation when I realized from my interrogators' questions that the others must have gotten away safely. Over and over again the men around me screamed out the same questions: "Where are the others? How many were in the building with you? How did they get out?" Apparently, the charge in the grease pit had successfully obliterated the tunnel entrance. The questions were punctuated with repeated slaps and kicks, until I finally sagged to the floor, mercifully unconscious again.

When I came to, I was still lying where I had fallen, on the bare, concrete floor. The light was on, no one else was in the room, and I could hear the chattering of pneumatic hammers and other sounds being made by repairmen working in the corridor beyond my cell door. I ached all over, with the handcuffs causing me particular agony, but my head was nearly clear.

My first thought was one of regret that I no longer had my poison capsule. The secret police, of course, had taken my little necklace away as soon as they had found my unconscious body in the wreckage of the garage. I cursed myself for having failed to take the precaution of carrying the capsule in my mouth before the explosion. Probably it wouldn't have been found there, and I could have bitten it as soon as I woke up in the hospital. In the days to come, this regret was to recur again and again.

My second thought was also one of regret and self-recrimination. I was tormented by a suspicion so strong that it nearly amounted to certainty that my ill-advised visit to Elsa two days earlier was responsible for my predicament. Evidently, someone from Elsa's group had followed me home and then had informed on me. This suspicion was later confirmed indirectly by my captors.

I was alone with my aches and somber thoughts for only a few minutes before my second interrogation session began. This time two FBI agents came into my cell, followed by a physician and three other men, two of the last three being large, muscular-looking Negroes. The third man was a stooped, white-haired figure of about 70. A nasty little smile flickered around the corners of his coarse-looking mouth, which occasionally split into a leering grin, revealing the gold caps on his tobacco-stained teeth.

After the physician had quickly checked me over, pronounced me reasonably fit, and left, the two FBI agents jerked me to my feet and then took up positions near the door. The session was turned over to the sinister-looking fellow with the gold teeth.

Speaking with a thick Hebrew accent and a disarmingly mild, professorial manner, he introduced himself to me as Colonel Saul Rubin, of Israeli Military Intelligence. Before I could even wonder what business a representative of a foreign government had questioning me, Rubin explained:

"Since your racist activities are in violation of the International Genocide Convention, Mr. Turner, you will be tried by an international tribunal, with representatives from both your country and mine. But first we need some information from you, so that we can also bring your fellow criminals to justice at the same time.

"I understand that you were not very cooperative last night. Let me warn you that it will go very hard for you if you fail to answer my questions. I have had a great deal of experience over the last 45 years in extracting information from people who did not wish to cooperate with me. In the end they all told me everything I wanted to know, both the Arabs and the Germans, but it was a very unpleasant experience for those who were stubborn."

Then, after a brief pause: "Ah yes, some of those Germans, back in 1945 and 1946 — particularly the ones from the SS — were quite stubborn."

The apparently satisfying recollection brought another hideous grin to Rubin's face, and I could not suppress a shudder. I remembered the horrible photographs one of our members who was a former Army intelligence officer had shown me years ago of German prisoners who had had their eyes gouged out, their teeth pulled, their fingers cut off, and their testicles smashed by sadistic interrogators, many wearing U.S. Army uniforms, prior to their conviction and execution by military courts as "war criminals."

I wanted nothing so much as to be able to smash the leering Jewish face before me with my fists, but my handcuffs would not permit me that luxury. I settled for spitting into Rubin's face and simultaneously aiming a kick at his crotch. Unfortunately, my stiff, aching muscles ruined my aim, and my kick only caught Rubin's thigh, sending him staggering back a couple of paces.

Then the two Negro orderlies seized me. Under Rubin's instructions, they proceeded to give me a vicious, thorough, and scientific beating. When they finished my whole body was a throbbing, searing mass of pain, and I was writhing on the floor, whimpering.

91

The subsequent interrogation sessions were worse — much worse. Because a public "show trial" was planned for me, presumably in the Adolf Eichmann manner, Rubin avoided the eye-gouging and finger-cutting, which would have disfigured me, but the things he did were fully as painful. (*Note to the reader:* Adolf Eichmann was a middle-level German official during World War II. Fifteen years after the war, in 39 BNE, he was kidnapped in South America by Jews, flown to Israel, and made the central figure in an elaborately staged, two-year propaganda campaign to evoke sympathy from the non-Jewish world for Israel, the only haven for "persecuted" Jews. After fiendish torture, Eichmann was displayed in a soundproof glass cage during a four-month show trial in which he was condemned to death for "crimes against the Jewish people.")

For days at a time I was completely out of my mind, and, as Rubin had predicted, I eventually told him everything he wanted to know. No human being could have done otherwise.

During the torture sessions the two FBI agents who were always present as spectators sometimes turned a bit pale — and when Rubin had his two Black assistants thrust a long, blunt rod up into my rectum, so that I was screaming and wriggling like a skewered pig, one looked as if he were going to be sick — but they never raised an objection. I guess it was much the same after World War II, when American officers of German descent calmly watched Jewish torturers work over their racial brothers who had been in the German army and likewise saw nothing amiss when Negro G.I.'s raped and brutalized German girls. Is it that they have been so brainwashed by the Jews that they hate their own race, or is it that they are just insensitive bastards who will do whatever they're told as long as they keep drawing their salaries?

Despite Rubin's exquisitely painful expertise, I am now thoroughly convinced that the Organization's interrogation techniques are much more effective than the System's. We are scientific, whereas the System is merely brutal. Although Rubin broke my resistance and got answers to his questions, fortunately he failed to ask many of the right questions.

When he had finally finished with me, after nearly a month-long nightmare, I had told him the names of most of the members of the Organization that I knew, the locations of their hideouts, and who had been involved in various operations against the System. I had described in detail the preparation for the bombing of the FBI building and my role in the mortar assault on the Capitol. And, of course, I explained exactly how the other members of my unit had escaped capture.

All these disclosures certainly caused problems for the Organization. But since they were able to anticipate exactly what the political police would learn from me, they were able to nullify any potential damage. Mainly it meant hastily abandoning several perfectly good hideouts and establishing new ones.

But Rubin's interrogation technique elicited only information in the form of answers to direct questions. He asked me nothing about our communications system, and so he found out nothing about it. (As I learned later, our legals inside the FBI kept the Organization informed as to just what information my interrogation was yielding, so we retained confidence in the security of our radio communications.)

He also found out nothing about the Order or about our philosophy or long-range goals, which knowledge might have helped the System understand our strategy. As it was, everything Rubin got from me was of a tactical nature only. I believe the reason for this to be the System's arrogant assumption that the task of liquidating the Organization would be a matter of only weeks. We were regarded as a major problem but not as a mortal danger.

After my period of interrogation was over, I was kept in the FBI building for another three weeks, apparently in anticipation of having me handy to identify various Organization members who might be arrested on the basis of the information I had furnished. None were arrested during this time, however, and I was eventually transferred to the special prison compound at Fort Belvoir where nearly 200 other Organization members and about the same number of our legals were being held.

The government was afraid to put us into ordinary prisons because of the danger that the Organization might free us — and also, I suspect, because they were afraid we might indoctrinate other White prisoners. So all captured Organization members were taken to Fort Belvoir from all over the country and kept in solitary-confinement cells in buildings surrounded by barbed wire, tanks, guard towers with machine guns, and two companies of MP's — all in the center of an Army base. And there I spent the next 14 months. What happened to the plans for my trial I cannot say.

Many people consider solitary confinement to be especially harsh treatment, but it was a blessing for me. I was still in such a depressed and abnormal frame of mind — partly the result of Rubin's torture, partly from a sense of guilt at having yielded to that torture, and partly just from being locked up and unable to participate in the struggle — that I needed some time alone to straighten myself out again. And, of course, it was nice not to have to worry about Blacks, which would have been a real curse in any ordinary prison.

No one who has not been subjected to the terror and agony to which I was can understand the profound and lasting effect of such an experience. My body has healed completely now, and I have recovered from the peculiar combination of depression and nervous jitters with which my interrogation left me, but I am not the same man I was. I am more impatient now, more serious-minded (even somber, perhaps), more determined than ever to get on with our task.

And I have lost all fear of death. I have not become more reckless — less so, if anything — but nothing holds any terror for me now. I can be much harder on myself than before and also harder on others, when necessary. Woe betide any whining conservative, "responsible" or otherwise, who gets in the way of our revolution when I am around! I will listen to no more excuses from these self-serving collaborators but will simply reach for my pistol.

All the time I and the others were at Fort Belvoir we were supposed to be incommunicado and were allowed no reading material, newspapers or otherwise. Nevertheless, we soon learned how to communicate to a limited extent with one another, and we established an oral news pipeline from the outside through our guards, who were not an altogether unsympathetic lot.

The news we all wanted to hear, of course, was of the war between the Organization and the System. We were especially cheered up whenever there was news of a successful action against the System — an "atrocity," in the jargon of the news media — and we became depressed if the period between news of major actions stretched to more than a few days.

As time passed, news of actions *did* become considerably less frequent, and the media began predicting with greater and greater confidence the imminent liquidation of the remnants of the Organization and the return of the country to "normalcy." That worried us, but our worry was tempered by the observation that fewer and fewer new prisoners were joining us at Fort Belvoir. An average of one a day was being brought in when I first went there, but that number had declined to less than one a week by August of last year.

Then came the great Houston bombings of September 11 and 12, 1992. In two earthshaking days there were 14 major bombings, which left more than 4,000 persons dead and much of Houston's industrial and shipping facilities smoldering wreckage.

The action began when a fully loaded munitions ship, carrying aerial bombs to Israel, detonated in the crowded Houston ship channel in the pre-dawn hours of September 11. That ship took four others to the bottom of the channel with her, thoroughly blocking it, and also set fire to an enormous refinery nearby. Within an hour eight other massive explosions had occurred along the ship channel, putting the nation's second-busiest port out of business for more than four months.

Five later explosions closed the Houston airport, destroyed the city's main power-generating station, and collapsed two strategically located overpasses and a bridge, making two of the most heavily traveled freeways in the area impassable. Houston became an instant disaster area, and the Federal government rushed in thousands of troops — as much to keep an angry and panic-stricken public under control as to counter the Organization.

The Houston action won us no friends, but neither did it help the government's case. And it thoroughly dispelled the growing notion that our revolution had been stifled.

And, after Houston, there was Wilmington, then Providence, then Racine. Actions were fewer than before, but they were much, much bigger. It became apparent to us last fall that the revolution had entered a new and more decisive phase. But more of that later.

Last night was the most important action of all for those of us at Fort Belvoir. Just before midnight, as usual, two olive-drab buses pulled up in front of the gate to our prison compound. Ordinarily they bring in about 60 MP's for the midnight guard shift and take away the evening shift. This time it was different.

My first inkling that a breakout was in progress came when I was wakened by the sound of a machine gun being fired from one of the guard towers. It was quickly silenced by a direct hit from the 105-mm gun on one of the four tanks in our compound. After that there was intermittent small-arms fire and a lot of shouting and the sound of running feet. Finally, the wooden door of my cell burst inward under the blow of a sledgehammer, and I was free.

I was one of the lucky 150 or so who squeezed into the two MP buses and rode out in them. Several dozen others clung to the outside of the four captured tanks, whose inattentive crews had been the first targets of our rescuers. The rest had to go on foot, slogging through a downpour which providentially kept the Army's helicopters grounded.

Altogether we lost 18 prisoners and four rescuers killed and 61 prisoners recaptured. But 442 of us — according to the news report on the radio — made it to the waiting trucks outside the base, while the tanks kept our pursuers at bay.

That wasn't the end of the excitement, but let it suffice to say that by four o'clock this morning we had successfully dispersed to more than two dozen preselected "safe houses" in the Washington area. After a few hours rest, I slipped into a set of civilian work clothes, took the set of false identification cards that had been carefully and masterfully prepared for me, and, carrying a newspaper and a lunch pail, made my way among the morning job-goers to the rendezvous point I was assigned.

Within two minutes a pickup truck carrying a man and a woman pulled up to the curb beside me. The door opened and I squeezed in. As Bill drove off into the rush-hour traffic, I held my beloved Katherine in my arms once again.

XIV

March 24, 1993. Today I was tried on the charge of Oath-breaking — the most serious offense with which a member of the Order can be charged. It was a harrowing experience, but I knew it was coming, and I am enormously relieved to have it behind me, despite the outcome.

All during the months in my prison cell, I agonized over the question: Did I, by failing to kill myself before I was captured, break my Oath to the Order? I must have reviewed in my mind a hundred times the circumstances of my capture and the subsequent events, trying to convince myself that my behavior had been blameless, that I had fallen alive into the hands of my captors through no fault of my own. Today I related the whole sequence of events to a jury of my peers.

The summons came this morning, via radio, and I knew immediately what it was for, although I was surprised at the address to which I was ordered to report: one of the newest and largest office buildings in downtown Washington. As an attractive receptionist ushered me into a conference room in a large suite of law offices, my apprehension was mixed with gratitude for the three-day period of recuperation I had been allowed since the breakout.

I had just slipped into the robe which I found waiting for me on a coatrack, when another door opened and eight other robed and hooded figures walked into the room and silently took seats around a large table. The last of the eight had his hood pushed back, and I recognized the familiar features of Major Williams.

The proceedings were brisk and bathed in an air of formality. After a little more than an hour of questioning, I was told to wait in a smaller, adjoining room. I waited there for nearly three hours.

When the others had finally finished discussing my case and had reached a decision, I was summoned back into the conference room. While I stood at one end of the table, Major Williams, seated at the other end, announced the verdict. His words, to the extent I can remember them, were as follows:

"Earl Turner, we have weighed your performance as a member of this Order on two grounds, and we have found you wanting on both.

"First, in your conduct immediately prior to the police raid in which you were seized and imprisoned, you gave evidence of a shocking lack of maturity and sound judgment. Your indiscretion in visiting the girl in Georgetown — an act which, although not specifically forbidden, was not within the realm of your assigned duties — led directly to a situation in which you and the members of your unit were placed in extreme jeopardy, and a valuable facility was lost to the Organization.

"Because of this failure of judgment on your part, your period as a probationary member of the Order is being extended for six months. Furthermore, your time as a prisoner will not count as a part of your probation. Therefore, you will not be permitted the rite of Union before March of next year, at the earliest.

"We find, however, that your conduct prior to the police raid does not constitute a violation of your Oath."

I breathed an inaudible sigh of relief upon hearing this last statement. But then Williams continued, with a grimmer note in his voice:

"The fact that you were taken alive by the political police and remained alive during nearly a month of interrogation is a far more serious matter.

"In swearing your Oath, you consecrated your life to the service of the Order. You undertook to place your duty to the Order ahead of all other things, including the preservation of your life, at all times. You accepted this obligation willingly and with the knowledge that, for the duration of our struggle, it entails a very substantial possibility of your actually having to give up your life in order to avoid breaking your Oath.

"And you were specifically warned against falling alive into the hands of the political police and were given the means to avoid this. Yet you did fall into their hands and remained alive. The information they extracted from you seriously hampered the work of the Organization in this area and placed many of your comrades in very grave danger.

"We understand, of course, that you did not make a conscious decision to violate your Oath. We have carefully looked into the circumstances of your capture, and we are aware of the interrogation techniques the political police now use against our people. If you were merely a soldier in any other army in the world, you would be held blameless.

"But the Order is not like any other army. We have claimed for ourselves the right to decide the fate of all our people and, eventually, to rule the world in accord with our principles. If we are to be worthy of this right, then we must be willing to accept the responsibility which goes with it.

"Each day we make decisions and carry out actions which result in the deaths of White persons, many of them innocent of any offense which we consider punishable. We are willing to take the lives of these innocent persons, because a much greater harm will ultimately befall our people if we fail to act now. Our criterion is the ultimate good of our race. We can apply no lesser criterion to ourselves.

"Indeed, we must be much sterner with ourselves than with others. We must maintain for ourselves a standard of conduct much higher than we demand of the general public or even of ordinary members of the Organization. In particular, we must never accept the idea, born of the sickness of our era, that a good excuse for non-performance of a duty is a satisfactory substitute for performance.

"For us, there can be no excuses. Either we perform our duty, or we do not. If we do not, we need no excuse; we simply accept the responsibility for failure. And if there is a penalty, we accept that too. The penalty for Oath-breaking is death."

The room was perfectly still, but I could hear a buzzing in my ears, and the floor seemed to sway under my feet. I stood in stunned silence until Williams began speaking again, this time in a somewhat softer voice:

"The duty of this tribunal is clear, Earl Turner. We must act in your case in such a way that every member of this Order who may, at some time in the future, find himself in circumstances similar to yours during the police raid on your headquarters, will know that death is inevitable if he cannot avoid capture — either an honorable death by his own hand or a less-than-honorable death at the hands of his comrades later. There must be no temptation for him to avoid his duty, in the hope that a 'good excuse' later will preserve his life.

"Some of us here today have argued that this consideration — setting a firm example for others — should be the sole determinant of your fate. But others of us have argued that, because you had not yet achieved full membership in this Order at the time in question — because you had not yet participated in the rite of Union — your conduct can be reasonably judged by a different standard than would be applied to someone who had completed his probationary period and achieved Union.

"Our decision has not been easy, but now you must hear it and you must abide by it. First, you must satisfactorily complete your extended period of probation. Then, at some time after the end of that period, you will be permitted Union — but only on a conditional basis, something we have never allowed before. The condition will be that you undertake a mission whose successful completion can reasonably be expected to result in your death.

"Unfortunately, we are all too often presented with the painful task of assigning such 'suicide missions' to our members, when we can find no other way to achieve a necessary goal. In your case, such a mission will serve two ends.

"If you complete it successfully, the act of completion will remove the condition from your Union. Then, even though you die, you will continue to live in us and in our successors for as long as our Order endures, just as with any other member who achieves Union and then loses his life. And if, by some chance, you should survive your mission, you may then take your place in our ranks with no stain on your record. Do you understand everything I have said?"

I nodded, and answered: "Yes, I understand, and I accept your judgment without reservation. It is just and proper. I have never expected to survive the struggle in which we are now engaged, and I am grateful that I will be allowed to make a further contribution to it. I am also grateful that the prospect of Union remains before me."

March 25. Today Henry came over, and he, Bill, and I had a long talk. Henry is heading for the West Coast tomorrow, and he wanted to help Bill fill me in on the developments of the past year before he leaves. Apparently he will be engaged in training new recruits and handling some of the Organization's other internal functions in the Los Angeles area, where we are especially strong. When he greeted me he showed me the Sign, and I knew that he had also become a member of the Order.

99

In essence, what I learned today is what I had already concluded in my prison cell: the Organization has shifted the main thrust of its attacks from tactical, personal targets to strategic, economic targets. We are no longer trying to destroy the System directly, but are now concentrating on undermining the general public's support for the System.

I have felt for a long time that this change is necessary. Apparently two things forced Revolutionary Command to the same conclusion: the fact that we were not recruiting enough new members to make up our losses in the war of attrition against the System, and the fact that neither our blows against the System nor the System's increasingly repressive responses to those blows were having any really decisive effect on the public's attitude toward the System.

The first factor was mandatory. We simply could not keep up our level of activity against the System as our casualties steadily mounted, even if we wanted to. Henry estimated that the total number of our front-line combat troops for the whole country — those ready and able to use knife, gun, or bomb against the System — had declined to a low point of about 400 persons last summer. Our front-line troops make up only about a fourth of the Organization's membership, and they have been suffering a greatly disproportionate casualty rate.

So, the Organization was forced to de-escalate the level of the war temporarily, while we still preserved a strong enough nucleus for another approach. Our whole strategy against the System was failing.

It was failing because the great bulk of White Americans were not responding to the situation in the way we had hoped they would. That is, we had counted on a positive, imitative response to our "propaganda of the deed," but it was not forthcoming.

We had hoped that when we set the example of resisting the System's tyranny, others would resist too. We had hoped that by making dramatic strikes against top System personalities and important System facilities, we would inspire Americans everywhere to initiate similar actions of their own. But, for the most part, the bastards just sat on their asses.

Sure, a dozen or so synagogues were burned, and there was an overall rise in the level of politically motivated violence, but it was generally misdirected and ineffective. Without organization such activities have little value, unless they are very widespread and can be sustained over a long period.

And the System's response to the Organization irritated many people and caused a lot of grumbling, but it didn't even come close to provoking a rebellion. Tyranny, we have discovered, just isn't all that unpopular among the American people.

What is really precious to the average American is not his freedom or his honor or the future of his race, but his pay check. He complained when the System began busing his kids to Black schools 20 years ago, but he was allowed to keep his station wagon and his fiberglass speedboat, so he didn't fight.

He complained when they took away his guns five years ago, but he still had his color TV and his backyard barbeque, so he didn't fight.

And he complains today when the Blacks rape his women at will and the System makes him show an identity pass to buy groceries or pick up his laundry, but he still has a full belly most of the time, so he won't fight.

He hasn't an idea in his head that wasn't put there by his TV set. He desperately wants to be "well adjusted" and to do and think and say exactly what he thinks is expected of him. He has become, in short, just what the System has been trying to make of him these past 50 years or so: a mass-man; a member of the great, brainwashed proletariat; a herd animal; a true democrat.

That, unfortunately, is our average White American. We can wish that it weren't so, but it is. The plain, horrible truth is that we have been trying to evoke a heroic spirit of idealism which just isn't there any more. It has been washed right out of 99 per cent of our people by the flood of Jewish-materialist propaganda in which they have been submerged practically all their lives.

As for the last one per cent, there are various reasons why they aren't doing us much good. Some, of course, are too ornery to work within the confines of the Organization — or any organized group; they can only "do their own thing," as a number, in fact, are. The others may still have different ideas of their own, or they simply may not have been able to make contact with us since we were forced underground. Eventually we could recruit most of these, but we no longer have the time.

What the Organization began doing about six months ago is treating Americans realistically, for the first time — namely, like a herd of cattle. Since they are no longer capable of responding to an idealistic appeal, we began appealing to things they can understand: fear and hunger.

We will take the food off their tables and empty their refrigerators. We will rob the System of its principal hold over them. And, when they begin getting hungry, we will make them fear us more than they fear the System. We will treat them exactly the way they deserve to be treated.

I don't know why we held back from this approach for so long. We have had the example of decades of guerrilla warfare in Africa, Asia, and Latin America to instruct us. In every case the guerrillas won by making the people fear them, not love them. By publicly torturing to death village leaders who opposed them and by carrying out brutal massacres of entire village populations which refused to feed them, they inspired such terror in neighboring villages that everyone was afraid to refuse them what they asked.

We Americans observed all this but failed to apply the lesson to ourselves. We regarded — correctly — all those non-Whites as mere herds of animals and were not surprised that they behaved as they did. But we regarded ourselves — incorrectly — as something better.

There was a time when we were better — and we are fighting to insure that there will be such a time again — but for now we are merely a herd, being manipulated through our basest instincts by a pack of clever aliens. We have sunk to the point where we no longer hate our oppressors or try to fight them; we merely fear them and attempt to curry favor with them.

So be it. We will suffer grievously for having allowed ourselves to fall under the Jewish spell.

We stopped wasting our resources in small-scale terror attacks and shifted to large-scale attacks on carefully selected economic targets: power stations, fuel depots, transportation facilities, food sources, key industrial plants. We do not expect to bring down the already creaky American economic structure immediately, but we do expect to cause a number of localized and temporary breakdowns, which will gradually have a cumulative effect on the whole public.

Already a sizable portion of the public has been made to realize that it will not be allowed to sit back and watch the war on TV in safety and comfort. In Houston, for example, hundreds of thousands went for nearly two weeks without electricity last September. The food in their refrigerators and freezers quickly spoiled, as did the perishables in their supermarkets. There were two major food riots by hungry Houstonians before the Army was able to set up enough relief stations to handle everyone.

In one instance Federal troops shot 26 persons in a mob trying to storm a government food depot, and then the Organization got another riot started with the rumor that the emergency rations the government was handing out were contaminated with botulism. Houston isn't back to normal yet, with most of the city still subject to a staggered six-hour-a-day power blackout.

In Wilmington we put half the city on the dole by blowing up two big DuPont plants. And we turned the lights off for half of New England when we knocked out that power-generating station just outside Providence.

The electronics manufacturer we hit in Racine wasn't very big, but he was the sole supplier of certain key components for other manufacturers all across the country. By torching his plant, we eventually caused twenty others to shut down.

The effects of these actions are not decisive yet, but, if we can keep it up, they will be. The public reaction has already convinced us of that.

That reaction can certainly not be considered friendly to us, on the whole. In Houston a mob took two prisoners — suspects arrested for questioning in one of the bombings — away from the police and tore them limb from limb. Fortunately, they were not our people — just two hapless fellows who were in the wrong place at the wrong time.

And the conservatives, of course, have redoubled their squawking and cackling that we're ruining all chances for an improvement in conditions by "provoking" the government with our violence. What the conservatives mean when they talk of an "improvement" is a stabilization of the economy and another round of concessions to the Blacks, so that everyone can return to consuming in multi-racial comfort.

But we learned long ago not to count our enemies, only our friends. And the number of the latter is growing now. Henry indicated that we have increased nearly 50 per cent in membership since last summer. Apparently our new strategy has knocked a lot of spectators off the fence — some on our side and some on the other. Perceptive people are beginning to realize that they won't be able to sit this war out. We are forcing them into the front lines, where they must choose sides and participate, whether they like it or not.

XV

March 28, 1993. I'm finally back in the swing of things now. Over the weekend Katherine answered many questions for me and gave me the details, especially about local developments, which I failed to get from Henry Friday.

While I was locked up the work on our communications equipment had to go on, of course, and now there are two other well-qualified people in the area handling that task. But there's

103

still plenty of technical work left for me. Bill is a fine mechanical craftsman and gunsmith, but he can't handle the ordnance jobs that require chemical or electronic techniques. He gave me a long list of requests for special devices which came into our unit while I was in prison and which he had been obliged to put aside.

We went over the list carefully last night and decided which items are most important for the current needs of the Organization. I then made up my own list of supplies and equipment needed to begin work.

The top-priority items on Bill's list of requests are radio-controlled detonators and time-delay detonators and igniters. The Organization has been improvising in the latter category — and getting too high a percentage of misfires. We want a time-delay device which is adjustable from a few minutes to a day or more and which is 100 per cent certain.

Another category of items requested is disguised bombs and incendiary devices. It is now just about impossible to get into any government or media facility without walking through a metal-detector, and all packages and mail are routinely scanned by x-ray. This will require some cleverness, but I already have a few ideas.

And then there is Bill's own project, on which he needs some technical assistance: counterfeiting! The Organization is already successfully printing money on a fairly large scale on the West Coast, Bill said, and they want him to begin doing the same thing here.

I understand now why the economic status of the Organization seems to have improved so much in the last year! Actually, since we switched to large-scale actions we've begun tapping some new sources of contributions — mostly fat cats buying "insurance," I suspect — but we are apparently still finding it useful to print some of our own money.

Whatever genius is running our West Coast counterfeiting operation made up a very thorough set of instructions, which Bill showed me. The guy must have worked for the Secret Service or the Bureau of Engraving and Printing. He really seems to know his business. (*Note to the reader:* The "Bureau of Engraving and Printing" was the government agency which produced paper money in the United States, and the "Secret Service" was a police agency which combatted counterfeiting, among other things. As we know, counterfeiting was later used by the Organization not only to supply its units with funds but also to disrupt the general economy. In the last days of the Great Revolution, the Organization was dumping such huge quantities of counterfeit money that the government, in desperation, outlawed *all* paper money, requiring all monetary transactions to take place either in coin or by check. This move played havoc with public morale and was one of the factors leading to the final success of the Revolution.)

Bill has already finished setting up nearly everything; he has a really fine shop for precision printing. He just needs help with the fluorescence problem. The instructions tell him what chemical additives to put in his ink, but not where to get them. And he is not sure about how to make and use an ultraviolet inspection unit for checking the finished product. That won't be hard.

Our new working and living arrangement is radically different from the one we had before. Instead of sneaking around "underground," we are right out in the open now. There's a neon sign in the window of the printing shop, and it's listed in the Yellow Pages. During the day the shop is "open for business," with Carol behind the counter, but Bill keeps his prices so high that just enough work to maintain appearances comes in. His real work takes place after hours, usually in the basement, where the armory is.

The four of us live above the shop, like we did over the old place, but we don't have to keep the windows blacked out. And Bill's pickup truck stays parked right on the street in front. So far as the world is concerned, we are just two young couples in the printing business together.

The trick, of course, was in establishing false identities that would stand up to System scrutiny, but the Organization has developed an admirable degree of expertise along that line. We all have Social Security cards, and two of us have driver's licenses. The cards and licenses are genuine (I have heard some unpleasant stories about how the Organization obtained them), so we can open bank accounts, pay taxes, and do other things like anyone else.

I just have to remember that my new name is — ugh! — "David J. Bloom." I am really being ribbed about that. Fortunately, the photograph on the driver's license is indistinct enough to pass for me, as long as I keep my hair dyed.

The Organization had no choice about establishing new identities for all of us who are underground. A person without a documented identity simply can't function in this society any longer. One can't buy groceries or even ride a bus without showing either a driver's license or one of the new identity cards the government has begun issuing.

105

It's still possible to get by with a fake in most cases, but the computerized system will be completed in another few months, and then fakes will automatically be detected. So the Organization decided to do it right and give us "genuine" credentials, even though that's a slow and difficult job. A few special units handle that task with coldblooded ruthlessness, but the demand for new credentials still far exceeds the supply.

It also appears that the System has become even more ruthless in its campaign against us. A number of our people — perhaps as many as fifty for the whole country — have been murdered by professional killers in the last four months. It's hard to fix the exact total, because some we suspect have been killed have just disappeared, and no body has been found.

When our people first began to disappear or to be found floating in the river with their hands tied behind their backs and six or seven bullet holes in their heads, there was a widespread assumption among the Organization rank and file that these killings were internal disciplinary actions by the Organization itself. In fact, there was a period last fall when we were losing more members because of disciplinary executions than anything else. That was a time when morale was very low, and it was necessary to use extreme methods to convince waverers to remain steadfast in their obligations to the Organization.

But it was immediately apparent to Revolutionary Command — and it soon became apparent to everyone else — that a new element had entered the picture. From our contacts inside one of the Federal police agencies we learned that our people are being killed by two groups: a special Israeli assassination squad and an assortment of Mafia "hit men" under contract to the government of Israel. Where both these groups are concerned, U.S. police have been given a "hands off" order by the FBI. (*Note to the reader:* The "Mafia" was a criminal confederation, composed primarily of Italians and Sicilians but usually masterminded by Jews, which flourished in the United States in the eight decades prior to the Great Revolution. There were several half-hearted governmental efforts to stamp out the Mafia during this period, but the unrestricted capitalism then flourishing provided ideal conditions for large-scale, organized crime and its concomitant political corruption. The Mafia remained in existence until virtually all its members — more than 8,000 men — were rounded up and executed in a single, massive operation by the Organization during the mopping-up period which followed the Revolution.)

All the victims so far have been among our "legals." Apparently someone in the FBI gives the names of persons suspected of being members of the Organization but not yet under arrest to someone in the Israeli embassy, and they take it from there.

We have made some reprisals — in New Orleans, for example. After two of our "legals," one a prominent attorney there, were murdered Mafia-style about six weeks ago, we mined the nightclub which served as the local Mafia hangout. When the bombs went off and the place burst into flames during a birthday celebration for one of their "underbosses," the fleeing patrons were met with merciless hails of machinegun fire from our people, who were stationed on rooftops across from the only two exits. More than 400 persons lost their lives there that night, including approximately 60 members of the Mafia.

But this new threat still remains very much with us, and it has severely damaged the morale of those of our members and partisans who are exposed to it — namely those who, by retaining their status as law-abiding citizens and operating under their own identities, do not enjoy the anonymity of us in the underground. It is clear that we will soon have to move against the source of the threat.

April 2. Supply problem solved — at least temporarily. It required another one of those stickup operations which I really detest. I wasn't as nervous this time as when Henry and I pulled our first one — that seems half a lifetime ago — but I still didn't like it.

Bill and I broke our list of needed items up into three categories, according to their source. About two-thirds of the chemical items we needed were not readily available on the general-consumer market and would have to come from a chemical supply house. Then, I wanted at least 100 wristwatches for timing devices, and they would cost us too much if we simply purchased them. Finally, there were a number of electronic and electrical components, some items of general hardware, and a few readily available chemicals, all of which could be purchased without difficulty and within the resources of our budget.

I spent most of Tuesday and Wednesday gathering up the items in the last category.

The chemical problem was also solved Wednesday. That had been a worry, because suppliers of laboratory and industrial chemicals are now required to check out all new customers with the political police, just as are suppliers of explosives. I'd just as soon avoid that sort of scrutiny. But I checked with WFC and found that one of our "legals" in Silver Spring has a small electroplating shop and could order what I need from his regular supplier. I'll pick the stuff up from him Monday.

But the watches! I knew exactly what I wanted for our timers, and I wanted enough of the same style so that the timers could be standardized, both for efficiency in building them and precisely known behavior in operation. So Katherine and I robbed a warehouse in northeast D.C. yesterday and got 200 of them.

It took two days of telephoning just to find the watches I was looking for. Then they had to be sent down to the Washington warehouse from Philadelphia. I told the man in Washington I was in a big hurry for them and would send someone out right away with a certified check for $12,000 to pick them up. He said they would be waiting for me in the front office. And they were.

I wanted Bill to go with me, but he has been tied down with work at the shop all week. And Katherine really wanted to go. The girl has a wild streak in her that someone who doesn't know her well would never suspect.

First, one of Katherine's makeup jobs, to protect my "David Bloom" identity and her own. Identity under identity under identity — I've almost forgotten who Earl Turner is or what he actually looks like!

Then we had to swipe a vehicle. That only took a few minutes, and we followed the usual procedure: Park the pickup in a big shopping center, walk to the other side of the parking lot, find a car which is unlocked, and get in. I used a small boltcutter to cut the armored cable to the ignition switch under the dashboard, and then it was a matter of only a few seconds to find the right wires in the cable and attach clip leads.

I had hoped there would be no violence at the warehouse, but my wish was not to be granted. We presented ourselves to the manager and asked for our package. He asked for the certified check. "I have it," I said, "and I'll give it to you as soon as I check to see that the watches are the ones I ordered."

My plan was to take the watches and just walk out the door, leaving the manager yelling for his check. But when the man came back with our package, two husky warehouse workers came with him, and one took up a position between us and the door. They were taking no chances.

I opened the package, checked the contents, and drew my pistol. Katherine also drew her gun, and she waved the man near the door away. But then the door would not open when she tried it!

She turned her gun on the worker and he quickly explained: "They have to push the buzzer in the office to unlock the door."

I whirled back toward the manager and snarled at him, "Get this door open now, or I'll pay you for these watches with hot lead!" But he nimbly ducked out another doorway, from the office into the storage area, and slammed a heavy metal door behind him before I could react.

I then ordered the female clerk at the desk to push the buzzer for the door. She, however, continued to sit as rigidly as a statue, her mouth wide open in an expression of horror.

Beginning to feel desperate, I decided to shoot the lock off the door. It took four shots to do it, partly because my nervous haste spoiled my aim.

We ran to the car, but the warehouse manager was already there. The bastard was letting the air out of our tires!

I slammed the barrel of my revolver down on his head and sent him sprawling in the gravel. Fortunately, he had only partially deflated one tire, and the car could still be driven. Katherine and I wasted no more time getting away from there.

What a life!

It wasn't until this afternoon, when I had finished assembling and testing the first timer, that I was convinced that the fancy watches I wanted were worth the hassle it took to get them. The new timer works perfectly; it makes a positive, low-resistance contact every time, and I am sure it will reduce our percentage of misfires to practically zero.

I also got Bill's UV inspection unit working for him, and he will be ready to print his first greenbacks as soon as I pick up his ink additives Monday. His product won't be perfect, but it should be close enough. In particular, it should pass all the standard tests used in banks to spot counterfeit bills. They'll have to take it to a lab to tell it's phony.

And I finished designing three different bomb mechanisms that should pass an X-ray examination without arousing suspicion. One of them fits into an umbrella handle — batteries, timer, and all. The main shaft of the umbrella can be filled with thermite if one wants an incendiary device, or the handle can be detached and used as a detonator. Another timer-detonator combination will be built into a pocket transistor radio (that one can also be fired by a tone-coded radio signal), and the third will be an electric wristwatch, with the detonator and booster molded into the wrist band and fired by the watch's built-in battery. In each case, of course, the bulk explosives must be brought into an area separately, but they can be disguised in many different ways —

cast like plaster, for example, into the shape of any familiar
object, even painted the right color.

XVI

April 10, 1993. This is the first time in a week I've had some
time to myself and have been able to relax. I'm in a Chicago
motel with nothing to do until tomorrow morning, when I'll take
a tour of the Evanston Power Project. I flew out here Friday
afternoon for two things: the Evanston tour and a delivery of hot
money to one of our Chicago units.

Bill started his press up Monday night, as soon as we had mixed
the chemical additives into the ink, and he kept it going almost
continuously until the wee hours of Friday morning, with Carol
spelling him twice for a few hours of sleep. He didn't shut down
until he had used the last of the banknote paper acquired for the
purpose. Katherine and I helped by doing the cutting and by
handling the paper at both ends of the press. The work nearly
killed all of us, but the Organization wanted the money in a
hurry.

They really have a pile of it now! I had never dreamed of seeing
so much money in my life. Bill printed just over ten million
dollars in $10 and $20 bills — more than a ton of crisp, new
banknotes. And they look good! I compared one of Bill's new
tens with a genuine, new one, and I couldn't tell which was
which, except by the serial numbers.

Bill really did a professional job all around. Every bill even has
a different serial number. This project just shows what can be
accomplished with careful planning, dedication, and hard work.
Of course, Bill had six months to set things up and practice with
dry runs, before I was available to help him with the ink additives
and the UV unit. He had all the bugs worked out of the process
before beginning his three-and-a-half-day run.

I brought 50,000 of the new 20's with me and delivered them to
my Chicago contact yesterday. His unit has the job of
"laundering" the bills, so that an equivalent amount of genuine
currency will be available for the Organization's expenses in this
area. That's really a much trickier and more time-consuming
operation than the printing.

At the same time I left for here, Katherine was boarding a
flight for Boston with $800,000 in her luggage. Later this week we
will be making deliveries in Dallas and Atlanta. Getting through
the airport security checks with all that hot money is a little

ticklish, but as long as they don't do anything other than x-ray our luggage we'll be all right. The only things they seem to be looking for now are bombs and firearms. But just wait until they begin picking up our hot bills all over the country!

I had a chance to do some thinking on the plane from Washington. From 35,000 feet one gets a different perspective on things. Seeing all those sprawling suburbs and freeways and factories spread out below makes one realize just how big America is and what an awesomely difficult task we have undertaken.

Essentially, what we are doing with our program of strategic sabotage is hastening along somewhat the natural decay of America. We are chipping away at the termite-eaten timbers of the economy, so that the whole structure will collapse a few years sooner — and more catastrophically — than without our efforts. It is depressing to realize what a relatively small influence all our sacrifices are having on the course of events.

Consider our counterfeiting for example. We will have to print and distribute in a year's time at least a thousand times as much money as Bill printed last week — at least $10 billion a year — before we will make even a barely measurable effect on the national economy. Americans spend three times that much just on cigarettes.

Of course, we have two other money presses running on the West Coast, and we'll be setting up others in the near future. And if I can figure a way to take out the Evanston Project, that'll be a capital loss of nearly $10 billion in one stroke — not to mention the economic damage which will result from the loss of electrical power to industrial plants throughout the Great Lakes region.

But we are doing something else which is really more important than our campaign against the System. In the long run, it will be infinitely more important. We are forging the nucleus of a new society, a whole new civilization, which will rise from the ashes of the old. And it is because our new civilization will be based on an entirely different world view than the present one that it can only replace the other in a revolutionary manner. There is no way a society based on Aryan values and an Aryan outlook can evolve peacefully from a society which has succumbed to Jewish spiritual corruption.

Thus, our present struggle is unavoidable, completely aside from the fact that it was forced on us by the System and was not of our choosing. Looking at the events of the past 31 months from this viewpoint — that is, considering our constructive task of building a new social nucleus rather than our purely

111

destructive war against the System — it appears to me that our initial strategy of hitting System leaders instead of the general economy was not really as bad a way to *start* as I had thought.

It shaped the character of the battle from the beginning as *us vs. the System*, rather than us vs. the economy. The System responded represssively to protect itself from our attacks, and this caused it to isolate itself to a certain extent from the public. When we weren't doing much but assassinating Congressmen, Federal judges, secret policemen, and media masters, the people themselves did not feel especially threatened, but they resented the inconveniences caused by all the System's new security measures.

If we had hit the economy from the beginning, the System could have more easily painted the struggle as one of *us vs. the people*, and it would have been easier for the media to convince the public of the necessity of collaborating with the System against a common menace — namely us. So our initial error in strategy has providentially made it easier for us to recruit now, when we are deliberately working to make things as uncomfortable for everyone as we can.

And it isn't just the Organization which has been doing a lot of recruiting lately. The Order is also growing at a rate unprecedented in the last 48 of its nearly 68 years of existence. I surreptitiously made the Sign when I met our pickup man here yesterday — as I always do when I meet new Organization members now — and I was pleasantly surprised when he responded in kind.

He invited me to be a guest at an induction ceremony last night for new probationary members in the Chicago area. I gladly accepted, and I was astounded to count approximately 60 persons at the ceremony, nearly a third of whom were inductees. That's more than three times the total number of members the Order has in the Washington area. I was nearly as moved by the ceremony as I was by my own induction a year and a half ago.

April 14. Problems, problems, problems! Nothing has gone right since I got back from Chicago.

Bill can't find any more of the paper he used for the last batch of money, and he asked me to help him improvise. We tried tinting some slightly off-color paper of the same basic texture and composition, but the result was unsatisfactory. Bill will keep looking for another supply of the original paper, while I continue trying different tinting processes.

Then there was the delegation from the local Human Relations Council which visited the shop yesterday. Four Blacks and a sick, sick, sick White male, all wearing Council armbands, came into the print shop. They wanted to put a big poster in the shop window — the same kind one sees everywhere now, urging citizens to "help fight racism" by reporting suspicious persons to the political police — and leave a container for donations on the counter. Carol was behind the counter at the time, and she told them, in effect, to go to hell.

That, of course, wasn't the right thing to do, under the circumstances. They would have reported *us* to the political police, if I hadn't heard the commotion and intervened. I came up the basement stairs with what I hoped was a convincingly Jewish expression on my face and went into a "So, vot's goink on here, already?" routine. I laid it on thick — not *too* thick, I hope — so they would get the message: the shop manager here was himself a member of a minority group, a *very special* minority group, and could hardly be suspected of harboring any hostility for the Human Relations Councils or their commendable efforts.

The head nigger began complaining indignantly to me about Carol's rebuff. I cut him off with an impatient wave of my hand and directed a look of mock shock at Carol. "Of course, of course," I said, "leave your collection box here. It's for a good cause. But no vindow poster — not enough room. I vouldn't even let my cousin Abe put vun of his United Jewish Appeal posters there. Come! I show you where."

As I officiously led the delegation toward the door, I ordered Carol back to work in my best Simon Legree manner. "Yes, Mr. Bloom," she said meekly.

Out on the sidewalk I overcame my revulsion while I chummily put an arm around the shoulders of the Black spokesman and directed his attention to a store directly across the street. "Ve don't have so many customers here," I explained. "But my good friend Solly Feinstein has many people going in and out. And he has a big vindow. He vill be happy for your poster to be there. You can put it right under where it says 'Sol's Pawn Shop,' and everybody vill see it. And be sure to leave him a donation box — two donation boxes; he has a big store."

They all seemed pleased by my friendly suggestion and started across the street. But the White, a sorry-looking specimen with pimples and an imitation Afro, hesitated, turned, and said to me: "Maybe we ought to get that girl's name. Some of the things she said to us sounded definitely racist."

113

"Don't vaste your time on her," I responded brusquely, dismissing his suspicion with a wave. "She is just a dumb shiksa. She talks that way to everybody. I get rid of her soon."

When I re-entered the shop Bill, who had overheard the episode from the basement stairs, and Carol were convulsed with laughter. "It's not really that funny," I admonished them with an effort at sternness. "I had to do something right away, and if my pucker and my phony accent hadn't fooled that crew of sub-humans we'd be in real trouble now."

Then I lectured Carol: "We can't afford the luxury of telling these creatures what we think of them. We have a job to do first, and then we will settle with that bunch once and for all. So, let's swallow our pride and play along as long as we have to. Those who don't have our responsibilities can get themselves investigated for racism if they want — and more power to them."

But I could not repress a grin when I saw the poster go into place in the pawn shop window across the street, blotting out most of Sol's display of used cameras and binoculars. He must really have had to bite his tongue! And now all the people who see that particular poster will make the correct mental association between the Council's thought-control program and the people behind it.

The last thing to go wrong was Katherine coming down with the flu last night. She was scheduled to take a load of money to Dallas this morning, but she was too sick to go, and it looks like she'll be in bed for another two or three days. Which means that I'll be stuck not only with a trip to Atlanta tomorrow, but I'll also have to make the Dallas delivery. That'll be a whole day wasted on planes and at airports, and I need the time badly for getting ready for the Evanston operation.

We want to hit the new nuclear power complex at Evanston during the next six weeks, while they're still guiding tourists through it. After the first of June, when it will be closed to the public permanently, knocking it out will become much more difficult.

The Evanston Power Project is an enormous thing: four huge nuclear reactors surrounded by the biggest turbines and generators in the world. And the whole thing sits on concrete pilings a mile out in Lake Michigan, which supplies the cooling water for the reactors' heat exchangers. The Project generates 18,000 megawatts of electrical power — almost 20 *billion* watts! Incredible!

The power is fed into the power grid which supplies the entire Great Lakes region. Before the Evanston Project went into

114

operation two months ago, the whole Midwest was suffering from a severe power shortage — much worse than we have here, which is bad enough. In some areas factories were restricted to operating only two days a week, and there were so many unexpected blackouts in addition that the region was on the verge of a real economic crisis.

If we can take out the new power plant, things will be even worse than they were before. In order to keep the lights on in Chicago and Milwaukee, the authorities will have to steal power from as far away as Detroit and Minneapolis, where there is none to spare. All of that part of the country will be hit hard. And it took 10 years to design and build the Evanston Project, so they won't be able to remedy the situation very soon.

But the government has thought about the consequences of losing the Evanston Project too, and the security there is pretty formidable. One can't get near the place except by boat or airplane. And there are searchlights, patrol boats, and strings of buoys with nets of cable between them all around it, which makes the approach by water almost out of the question.

The shore for miles in either direction is fenced off, and there are a number of military radar and anti-aircraft installations behind the fence, making any attempt to crash an airplane loaded with explosives into the plant very unlikely to succeed.

It seems to me that about the only way we could mount an attack on the place by conventional means would be to sneak some heavy mortars within range, somewhere near the shore where there is a possibility for concealment. But, to my knowledge, we don't have that kind of weaponry available at the moment. Anyway, the really vital parts of the power station are in such massive buildings that I doubt a mortar attack could inflict more than superficial damage.

So, Revolutionary Command asked me to tour the place and come up with some unconventional ideas — which I have done, but there are still several tough problems to be solved.

My visit there last Monday gave me a pretty good idea of the strengths and weaknesses of the security arrangements. Some of the weaknesses are really quite astounding. Most astounding of all is the government's decision to let tourists into the place, even temporarily. The reason for that decision, I am sure, is the big fuss the anti-nuclear crazies have been making about the plant. The government feels obligated to show the public all the safety features which have been built into it.

When I signed up for the tour, I deliberately loaded myself down with all sorts of paraphernalia, just to see what I could get into the plant. I carried an attache case, a camera, and an umbrella, and I filled my pockets with coins, keys, and mechanical pencils.

On the ferry boat which takes tourists out to the plant there is very little security. They merely made me open my attache case for a cursory inspection. But when I got into the guard station at the plant itself, they divested me of my case, camera, and umbrella. Then I had to walk through a metal detector, which picked up all the metal junk in my pockets. I emptied my pockets for the guards, but then they handed the stuff back to me. They didn't look closely at any of it. So, one can at least sneak an incendiary pencil in.

What really interested me, though, was that one old gentleman in my group was carrying a cane with a metal head, and the guards let him keep it during the tour.

In essence, my idea is this: Since there's no way a single tourist can sneak in enough explosive material to wreck the place — nor any way he can position the small amount he could sneak in so it would be really effective, like punching a hole in one of the reactor pressure vessels, we may as well forget about explosives. Instead, we'll try to contaminate the plant with radioactive material, so that it can't be used.

What makes this idea feasible is that we have a source, inside the Organization, for certain radioactive materials. He's a chemistry professor at a university in Florida, and he uses the materials in his research.

We can easily pack enough of a really hot and nasty radionuclide — something with a half-life of a year or so — into a cane or a crutch, together with a small explosive charge for dispersing it, to make the entire Evanston Power Project uninhabitable. The plant won't be damaged physically, but they'll have to shut it down. Decontamination will be such an enormous task that the plant may very well stay closed permanently.

Unfortunately, this will be a suicide mission. Whoever carries the radioactive material into the plant will already have been exposed to a lethal dose of radiation before he gets to the plant gate with it. There's just no practical way to provide for any shielding.

The biggest worry is the radiation detectors which are all over the plant. If one of those gets a whiff of our man before he's ready to do his thing, it could get sticky.

I noticed, however, no detectors in the entrance station of the plant, where the guards check the incoming tourists. There are several in the huge turbine-and-generator room, where the tourists are taken, and there is one beside the exit gate used by the tourists — presumably to guard against the unlikely event of a visitor somehow pocketing a piece of nuclear fuel and trying to sneak it out. But it seems not to have occurred to them that someone might try to sneak radioactive material into the plant.

I remember pretty well where all the detectors are, and I'll have to consult with our man in Florida on the likelihood of one of them picking up something at a given distance from the material he will supply us. If an alarm goes off after our carrier is in the plant but before he gets to the generator room, he'll just have to make a run for it. But we'll try to design our gadget so as to give him the best possible chance.

The whole plan is pretty scary, but it has one big advantage: the psychological impact on the public. People are almost superstitious in their fear of nuclear radiation. The anti-nuclear lobby will have a field day with it. It will catch people's imagination to a far greater extent than any ordinary bombing or mortar attack. It will horrify many people — and it will knock more of them off the fence.

I must confess that I'm glad at this point that my probationary period still has 11 months to run and that I won't be asked to volunteer for this particular mission.

XVII

April 20, 1993. A beautiful day, a day of rest and peace, after a hectic week. Katherine and I drove to the mountains early this morning and spent the day walking in the woods. It was cool and bright and clear. After a picnic lunch we made love in a little meadow under the open sky.

We talked of many things, and we were both happy and carefree. The only shadow which fell on our happiness was Katherine's complaint about the number of out-of-town trips the Organization has sent me on recently, even though I have been out of prison for less than a month. I didn't have the courage to tell her that in the future we will have even less time together.

I only found that out myself yesterday. When I reported to Major Williams last night after returning from Florida, he told me that I'll be traveling a lot in the next few months. I didn't get all the details from him, but he hinted that the Organization is preparing for an all-out, nationwide offensive this summer, and I am to be a sort of roving military engineer.

But today I put that out of my mind and just enjoyed being alive and free and alone with a lovely girl in the midst of Nature's beauty.

As we were driving home this evening, we heard the news on the radio which capped a perfect day: the Organization hit the Israeli embassy in Washington this afternoon. No better date in the year could have been chosen for such an action!

For months an Israeli murder squad, working out of their embassy, has been picking off our people around the country. Today we settled the score — for the moment.

We struck with heavy mortars while the Israelis were throwing a cocktail party for their obedient servants in the U.S. Senate. A number of Israeli officials had flown in for the occasion, and there must have been more than 300 people in the embassy when our 4.2-inch mortars began raining TNT and phosphorus onto their heads through the roof.

The attack only lasted two or three minutes, according to the news report, but more than 40 projectiles struck the embassy, leaving nothing but a burned-out heap of wreckage — and only a handful of survivors! So, we must have had at least two mortars firing. That confirms what I was told last week about our new weapons acquisitions.

One fascinating incident in the news story, which the censors somehow failed to cut before it was broadcast, was the murder of a group of tourists by an embassy guard. During the attack an Israeli came running out of the crumbling building with a submachine gun, his clothing in flames. He spotted a group of a dozen tourists, all women and small children, gawking at the scene of destruction from across the street. Shrieking out his hatred in guttural Hebrew, the Jew opened fire on them, killing nine on the spot and critically wounding three others. Of course, he was not charged by the police. Your day is coming, Jews, your day is coming!

I should be getting to bed early tonight in order to be ready for a long day tomorrow, but the excitement of our achievement this afternoon makes it impossible for me to sleep yet. The Organization has demonstrated once again what an incomparable weapon the mortar is for guerrilla warfare. I am much more enthusiastic now about our new plan for Evanston, and I'll be better braced for overcoming any more balkiness on the part of our professor in Florida.

Last Saturday, when I was discussing my plan for getting radioactive material into the Evanston plant with Henry and Ed Sanders, they convinced me that a mortar could do the job better, and that we are now well supplied in that department. So I redesigned the delivery package, changing it from a walking cane to a 4.2-inch mortar projectile.

We will replace the phosphorus in three WP rounds with our radioactive contaminant. After we have zeroed in the target with conventional rounds, we'll fire our three modified projectiles, which will be adjusted to exactly the same weight, of course.

This way of doing it has three advantages over my original plan. First, it is surer; there is much less chance of something going wrong. Second, we will be delivering approximately 10 times as much contaminant, and the bursting charges in the projectiles will disperse it better than anything we could hope for with a loaded walking cane. And third, it need not be a suicide mission. We can keep the "hot" projectiles shielded until the moment they are to be fired, so the mortar crew will not be exposed to a lethal dose of radiation.

My big worry was whether we would be able to get our projectiles *inside* the power station, instead of just on the roof. The building is so heavily constructed that I doubt that they would penetrate, even with delayed-action fuzes. Ed Sanders convinced me, though, that once a 4.2-incher is zeroed in and firmly seated it will deliver rounds with sufficient accuracy and a low enough trajectory so that we will have an excellent hit probability on the side of the generator building facing the shore, which is practically one, huge window, 10 stories high and more than 200 yards wide.

Armed with this new plan, I went to talk to Harrison, our Florida chemist. I explained to him that his part of the job is to procure a suitable radioactive material and then, using his special facilities, safely load it into the mortar projectiles I will bring him.

Harrison had a fit. He complained that he had only offered to supply the Organization with small quantities of radionuclides and other hard-to-obtain materials. He did not want to become involved in actually handling any ordnance, and he especially objected to the quantity of material required by our plan. Not many people in the country have access to so much radioactive material, and he is afraid it will be traced to him.

I tried reasoning with him. I explained that if we try to load the projectiles ourselves, without the shielded handling facilities he has, one or more of our people will surely be exposed to a lethal dose of radiation. And I told him that he is free to choose a radionuclide, or a mixture of radionuclides, which will cast the least suspicion on him — so long as it is suitable for our purpose.

But he flatly refused. "It's out of the question," he said. "It would jeopardize my entire career."

"Dr. Harrison," I replied, "I am afraid you do not understand the situation. We are at war. The future of our race depends upon the outcome of this war. As a member of the Organization you are obliged to put your responsibility to our common effort ahead of all personal considerations. You are subject to the Organization's discipline."

Harrison turned white and began stammering, but I continued relentlessly: "If you continue to refuse my request, I am prepared to kill you on the spot." As a matter of fact, I was unarmed, because I had flown down on a commercial airliner, but Harrison didn't know that. He swallowed a couple of times, found his voice, and said he will do what he can.

We went over our figures and our requirements again and settled on an approximate timetable. Before I left I assured Harrison that if he feels this operation will place him in too much jeopardy to continue as a "legal" we can bring him underground after it is completed.

He is obviously still very nervous and unhappy, but I don't think he will try to betray us. The Organization has established a very high degree of credibility for its threats. Just to be on the safe side, however, we will use another courier when the time comes to drive the modified projectiles down to Florida to be loaded and brought back. No technical knowledge is required for that.

I don't like to act like a "tough guy" and threaten people; that is an unnatural role for me. But I have very little sympathy for people like Harrison, and I am sure that if he had not agreed to cooperate, I would have leaped on him and strangled him with my bare hands.

I guess there are a lot of other people who think they are playing it smart by looking out for themselves and letting us take all the risks and do all the dirty work. They figure they will reap the benefits with us if we win, and they won't lose anything if we lose. That's the way it has been in most other wars and revolutions, but I don't believe it will work out that way this time. Our attitude is that those whose only concern is to enjoy life in these times of trial for our race do not deserve life. Let them die. In the conduct of this war we certainly will not concern ourselves with looking out for their welfare. More and more it will be a case of either being for us, all the way, or against us.

April 25. Off to New York tomorrow for at least a week. Several things cooking up there which require my attention. The business down in Florida should have been taken care of by the time I return, and, if so, it'll be another trip to Chicago for me, this time by car.

The Yids are really screaming about the attack on their embassy. They are giving far more emphasis in the news media to this attack than they did to either the attack on the Capitol or the bombing of the FBI building. Each day on TV it gets worse, with more and more of the old "gas chamber" propaganda that has worked so well for them in the past. They are really pulling their hair and rending their garments: "Oy, veh, how we are suffering! How we are persecuted! Why did you let it happen to us? Weren't six million enough?"

What an act of outraged innocence! They are so good at it that they almost have me weeping along with them. But, strangely, there has not been another mention of the murder of those nine tourists by the Israeli guard. Ah, well, they were only Gentiles!

One unexpected benefit to us from the embassy action has been a major quarrel between the Blacks and their Jewish patrons. Purely by coincidence the attack came three days before the date which had been set for a nationwide "strike for equality" — another of those giant media affairs to be stage-managed by the Human Relations Councils, in which "spontaneous" demonstrations were to be held simultaneously in a number of large cities, with Black and White citizens joining together in a call for the government to break down the last of the barriers between the races and assure the Blacks of "full equality."

But then last Thursday, the day after we hit the Israelis, the big boys in the Councils — Jews, of course — called it all off. They decided they can't afford to share the media spotlight with the Blacks until they have finished milking their own "martyrdom" in the embassy raid for all it is worth.

A few of the more militant Black leaders, who spent a long time working on the preparations for the equality strike, didn't see it that way. They have long resented the high-handed way in which the Jews manipulate and exploit the entire "equality" movement for their own ends, and this was the last straw for some of them. There were angry accusations and counter-accusations, which culminated Saturday in the Jews' number-one house nigger, the nominal "chairman" of the National Association of Human Relations Councils, giving a press interview at which he denounced his Jewish masters. From now on, he said, the Human Relations Councils will not recognize the

Jewish claim to minority status. They will be treated just like the White majority and will no longer be exempt from investigation and punishment for "racism."

He was out on his ear before he knew what happened, of course, and his place has been taken by a better-housebroken Black, but the fat is already in the fire. On the streets the roving bands of Black "deputies" have gotten the word, and woe betide any member of the self-chosen tribe who falls into their hands! Several have already died while being "questioned," just in the last two days.

The "Toms" will eventually get their more militant and resentful brethren back into line, but meanwhile Izzy and Sambo are really at one another's throats, tooth and nail, and it is a joy to behold.

May 6. It's nice to be home again, even if only for a day. But New York was interesting! I saw more ordnance up there than I ever imagined we'd have at our disposal.

One of our specialized units in New York has been acquiring military materiel of all sorts and stockpiling it. The purpose of my visit was to survey the types of military gadgets available which might be useful to me in designing and building special weapons and sabotage devices, so that I can make recommendations for future procurement priorities.

I was met at the airport by a girl, who drove me to a wholesale plumbing supply store in an incredibly filthy industrial and warehouse area in Queens, near the East River. Garbage, old newspapers, and empty liquor bottles were strewn all over. We had to navigate around the stripped and rusting hulks of several abandoned autos which nearly blocked the narrow street before the girl finally pulled into a small, muddy parking area behind a tall, chain-link fence.

She knocked at a steel door marked "employees only," and we were quickly admitted to a gloomy, dusty storeroom filled with bins of pipe fittings. There she turned me over to a cheerful young man, about 25 years old, dressed in greasy coveralls and carrying a clipboard. He introduced himself only as "Richard" and offered me a cup of coffee from a disreputable-looking electric urn at one end of a long counter near the door.

Then we took an old and rickety freight elevator to the second floor of the building. When we stepped out of the elevator, I gasped in surprise. In a huge, low-ceilinged room, more than a hundred feet on a side, there were immense heaps of every sort of military weaponry imaginable: automatic rifles, machine guns,

122

flame throwers, mortars, and literally thousands of cases of ammunition, grenades, explosives, detonators, boosters, and spare parts. I don't know how the floor supported it all.

In one corner of the room four men and a woman worked at two long benches under fluorescent lights. One man was grinding the serial numbers off automatic rifles, which he took one at a time from a stack of approximately 50, while the others oiled and reassembled the rifles and then carefully packed them inside a large hot-water heater from which the top had been removed. I saw a dozen large cartons nearby which contained other water heaters.

"That's the way we store and ship the weapons," Richard explained. "We remove the serial numbers just to make it harder for the authorities to figure out where we're getting the stuff, in case they ever find any of it. And once the water heaters leave here, there's no way they can be traced back to us. The phony shipping tags we put on the cartons are coded to tell us what the contents are. You'll find that our rather special water heaters have been installed in the headquarters of quite a few of our combat units along the east coast, but we ship them everywhere in the country."

Almost in a daze, I wandered among the heaps of weaponry. I stopped beside a ceiling-high stack of large, olive-drab crates. Stencilled on each crate were the words: "Mortar, 4.2 inch, M 30, Complete," and under that, "Gross Wt. 700 lbs."

"Where did you get these?" I asked. I remembered all the work we had done a year and a half ago modifying just one mortar of ancient vintage.

"Those came in last week from Fort Dix," Richard answered. "The people in one of our units just outside Trenton paid a Black supply sergeant on the base $10,000 to swipe a truck with those things on it and deliver it to them. Then they brought them up here two at a time in the back of a pickup.

"We receive materiel here from more than a dozen bases and arsenals in New York, New Jersey, and Pennsylvania. Look what we got last month from Picatinny Arsenal," he said, throwing back a tarpaulin covering a nearby stack of cylindrical objects.

I leaned over to examine them. They were fiberboard tubes about two feet long and five inches in diameter. Each one contained an M329 high-explosive mortar projectile. There must have been at least 300 of them in that one pile.

Richard continued his explanation: "It used to be that most of our new weapons were smuggled off military bases one at a time, by our own people who were stationed there. But lately we've switched to hiring Black service personnel to hijack the stuff for us by the truckload. We don't always get exactly what we want that way, but we get a lot more of it.

"We've set up a couple of phony fronts posing as Mafia buyers for the illegal weapons-exporting business. Our people on the bases steer the buyers to Blacks in charge of the weapons storage areas. For enough money they'll walk off with the whole base for us. They just have to share some of the money we give them with a few of their 'soul brothers' on guard duty.

"There are several advantages for us. First, it's easier for the Blacks to swipe the stuff without getting caught. The political police aren't watching them as closely as they are the White service personnel, and the Blacks already have organized networks on all the bases for siphoning off and selling tires, gasoline, PX supplies, and other things for which there is a civilian demand. And it allows our people in the service to concentrate on their main task, which is recruiting other White servicemen and building our strength inside the military."

I spent the rest of the day going through everything in the room and mentally cataloguing it. When I left I took samples of a couple dozen different types of high-explosive fuzes, igniters, and other odds and ends I wanted to experiment with. Which meant I had to come back on the train.

The situation in the military is double-edged. With more than 40 per cent Blacks in the Army and nearly that many in the other services, morale, discipline, and efficiency are shockingly low. That makes it enormously easier for us to steal weapons and also to recruit, especially among the career personnel, who resent what has been done to their services.

But it also poses a fearful danger in the long run, because the day will come when we must make our move inside the military. With so many Blacks under arms, there is bound to be a bloody shambles. While we are cleaning out the Blacks and reorganizing the services, the country will be virtually defenseless.

Well, I guess it has been planned that way.

XVIII

May 23, 1993. This is my last night in Dallas. I've been here two weeks now, and I'd hoped to be heading back to Washington tomorrow, but orders came in this afternoon to go to Denver instead. It looks like I'll be doing approximately the same thing there I've been doing here, which is teaching.

124

I have just finished conducting a crash course in the technology of sabotage for eight selected activists here, and I do mean "crash"; this is the first free hour I've had since I arrived here when I wasn't too tired to think. We've been at it from eight in the morning until eight at night every day, with only a few minutes off for meals.

I have taught the people here virtually everything I know. We started by learning how to build improvised detonators, timers, igniters, and other gadgets from scratch. Then we studied the structure, properties, and performance characteristics of currently available military devices which can be adapted for various purposes. All my students can now disassemble and reassemble every type of fuze and delay device we studied, blindfolded.

After that we examined a large number of hypothetical targets and worked out detailed plans for attacking them. We considered reservoirs, pipelines, fuel depots, rail lines, air terminals and aircraft, telephone exchanges, oil refineries, power transmission lines, generating stations, highway interchanges, grain elevators, warehouses, and various types of machinery and other manufacturing equipment.

Finally, we picked a real target and destroyed it: Dallas's central telephone exchange. That was yesterday. Today we held a post mortem and criticized the operation in detail.

Actually, everything went extraordinarily well; my students all passed their final examination with flying colors. But I did everything possible to guarantee there would be no slipups. We spent three full days preparing specifically for the telephone exchange.

First we thoroughly pumped one of our local members who had formerly worked in the building as an operator. She described the layout for us, giving us the approximate location of the rooms on each floor which held the automatic switching equipment. With her help we made a rough map, showing the stairwells, the employees' entrances, the guard room, and other pertinent details.

Then we prepared our equipment. I decided we would use surgical precision on this job rather than brute force; besides, we didn't have a sufficiently large quantity of explosives for a brute-force demolition job. What we did have were three 500-foot spools of PETN-filled detonating cord and a little over 20 pounds of dynamite.

I broke our eight activists up into four two-man teams. One man in each team carried a sawed-off, autoloading shotgun, and the other carried demolition equipment. Three of the teams were assigned to the three floors of switching equipment, one to a floor. Each of these teams was given one of the spools of detonating cord; a five-gallon can of a homemade, napalm-like mixture of gasoline and liquid soap; and a delayed-action detonator. The fourth team was given a 20-pound satchel charge and a homemade thermite grenade and assigned to the transformer vault in the basement. The dynamite would wreck the transformers, and the thermite would set the transformer oil afire.

About ten o'clock last night we were parked in two automobiles on a dark side street two blocks from the telephone exchange. Every few minutes a telephone company service truck went through the intersection directly in front of us.

Finally the situation for which we had been waiting occurred: a service truck came to a stop for the red light at the intersection, and there were no other vehicles or pedestrians in sight. We sped out of the side street, blocking the truck fore and aft while two of our men jerked open the truck doors and ordered the driver into the back at gunpoint. Then we drove all three vehicles back onto the side street and transferred everyone and all our gear into the service truck.

That only took a few seconds, but we spent another half hour talking to the telephone serviceman we had kidnapped. With a minimum of prodding he answered a number of questions we still had about the location and layout of the switching equipment in the telephone building and about the security staff and procedures.

We were pleasantly surprised to learn that there was only one armed guard in the building at night and that he depended upon a direct line to the police substation five blocks away for backup in case of emergency. We relieved the serviceman of his uniform and his magnetically coded company security badge, which was needed to unlock the rear employees' entrance at night. Then we tied him securely with wire, gagged him, and drove the truck back to the rear entrance of the telephone building.

I was wearing the uniform. Following the serviceman's instructions, I gained entrance to the building while the others remained hidden in the truck. It was then only a matter of a moment to relieve the surprised guard of his gun and beckon to the others to enter. While our four teams fanned out through the building I found a convenient janitor's closet and used the guard's own master key to lock him in it.

From that point the whole operation took less than five minutes. The three teams assigned to the switching equipment worked quickly and efficiently. While the man with the shotgun on each team herded any employees that were encountered into an office and kept an eye on them, the other man went to work on the equipment.

The detonating cord was unreeled and laced through two or three long banks of electronic panels on each floor. Then the demolition man took the five-gallon can of napalm and sloshed its contents over large sections of the equipment, both those which had been laced with the detonating cord and those which had not. Finally, a time-delay detonator was taped to one end of the detonating cord.

As our men came racing down the stairs to join me on the ground floor, three deafening explosions rocked the windowless building. A moment later our fourth team came running up the stairs from the basement.

We wasted no time in piling back into the truck. Just as we drove out of the parking lot, the satchel charge went off in the basement transformer vault with a roar which caused a huge section of the brick facade on one side of the building to split off and topple into the street, exposing the interior, which by now was filled with flames and smoke from the blazing napalm and burning switching gear.

The accounts of the operation in this afternoon's local newspaper indicated that the two dozen or so employees who were in the building managed to get out safely—all except the guard I locked in the closet, who died of smoke inhalation. I feel guilty about that, but it couldn't be helped; we were in a hurry.

Although our destruction of the equipment in the telephone building was pretty thorough, the telephone company has announced that it expects to have most essential telephone lines back in service within 48 hours and complete restoration of telephone service for the city within two weeks.

That announcement did not surprise us. We knew that the telephone company can fly in new equipment and teams of repair specialists to quickly undo the damage we did. Our attack on the telephone exchange would only make real sense as a blow against the System if it had been coordinated with an all-out assault on a number of other fronts.

The System has figured that out for itself, of course, and, not having any way of knowing that yesterday's operation was only a training exercise, it is bracing itself for the worst. There are tanks at nearly every downtown intersection, and troops and police

127

have set up so many vehicle checkpoints on all the main roads and freeways that automobile traffic is at a virtual standstill throughout the city. If it weren't for that, I'd be leaving for Denver tonight instead of tomorrow.

June 8. Received a note from Katherine today! It came enclosed in a box of equipment I had asked the Organization to have sent to me from the shop back home. I didn't discover the note until I unpacked the box, and so there was no chance to send a reply with the courier who made the delivery.

She and the others have all been working 70 to 80 hours a week in the shop, she reports, printing money mostly but also large quantities of propaganda leaflets. She suspects from the urgency with which the leaflets have been requested that a major new campaign is afoot in the Washington area. (She'll find out what's afoot soon enough!)

She thinks I am still in Dallas, and she says she is hoping she will be ordered to make another cash delivery to Dallas soon so she can see me. How my heart aches to be with her again, even if only for a few hours!

There's not much chance of my getting back to Washington again for at least another three weeks, though. Things have really mushroomed out here in the Rocky Mountain area. The Organization is not particularly strong here, and yet Revolutionary Command has designated 43 high-priority targets in the area — more than half of them military installations — which we must prepare ourselves to hit simultaneously when the order is given, probably early in July.

On top of that, there is practically no one out here with any experience in specialized ordnance, and so I am having to train everyone from scratch — 26 students altogether. They will have the responsibility for preparing and using all the incendiary and explosive devices required for the assigned targets in the area. Fortunately, we do have several military people here with an excellent grasp of guerrilla tactics, and so I am restricting my training to the technical end only and leaving the tactics to the military people.

Despite the narrower scope of my work here, it's still going more slowly than in Dallas, because things are so spread out. It was deemed inadvisable to try to hold classes for 26 people at a time, so I meet with six here in Denver; 11 in Boulder, a college town about 20 miles north of here; and nine in a farmhouse just south of here. I see each group every third day, but I give them plenty of homework to do between meetings.

128

We've initiated virtually no violent actions against the System in the Rocky Mountain area so far, and the general atmosphere here is quite a bit more relaxed than along the East Coast. Something very unpleasant happened last week, though, which serves as a grim reminder that the struggle here will be just as brutal and vicious as anywhere else.

One of our members, a construction worker, was caught trying to sneak a few sticks of dynamite off the construction site where he was employed. Apparently he had been smuggling a dozen or so out in his lunch box every day for quite a while.

The site guard turned him over to the local sheriff, who immediately searched the man's house and found not only a big cache of dynamite but also several guns — and some Organization literature. The sheriff figured he had stumbled onto something which could really give a boost to his career. If he could crack the Organization in the Rocky Mountain area, the System would be very grateful to him. He would have a good chance of winning a seat in the state legislature, perhaps even becoming lieutenant governor or being appointed to some other high post in the state government.

So the sheriff and his deputies began beating our man, trying to make him name other Organization members. They gave him a vicious working over, but he wouldn't talk. Then they brought in the man's wife and began slapping and kicking her around in his presence.

The outcome was that our man, in desperation, snatched a revolver from the holster of one of the deputies. He was shot dead by another deputy before he could pull the trigger. The wife was handed over to the FBI and flown back to Washington for interrogation. She should not be able to give them any significant information, but I shudder to think of the ordeal to which she is being submitted.

The sheriff's glory was short-lived, however. The evening of the day our member was killed, the sheriff appeared in a televised news interview, boasting of the blow he had struck in the name of law, order, and equality and pompously warning that he would treat with equal ruthlessness any other "racists" who fell into his hands.

When he arrived home that night after his TV interview, he found his wife on his living-room floor, with her throat cut. Two days later his patrol car was ambushed. His bullet-riddled body was found in its burned-out wreckage.

It is a terrible thing to kill women of our own race, but we are engaged in a war in which all the old rules have been scrapped.

We are in a war to the death with the Jew, who now feels himself so close to his final victory that he can safely drop his mask and treat his enemies as the "cattle" his religion tells him they are. Our retribution against the sheriff here should serve as a warning to the Jew's Gentile henchmen, at least, that if they adopt the Jew's attitude toward *our* women and children, then they cannot expect their own families to be safe. (*Note to the reader:* Several sets of books containing the Jewish religious doctrine, which was called "Judaism," are still extant today. These books, the Talmud and the Torah, do, indeed, refer to non-Jews as "cattle." Especially horrifying to us is the attitude the Jews had toward non-Jewish women. The word they used to designate a girl of our race was *"shiksa,"* which was derived from the Hebrew word meaning both "abomination" and "non-kosher meat" or "unclean meat.")

June 21. I was stopped at a police roadblock driving back from Boulder tonight. No problem getting through it; they just checked my driver's license (i.e., the late and unlamented David S. Bloom's license), asked me where I was going, and took a quick look in the car. But the roadblock had traffic backed up for miles, and other motorists were really fuming. One of them told me this is the first time they've used roadblocks in this area.

The roadblock and a couple of hints I've caught on news broadcasts in the last few days lead me to believe that the System knows something big is cooking. I hope they don't tighten up security out here the way they have back on the East Coast; it'll mess up our plans if they do.

On the other hand, it'll do these bumpkins around here a lot of good to get a full dose of Big Brother's loving care. Most of them hardly ever see a Black or a Jew, and they act as if there's not a war going on. They seem to think that they're far enough away from the things that are plaguing other parts of the country that they can keep on with their same old routine. They resent any hint that they may have to halt their pursuit of pleasure and affluence long enough to cut a cancer out of America that will surely destroy us all if it's not eliminated soon. But it's always been that way with Boobus Americanus.

I'm quite concerned that I've heard no news of Evanston. I've been expecting the raid there every day since the last week of last month. Has there been more trouble with Harrison? Or has Revolutionary Command decided to postpone the Evanston raid, perhaps until our big offensive next month?

There was no indication of such a postponement at my last briefing. More than likely the trouble is Harrison, damn him! When I recalculated the hit probability on the target at the range given me by our Chicago mortar team just before I left Washington for Dallas, I decided we should distribute our radioactive contaminant among five rounds instead of only three. That gives us a probability of nearly 90 per cent that we'll get one or more rounds into the generator building. But Harrison may have balked at having to handle that much ordnance. If that's the case, why hasn't someone told me?

I'm also becoming concerned that I've received no orders as to what I'm to do when I finish my work here next week. If I don't get back to Washington then, I'm afraid I may not make it before the big push starts. I want to be back there with Katherine and the others when everything hits the fan next month. And I can't see any reason why I shouldn't, because there will hardly be time to send me anywhere else to set up another training course in special ordnance.

XIX

June 27, 1993. So, I finally have my orders! It's to be California for me during our big summer offensive. At first I was very disappointed that I won't be able to go back to Washington, but the more I consider the implications of some of the things I was told this afternoon, the more I'm convinced that the real focus of our activity in the next few weeks will be on the West Coast. It looks like I'll be in the thick of things there, and that will be a welcome change from all this classroom work, at least.

Denver Field Command summoned me and six of my pupils to a meeting today on two hours' notice. We were told almost nothing, except that I and four of the others are to be in Los Angeles by Wednesday night at the latest. The last two were given a destination in San Mateo, just outside San Francisco.

I protested immediately and vehemently: "All these people have been trained especially to attack specific targets in this area. And they've been trained as teams. It doesn't make sense to break them up now and send some of them to California, when they can be so much more effective here. If they are sent away, our whole program for the Rocky Mountain area will be jeopardized."

The two DFC officers at the meeting assured me that their decision had not been made capriciously and that they are fully cognizant of the validity of my objections, but that more pressing

131

considerations must prevail. I finally forced them to reveal that they had received an urgent order from Revolutionary Command to transfer every activist they could spare to the West Coast immediately. Apparently other field commands all over the country have received similar orders.

They were reluctant to say more, but from the emphasis they put on our deadline for reporting to our California destinations, I strongly suspect that things are set to blow sometime next week.

I did accomplish one thing this afternoon: I arranged to have Albert Mason, who was to go to San Mateo but whose presence here is really essential to the success of the operations planned for this area, swapped for another man. But I had trouble gaining even that concession. I insisted on knowing exactly what criteria had been used in selecting the men to be transferred. It turned out that, except in my case, there were two: infantry combat experience and rifle marksmanship — which makes it look like they want snipers and barricade fighters out on the Coast, rather than saboteurs and demolition experts.

Al, it is true, qualified as an "expert" with the rifle when he was in the service, and he spent three years as a squad leader in Southeast Asia. (*Note to the reader:* Turner is referring to the so-called "Vietnam War," which had been over for two decades at the time but which played an enormously important role in laying the groundwork for the Organization's later success in dealing with the System's armed forces.) But he has also been my best pupil here. He is the one man I spent time with explaining some of the newer military gadgets we expect to acquire in our raids on the arsenals around here. He is the only one I am sure will be able to use the new M-58 laser range finders, for example, and teach our mortar teams how to use them too. And he is also the only one here to whom I taught enough basic electronics so that he can rig up the radio-controlled detonators which are an essential part of our plan for knocking out the highway network in this area and keeping it knocked out.

Only when I pointed out these things to DFC did they agree to let Al stay here. We then spent half an hour going over a list of all the other activists here before we found one I thought could go to California in Al's place without jeopardizing things here and who also satisfied their criteria.

My impression is that everything we planned for this area is still "go," and it is still considered important for us to achieve our objectives here, but the really critical theater of operations will be the West Coast. We are approximately doubling our manpower there with these last-minute transfers, but we are doing it in such a way that at least *most* of the operations planned for other areas can go ahead, though with fewer personnel.

Well, we only have 48 hours to drive more than 1,000 miles, and there's no telling how many checkpoints we'll be stopped at. The others will be by to pick me up in about two hours, and then it'll take me at least four hours to pack my gadgets in the car so they won't be found if we're searched. I think I'll take a quick nap now.

July 1. Wow! Are things tense here! We arrived yesterday, around one in the morning, after a trip I'd just as soon forget. The others are dispersed to their assigned units, but I'm staying with Los Angeles Northwest Field Command temporarily, in a place called Canoga Park, about 20 miles northwest of Los Angeles proper.

It is apparent that the Organization is much more solidly entrenched here than elsewhere, simply from the fact that there are eight different field commands in the Los Angeles metropolitan area, whereas one suffices for most other major cities in the country. That would indicate an underground membership here in the 500-700 range.

Mostly, I've been catching up on my sleep since I arrived, but the other people here don't seem to be doing any sleeping at all. Couriers are constantly coming and going, and conferences are being held at all hours. This evening I finally buttonholed someone and got at least a partial briefing on the situation.

A simultaneous assault on more than 600 military and civilian targets all over the country has been scheduled for next Monday morning, July 4. Unfortunately, however, one of our members here was picked up by the police on Wednesday, just a few hours before our arrival. It seems to have been just a fluke. He was stopped on the street for a routine identification check, and the cops became suspicious about something.

Since the man is not in the Order, he was neither prepared nor under an absolute obligation to kill himself if captured. The great worry for the last two days has been that, under torture, he will reveal enough of what he knows to tip off the System to the fact that a major assault is scheduled for Monday. Then, even though the authorities won't know just which targets we plan to hit, they'll tighten up security everywhere to the point that our casualties will be unbearably high.

Revolutionary Command has two choices: silence our man before he can be interrogated, or reschedule our entire offensive. The latter choice is almost unthinkable: too many things have been carefully arranged and synchronized in detail for next Monday to allow the date to be advanced, and a postponement might run into months — with enormous risks attendant on having so many people, already primed for Monday, knowing so much for so long.

So it was decided yesterday to act on the first choice. But even that presents a major problem: we can't hit our man here in Los Angeles without risking blowing the cover of one of our most valuable legals, a special agent in the FBI's Los Angeles office. That's because the prisoner is being held in a location which is supposed to be a big secret. If we raid the place, they'll only have half-a-dozen people to suspect as the one who leaked the information to us.

The System's customary procedure when they pick up one of our people is to perform only a very cursory interrogation in the field — just enough to determine whether there is any indication that the prisoner is connected in any way with the Organization. If there is, then he is flown back to Washington for a thorough working over by their Israeli torture specialists. And the latter is what we can't afford to let happen.

The interesting thing in this particular case — and the thing which has kept Revolutionary Command in a state of agonized indecision for two days now — is that the FBI has been holding the prisoner here, instead of flying him back to the Washington headquarters Thursday morning, as soon as they suspected they had an Organization member. No one seems to know exactly why, not even our FBI legal. It may just be an instance of organizational inefficiency on their part. Or perhaps they're bringing an interrogation team out here from Washington this time, contrary to their previous routine.

Anyway, RC has decided to hold off on the hit and see what happens. If no move is made to put the prisoner on a plane for Washington or to interrogate him further here within the next 36 hours, the problem will be solved; any information the System extracts from him will come too late to interfere with our Monday schedule. But if a transfer or an interrogation seems imminent before Sunday afternoon, we're prepared to launch a lightning raid on the FBI's secret prison here, even at the risk of losing our inside man in the local FBI office, whose information in coming months can be invaluable to us.

As for me, I still don't know why I'm here or what I'm supposed to do, and I'm not sure anyone else does either. I was just told to wait.

134

Well, I guess we're really facing a major test again, like we did in September 1991. It just seems incredible to me that the Organization is actually launching an all-out assault on the System in two days! The total number of men we can put on the firing line, for the whole country, can't be more than 1,500, despite the very rapid gains in recruiting we've made in the last few months. Altogether — including our support personnel, our female members, and our legals — our strength can't possibly exceed 5,000 people, and I'd estimate that nearly a third of them are concentrated here in California now. It just seems unreal — like a gnat planning to assassinate an elephant!

Of course, we're not expecting the System to collapse Monday. If it did we wouldn't know how to cope with the situation, because the Organization is still far too small to take over the running of the country and the rebuilding of American society. We'll need an infrastructure 100 times as large as we have now to even begin tackling that job.

What we will do Monday is escalate the conflict to a new level and forestall the System's latest strategy for dealing with us. We really have no choice in the matter; if the Organization is to survive and continue growing under the very difficult circumstances which have been imposed on us, we must maintain our momentum — especially our psychological momentum.

The danger in *not* constantly escalating the war is that the System will find a new equilibrium, and the public will become accustomed to it. The only way to maintain the present influx of recruits is to keep a substantial portion of the public psychologically off balance — keep them at least half convinced that the System isn't strong enough and efficient enough to wipe us out, that we are an irresistible force, that sooner or later the war will sweep them, too, up in it.

Otherwise, the worthless bastards will take the easy way out by just sitting back to see what happens. The American people have already proved that they can shamelessly continue their crass pursuit of pleasure under the most provocative conditions imaginable — so long as new provocations are introduced gradually enough for them to become accustomed to them. That's our greatest danger in not acting.

Besides that, however, the political police are continually tightening the screws. Despite our extraordinary security procedures, they will eventually succeed in penetrating the Organization and wrecking us — if we give them time. And it's becoming harder all the time for us to move around without being picked up. Very soon now, the new internal passport system

135

which we wrecked more than a year ago will be back on the tracks, twice as mean as before. I don't know how we'll survive when that becomes operational.

Thinking back over the last two years, though, it's amazing that we've survived even until now. There have been a hundred times when I didn't know how we'd be able to last another month.

Part of the reason we've been able to make it this far is something for which we really can't take credit — and that's the inefficiency of the System. They've made some bad mistakes and failed to follow up on a lot of things which could have hurt us badly.

One gets the impression that except for the Jews, who are really burning the midnight oil in their efforts against us, the rest of the System is a bunch of clock-watchers. Thank "equal opportunity" — and all those niggers in the FBI and in the Army — for that! The System has become so corrupt and so mongrelized that only the Jews feel at home in it, and no one feels any loyalty toward it.

But a bigger part of the reason is the way we've adapted to our peculiar circumstances. In just two years the Organization has learned a whole new way of existence. We're doing a number of things now which are absolutely vital to our survival but to which we had given almost no thought two years ago.

Our interrogation technique for checking out new recruits, for example; there's no way we could have lasted this long without that, and we didn't develop it until we absolutely *had* to have it. What we would have done without Dr. Clark to work out the technique, I don't know.

And then there's the matter of false identities. We had only the vaguest ideas about coping with this problem when we first went underground. Now we have a number of specialized units who do nothing but provide nearly foolproof false identities for our activists. They are real professionals, but they've had to learn their rather gruesome trade in a hurry.

And money — what a problem *that* was in the beginning! Having to count our pennies affected our whole psychology; it made us think small. So far as I know, no one in the Organization had ever given any serious thought to the problem of financing an underground movement before the problem became crucial. Then we learned the counterfeiting trade.

It was providential that we had someone in the Organization with the requisite technical knowledge, of course, but we still had to set up our distribution network for getting the counterfeit bills into circulation after we'd printed them.

136

In just the last few months this accomplishement has made an enormous difference for all of us. Having a ready supply of cash — being able to buy whatever we need instead of hijacking it, as in the old days — has made things much easier. It has given us greater mobility and greater safety.

There's been a certain element of luck in our success so far, and there's no doubt that Revolutionary Command has been doing a pretty good job of generalship. We've had good planning, a good strategy — but, more than that, we've shown the ability to meet new challenges and solve new problems. We've remained flexible.

I think the history of the Organization proves that no one can make a fixed plan for a revolution and then stick to it. The future is always too uncertain. One can never be sure how a given situation will develop. And totally unexpected things are always happening — things that no planner, however thorough, could have foreseen. So, in order to be successful, a revolutionary must always be ready to adapt to new circumstances and take advantage of new opportunities.

Our record in that regard is reassuring, but I cannot help being apprehensive about next week. I am sure we will knock hell out of the bastards Monday. We will throw a good-sized monkey wrench into the country's economic machinery if only half the things we have planned come off successfully. And we will force the System into a state of total mobilization, with the resulting psychological shock to the general public.

But what then? What about next month and the month after that? We're throwing everything we've got into next week's offensive, and there is just *no* way we can keep up such a level of activity for more than a few days. We are stretched too thin everywhere.

And yet my instinct tells me that the Organization is not acting purely from desperation now. We are not making one, last, desperate effort to wreck the System Monday. At least, I hope not. If we make an all-out effort, then have to retrench when it fails — as it surely will — the psychological effect will be as lethal for us as it will be helpful for the System.

So Revolutionary Command must have something up its sleeve I don't know about. I am sure the heavy concentration of our people in California is a clue, but I can't figure it out.

XX

July 7, 1993. Looks like I'll be here till morning, so I can take an hour or so now to record the events of the last few days.

This is really a swanky place. It's a penthouse apartment from which we can see most of Los Angeles — which is why we're using it as a command post. But the luxury is unbelievable: satin sheets; genuine fur bedspreads; gold-plated bathroom fixtures; wall taps which dispense bourbon, scotch, and vodka in every room; huge, framed, pornographic photographs on the walls.

The apartment belonged to one Jerry Siegelbaum, a business agent for the local Municipal Employees Union — and the star subject of the dirty photos on the walls. Looks like he preferred blonde, Gentile girls, although his partner in one picture is a Negress, and he's with a young boy in another. Some representative of the workers he was! I hope someone moves him from the hallway outside soon; there's been no air-conditioning since Monday, and he's beginning to stink pretty bad.

This huge city presents quite a different aspect now from the last time I had an overall view of it at night. The blaze of lights outlining all the main streets is gone. Instead, the general blackness is broken only by hundreds of fires randomly scattered through the city. I know there are thousands of vehicles moving down there, but they are driving without lights, so they won't be shot at.

For the last four days one has heard the practically continuous scream of sirens from police and emergency vehicles mixed with the sound of gunfire and explosions and the whirring clatter of helicopters. Tonight there is only the gunfire, and not much of that. It looks like the battle here has reached a decisive stage.

At two o'clock Monday morning more than 60 of our combat units struck simultaneously throughout the Los Angeles area, while hundreds of other units hit targets all across the country, from Canada to Mexico and from coast to coast. I haven't heard yet what we accomplished elsewhere, because the System has clamped a total censorship on all the news media — the ones we haven't seized ourselves, that is — and I haven't had a chance to talk to any of our own people who've been in contact with Revolutionary Command. But here in Los Angeles we've done surprisingly well.

Our initial assault cut off all water and electrical power into the metropolitan area, knocked out the main airports, and made all the major freeways impassable. We took out the telephone exchanges and blew up every gasoline storage depot. The harbor area has been almost a solid mass of flames for four days now.

We seized at least 15 police stations. Mostly we just took their weapons, destroyed their communications equipment and whatever vehicles were not on patrol at the time, and then pulled

138

out. But apparently our people are still holed up in several police buildings and are using them as local command posts.

At first the cops and the firemen were running around like chickens with their heads cut off — sirens and flashing lights everywhere. By Monday afternoon, however, communications had broken down so badly and there were so many fires and other emergencies that the police and fire departments were being much more selective in their responses. In many areas our teams were able to go about their work practically without interference. Now, of course, most emergency and police vehicles are out of fuel and can't move at all. And the ones which still have gas seem to be lying low.

The whole key to neutralizing the police — and to everything else, for that matter — was our work inside the military. It was apparent to everyone as early as Monday afternoon that something big was happening inside the military establishment. For one thing, other than the troops and tanks guarding power stations, TV transmitters, and so on — as always — no military units were deployed against us. For another thing, there were obvious signs of armed conflict *inside* all the military bases in the area.

We could see and hear jet fighter-bombers swooping low over the city, but they were not attacking us — at least, not directly. They were strafing and bombing the dozen or so California National Guard armories in the metropolitan area. Those jets were apparently from El Toro Marine Air Station south of here. Later we saw several dogfights in the sky over Los Angeles and heard that Camp Pendleton, the big Marine Corps base about 70 miles southeast of here, was being hit by heavy bombers from Edwards Air Force Base. All in all, a very confusing scenario for everyone concerned.

But Monday evening, quite by chance, I ran into Henry, of all people, and he explained quite a bit of the military situation to me. Good old Henry — how glad I was to see him again!

We met in the KNX transmitter building, where I was helping our broadcast team get the station back on the air after we seized it. That, by the way, is what I've been doing for four days: repairing shot-up transmitters, shifting transmitter frequencies, and improvising equipment. We now have one FM station and two AM stations on the air, all operating from emergency generators. In all three cases we cut the cables from the studios and installed our broadcast teams directly at the transmitter sites.

Henry came roaring up to KNX in a jeep, wearing a U.S. Army uniform with colonel's insignia and accompanied by three soldiers carrying machine guns and anti-tank rockets. He was bringing the text to be broadcast — a text directed primarily at military personnel.

As soon as I had finished splicing our microphone and audio equipment into the transmitter input, Henry and I stepped to the side to talk while his message was being read over the air by our announcer. It consisted of an appeal to all White military personnel who had not already done so to join our revolution, together with a warning to those who failed to heed the appeal. The message was very well designed, and I am sure its effect on both military and civilian listeners was powerful.

Henry, it turned out, has been in charge of the Organization's entire recruiting effort in the armed forces for over a year, and he has been concentrating his efforts on the West Coast since he was transferred here last March. The story he told me was a long one, but, together with what I have learned since then, its essence is this:

We have been recruiting inside the military on two levels since the Organization was formed. At the lower level we operated semi-openly before September 1991 and clandestinely afterwards. That involved the dissemination of our propaganda among enlisted personnel and non-coms, mostly on a person-to-person basis. But, Henry told me, we have also been recruiting at higher levels, in the utmost secrecy.

Revolutionary Command's strategy hinged on our success in winning over a humber of high-ranking military commanders, and on Monday we began playing that hidden trump. That's why the armed forces haven't been used against us and also why various military units have been shooting and bombing each other the last four days.

The intra-military conflict started with units commanded by our sympathizers on one side and those loyal to the System (by far the majority) on the other side. Another aspect to the conflict soon developed and overshadowed the first, however: Black against White.

Military units commanded by pro-Organization officers began disarming all Black military personnel as soon as we launched our Monday-morning attack. The excuse they used was that Black militants had launched a mutiny in other units and that their orders from higher up were to disarm *all* Blacks to prevent the spread of the mutiny. Generally, White servicemen were ready and willing to believe that story and did not need to be told twice to turn their guns against the Blacks in their units. Those few whose liberal predispositions made them hesitate were shot on the spot.

In other units our enlisted personnel simply began shooting any Blacks they saw in uniform and then deserted to units commanded by our sympathizers. The Blacks, naturally enough, reacted in such a way as to make the story about a Black mutiny come true. Even in those units commanded by pro-System officers heavy fighting between Blacks and Whites broke out.

And, since some of these units are nearly half Black, the fighting has been bloody and prolonged. The result has been that, although the units commanded by our sympathizers initially had only about five per cent of the strength of the pro-System units, most of the latter have been paralyzed by internal fighting between Blacks and Whites. And now Whites are coming over in increasing numbers to our units because of this.

Our broadcasts have helped this process along greatly. We have exaggerated our own strength, of course, and have told White servicemen who want to join our units where to go. And to help convince them — as well as to keep the niggers spooked and doing *their* thing — we have turned one of our transmitters into a phony "soul" station and been broadcasting a call for a Black revolution, telling the Blacks to shoot their White officers and non-coms before the Whites can disarm them.

About the only military units in the Los Angeles area able to offer any effective opposition to us have been some Air Force fighter and bomber units — and the Marine air unit at El Toro. They have been attacking military units believed to have come over to us. But, according to Henry, they have been doing about as much damage to the pro-System forces as to ours.

Henry chuckled as he explained to me that the Organization had been unable to make sufficient headway in its recruiting in the California National Guard to be able to count on any Guard units coming over to us. So the Organization kidnapped the local Guard commander, General Howell, just before the Monday morning attack, as a preventive measure.

When the System couldn't locate Howell, they were apparently afraid he had joined us. Their fears were undoubtedly confirmed when they heard that he had hurriedly left his home with three strangers after midnight Monday, less than an hour before everything hit the fan. Anyway, their suspicions got the better of them, and so they ordered all the National Guard armories and depots bombed by loyal air units Monday afternoon.

And at Camp Pendleton we were nowhere near having the upper hand before the System panicked and ordered in the bombers. I am sure that move is what tilted things in our favor. There is still heavy fighting in the Pendleton area, but we are apparently on top there now.

I don't know from which base the column of tanks came that neutralized the main Los Angeles police headquarters for us today, but they were certainly a godsend. We never could have done it without them.

From the beginning the L.A. cops have been our only really organized opposition. The smaller police forces in surrounding jurisdictions have not been a particular problem. Some we knocked out of action completely; others decided to lie low and mind their own business after a few early skirmishes. But the 10,000 or so men in the L.A.P.D. were very much in action against us until a few hours ago, and the going was very rough. We've had at least 100 KIA's here in the last four days — between 15 and 20 per cent of our local combat strength.

I don't know why we failed to do the same thing with the police here we seem to have done with the military. Perhaps it was just a shortage of cadres on our part, and military recruiting was given a higher priority than police recruiting. In any event, the main police headquarters here almost immediately became the center of counter-revolutionary resistance.

The L.A. city cops were joined by some sheriff's units from the county and even by some state highway patrol units, and they turned their main headquarters building into a fortress that was impregnable to anything we could bring to bear against it. In fact, it was almost certain death for any of our people to venture within a couple of blocks of the place. They had a large store of fuel, more than a thousand vehicles, and emergency power for their communications equipment, and they outmanned us by a large factor.

Using helicopters for reconnaissance, they pinpointed our various strongpoints and the buildings we had seized, and they sent out raiding parties involving as many as 50 vehicles and 200-300 men. Our demolition of virtually every highway overpass had limited their mobility to a large extent, but their airborne observers were able to route them around many obstacles.

We managed to protect certain really vital points — including the radio stations we had seized — only by having well-dug-in machine-gun crews covering the avenues of approach. Fortunately, the cops had only a few armored vehicles, because most of our people had no weapons for dealing with armor. It was only today that anti-tank weapons became generally available to our combat teams.

If the L.A. cops had been able to link up with any military units remaining loyal to the System, that would have been the end of us. Fortunately, a dozen old M60's from a unit which had come over to us got to them first. They rolled right over the roadblocks the police had set up around their headquarters, riddled the building with HE and incendiary shells, and liberally sprayed the hundreds of police vehicles in the area with machine-gun fire.

The cops' communications and power were knocked out, and their building was set afire in a dozen places. They had to evacuate the building, and we rained 81-mm mortar fire down on the surrounding parking lots and streets until the area became untenable for them. The place is deserted now and still burning. Most of the cops seem to have made their way to their homes and changed into civilian clothes.

Now that most of the organized resistance against us here has been neutralized, everything hinges on whether we can get this area effectively under our control before military units from other parts of the country are sent in. I don't understand why that hasn't already happened.

I was told just a couple of hours ago to report in the morning to a group of our technical people who will have the task of planning the details of restoring some electrical power and some water to the area, reestablishing routes for vehicular traffic, and locating and securing all remaining supplies of gasoline and diesel fuel. Sounds like more of a job for a civil engineer than for me.

It also sounds a little premature, but it is encouraging to know that Revolutionary Command seems to be confident of the future. Perhaps I'll find out more about the overall situation tomorrow.

July 10. Well, well, well! Things have really been happening — some good things and some bad things, but mostly good, so far.

The military-and-police situation seems to be essentially under control here — and, in fact, for most of the West Coast, although there is apparently a lot of fighting still going on around San Francisco and in a few other areas.

And there are still a few armed groups here — some cops and some military personnel — roving around and causing a little mischief. But we've secured all the bases and military airfields here and will round up stray personnel in another day or two. The order is out now to shoot on sight anyone carrying arms unless he is wearing one of our armbands.

143

That's a welcome switch from a few days ago, when we were the ones liable to be shot on sight. After years of hiding, slinking around in disguises, and getting sick with fear every time we saw a cop, it's a wonderful feeling to be out in the open — and to be the ones with the guns.

The big problem here has become a civilian one. The civilian population has gone completely amok. Actually, one can hardly blame them, and I'm surprised they behaved themselves — more or less — as long as they did. After all, they've been without electric power and without a water supply for a week. A very substantial portion of them have also been without food for several days.

For the first couple of days — Monday and Tuesday — the civilian population did just what we expected them to do. Hundreds of thousands of them piled into their cars and onto the freeways. They couldn't go very far, of course, because we had blown up a number of key interchanges, but they did manage to create a collection of the most monumental traffic jams imaginable, thus finishing our task for us of making ground travel almost impossible for the police.

By Tuesday afternoon most of the White population had returned to their homes — or, at least, to their own neighborhoods — many of them leaving their stalled cars on the roads and hiking back. They had discovered, first, that there was no feasible way for them to leave the Los Angeles area by automobile; second, that they couldn't buy gasoline, because the electric pumps at the filling stations weren't working; third, that most stores and businesses were closed up tight; and fourth, that something really *big* was happening. They stayed home, kept their transistor radios on, and worried. There was remarkably little crime or violence, except in the Black areas, where rioting, looting, and burning began early Monday afternoon and grew progressively more intense and widespread.

By early Thursday, however, there was a good bit of looting in White areas as well, mostly of grocery stores. Some people had not eaten for more than 48 hours by then and were acting from desperation rather than lawlessness.

Since it wasn't until Thursday night that we began to feel sure we had the police licked, we did nothing to discourage civilian disorder. The more of them in the streets, hungry and desperate, smashing store windows and stealing food, looking for drinkable water and fresh batteries for their radios, getting into fights with other people looking for the same things, the less time the police had for us. That, of course, was the principal idea behind our knocking out power, water, and transportation at the very beginning.

If the police had had only us to cope with, we couldn't have won. But they couldn't handle us *and* a general breakdown of public order at the same time.

Now, however, we're the ones with the job of restoring order, and it's going to be a bitch. The people are absolutely out of their minds with fear and panic. They are behaving in an entirely irrational manner, and a great number of lives are bound to be sacrificed before we get things under control. Partly, I'm afraid, starvation and exhaustion are going to have to do it for us, because our manpower and other material resources are entirely inadequate for the task.

Today I went out with a fuel recovery team, and I got a close look at our civilian problem. It really shook me. We were driving a big gasoline tank truck, with an armed jeep escort, from filling station to filling station in the Pasadena area, pumping the gasoline out of each station's tanks and into our truck. There's enough fuel in the area to meet our own needs for quite a while, but the civilians are just going to have to get along without their cars for the duration.

Pasadena used to be mostly White a few years ago, but it has become substantially Black now. In the Black areas, whenever we ran into Blacks near a filling station, we simply opened fire on them to keep them at a distance. In the White areas, we were mobbed by hungry Whites begging us for food — which, of course, we didn't have to give them.

It's a damned good thing they have no firearms, or we'd be in a hell of a jam now. Thank you, Senator Cohen!

Oops! No more time to write now — have to go to a meeting. We should get a briefing there on the national situation.

XXI

July 11, 1993. Busy day! We've got some electrical power coming back into the area now from one of the hydroelectric plants up north, but not much. Electricity has to be strictly rationed, and I spent all day mapping out the sections of the metropolitan area which were to be energized and then dispatching teams to cut or switch out power lines and reconnect others. Later, if the rationing is successful, we may also provide power to some other sections.

Last night I found out why Washington hasn't tried to send troops in here from other parts of the country: It's because we've got Vandenberg AFB and all the missile silos there!

For the first 48 hours after our Monday-morning attack last week, the System was in such a panic and the military situation was so uncertain that no major troop movements were possible. Although we were spread so thin that there was no hope of seizing and holding territory anywhere except here on the West Coast, we did create an enormous amount of disruption, disorder, and confusion everywhere.

Our people inside the military in other parts of the country had been instructed to carry out actions calculated to temporarily paralyze their units. This involved some sabotage, arson, and demolition, but to a much greater extent it involved selective shootings. In units with a high quota of non-Whites, our people shot down Blacks at random, shouting slogans such as "White power!," with the deliberate intention of provoking a Black reaction. This was followed up by the same tactic which we used here so successfully: seizing radio stations and broadcasting spurious calls for Blacks to turn their guns against their White officers.

In other units communications centers were seized and messages sent which created the false impression that the units had come over to us.

On top of all that, we wreaked real havoc on the civilian population. Power plants, communication facilities, dams, key highway interchanges, tank farms, gas pipelines, and everything else that could be blown up or burned down was hit Monday morning in an all-out effort, all across the country, to cause civilian panic and keep the System temporarily occupied with the attendant problems.

I also learned that, along with everything else, the raid on the Evanston Project took place Monday morning. I was immensely pleased to hear that it was a complete success.

So the net result was that, by the time the System had assessed the situation and had regained enough confidence in the loyalty of any of its military units to try to move against us, we had finished mopping up Vandenberg and had issued our ultimatum: any military move against us would result in our launching nuclear missiles targeted on New York City and Tel Aviv. And that's why things have been so quiet for the last few days!

And now I understand Revolutionary Command's whole strategy, which had eluded me for so long and caused me so many misgivings. RC realized all along that there was no way, with our

146

present numbers, that we could sustain a military assault against the System on a large enough scale for a long enough time to bring it down. We could have continued our guerrilla campaign of economic sabotage and psychological warfare for quite a while, of course, but time was ultimately on the side of the System. Unless we could make some really dramatic breakthrough which would increase our numbers substantially, the System's growing police powers would eventually paralyze us.

Well, we've made the breakthrough now. And we've got the potential, at least, for some very substantial growth; there are some twelve million people under our control in the Los Angeles metropolitan area alone. How large the total population base we have to draw from is still not clear, because of the anomalous situation in northern California.

Under direct Organization control at this moment is a strip of California which runs from the Mexican border to about 150 miles northwest of Los Angeles and from the coast inland for a distance varying from 50 to 100 miles. Included in this strip are San Diego, Los Angeles, and all-important Vandenberg AFB. The Sierras and the Mojave Desert form a natural eastern boundary to our territory.

In a further coastal strip which runs almost to the Oregon border and includes San Francisco and Sacramento, an anti-System military faction seems to be running things, but I gather that our own authority has not yet been established there. And the states of Oregon and Washington appear to be still firmly under System control, contrary to earlier rumors.

Elsewhere in the country, things are in a general uproar and our hit-and-run raids are continuing, but the System is in no immediate danger of collapsing. The main problem worrying the government seems to be whether or not it can trust its own armed forces. As a consequence of this worry, troops in some areas are still confined to their bases, even though they are badly needed to restore order among the civilian population.

In some of the worst areas of civilian rioting — primarily because of the disruption of food supplies — the government is using special military units made up of non-Whites only. They've rushed some of these all-nigger units into the border area around our California enclave.

The closest such unit seems to be in Barstow, about 100 miles northwest of here. Some White refugees from there have been trickling into our area, and their reports are pretty sickening: mass rape and terror from the Black troops, who are lording it over the local Whites. I hate to hear of such things happening to

147

White people, but the reaction can only be favorable to us. And it's good that we've forced the System to show its lack of confidence in the loyalty of the White population and its dependence on non-White elements.

What's most important for us now, though, is that the government isn't trying to force its way into our territory. Our Vandenberg threat is holding them off for the moment, although that situation certainly won't last forever. But at least it gives us a chance to try to get our civilian population under control here.

And what a mess things are in! There are more fires than ever, and rioting has become widespread. We simply don't have enough people, even including all the military personnel nominally on our side now, to maintain order while we restore essential utilities and set up an emergency food-distribution system.

We have altogether about 40,000 armed-forces personnel at our disposal, nearly two-thirds of them in the metro area here and the other third scattered from San Diego to Vandenberg. It is a ticklish situation, though, because they outnumber Organization members in this area by about 20 to one — which is actually not half as bad a ratio as I had thought earlier, but still quite bad enough! The great majority of these troops owe no loyalty to the Organization and, in fact, do not realize that their orders are coming from us.

So far we have been keeping them busy day and night, and they haven't had time to ask too many questions. Organization members have been assigned to every military unit, from the company level up, and Henry — whom I saw again briefly last night — seems to think we've got a pretty good grip on them. I hope so!

I have had a chance to chat with a few of the troops we have been using for fuel-recovery and utility-repair crews. They seem to be impressed by three facts: that the government in Washington has totally lost control out here; that the Blacks, both inside the military and outside, are a dangerous and unreliable element; and that they, with weapons and food, are a lot better off than the civilian population right now.

But ideologically they are in poor shape! Some of them are vaguely on our side; others are still chock-full of System brainwashing; and most are somewhere in between. The one thing that's keeping them in line now is the total absence of any alternate source of authority here.

The System hasn't even gotten around to broadcasting appeals for loyalty aimed at our troops — probably because that would constitute an admission to the rest of the country just how big our win here has been. The official System line at the moment is that the situation is well under control, and the "racist gangsters" in California (that's us) will soon be rounded up or liquidated. Since we have been broadcasting appeals to revolt aimed at *their* troops day and night and have also been giving a picture of the situation here much rosier than it actually is, the System's story sounds pretty hollow. Instead of denying our claims the System has simply started jamming our broadcasts, which is probably their shrewdest course.

July 14. The first substantial shipment of food entered the metro area today — a convoy of 60-odd big tractor-trailers full of fresh produce from the San Joaquin valley. They unloaded at 30 emergency distribution points we've now got manned in the White sections, but it was like trying to fill the ocean with a thimble. We need at least five times as much food every day, just to maintain the White population at a bare-subsistence level.

There are still large stocks of non-perishable food in warehouses here, even though all the grocery stores have been looted bare. As soon as we're a little better organized and have located and inventoried it all we can use this warehoused food to supplement the incoming fresh food. Meanwhile, there have been nasty incidents at several warehouses, where we've had to shoot a number of people who wouldn't take "no" for an answer.

The really nasty business is what we're running into in the Black and racially mixed areas, though. I've spent the last two days directing salvage crews in areas which the troops have just finished clearing.

The job of the troops is to separate the Blacks from the rest of the population and confine them in controlled-access areas until they can be convoyed out of our enclave. It's done in a quite simple and straightforward manner. A Black holding area is designated, having been chosen for its proximity to a freeway heading east and for the ease with which all exits from the area can be blocked. Tanks and machine-gun crews take up positions at these exits.

Then a sweep through surrounding neighborhoods begins, converging on the designated holding area. Groups of infantry are preceded by sound trucks which repeatedly broadcast an announcement, such as: "All Blacks must assemble immediately for food and water supplies at the Martin Luther King Elementary School on 47th Street. Any Black found north of

149

43rd Street after 1:00 PM will be shot on sight. All Blacks must assemble . . . ."

At first, groups of Blacks tried to stand their ground and defy the troops, apparently under the impression that the honkies wouldn't actually shoot them. (*Note to the reader:* "Honky" was one of many derogatory slang terms referring to a White person which was used by Negroes in the three decades prior to the Great Revolution. Its origin is uncertain.) They discovered their mistake quite soon, however, and the word spread quickly.

Most Blacks moved along the streets leading into the designated areas a block or two ahead of the slowly advancing infantry, who made quick searches of each building as they came abreast of it. Blacks who had not already vacated the premises were roughly driven into the streets at bayonet point. If they put up any resistance at all they were shot on the spot, and the sound of this occasional gunfire helped to keep the other Blacks moving along.

There have so far been only about half-a-dozen instances of Blacks with contraband firearms barricading themselves in buildings and shooting at our troops. Whenever this happens the troops bypass the occupied building and call in a tank, which riddles the building with cannon and machine-gun fire.

Once again, it's a damned good thing the civilian population was disarmed by the System years ago. If more Blacks had guns there'd be no way we could deal with them, considering the disparity in numbers.

My salvage crews move in right behind the infantry. Our job is to inventory and secure all essential supplies and facilities: gasoline and bulk quantities of other fuels, non-perishable food, medical supplies, heavy transport vehicles, certain industrial facilities, etc.

The Blacks have pretty well cleaned out all the food in their areas, and they've mindlessly destroyed a lot of the other things we're looking for — although we are finding a lot of things they've missed, including more than 40 tons of dried fish meal in a pet-food plant just this morning. The stuff doesn't taste very good, but this one batch will supply the minimum protein requirements of 100,000 people for a week. And yesterday we ran across 30,000 gallons of liquid chlorine, which is needed for water purification. We also recovered most of the drug inventories of a hospital and two clinics, in which the drug storerooms were still intact even after rioting Blacks had ransacked the buildings.

We also found gruesome evidence of one way in which the Blacks have solved their food shortage: cannibalism. They began by setting up barricades in one main street to stop cars driven by Whites, apparently as early as Tuesday of last week. The unfortunate Whites were dragged from their cars, taken into a nearby Black restaurant, butchered, cooked, and eaten.

Later the Blacks organized hunting parties and made raids into White areas. In the cellar of one Black apartment building we found a scene of indescribable horror attesting to the success of these raids.

I and a crew of my men noticed a commotion in front of the building as we finished checking the looted shambles of an adjacent warehouse and came out onto the street. A group of GI's milling around the entrance were obviously distressed about something. One of them came running out of the apartment building and began retching and vomiting on the sidewalk. Then another, with a grim expression on his face, led a young White girl out of the building. She was about 10 years old, naked, filthy, and in an obvious state of shock.

As soon as I pushed my way into the building I recoiled from the horrible stench which permeated the place. Putting a handkerchief over my nose and mouth didn't seem to help, but with the aid of my flashlight I descended the cellar stairs past two more GI's who were coming up. In the arms of one of them was a silently staring White child of about four, alive but apparently too weak to walk.

The cellar, which was illuminated by two kerosene lanterns hanging from steam pipes, had been converted into a human slaughterhouse by the Blacks in the apartment building. The floor was slippery with half-congealed blood. There were washtubs full of stinking entrails, and others filled with severed heads. Four tiny, human haunches dangled overhead from wires.

On a wooden workbench beneath one of the lanterns I saw the most terrible thing I have ever seen. It was the butchered and partially dismembered body of a teenaged girl. Her blue eyes stared emptily at the ceiling, and her long, golden hair was matted with the blood which had rushed from the gaping wound in her throat.

I retched and stumbled back up the stairs and out into the light again. I could not make myself go back into that awful cellar, but I sent two of my crew with cameras and lights down there to make a thorough photographic record. The photos will be useful for troop indoctrination.

From one of the GI's outside the building I learned that parts of at least 30 children, all White, had been found in the cellar, along with the two who were still alive. They had been tied to a pipe in one corner. In the rear courtyard of the building was an improvised barbecue grill and a large pile of small, human bones — thoroughly gnawed. We took photographs of the courtyard too.

I have been working in mostly Black areas, but I have also heard some pretty bad stories from our people who have been in White and Chicano areas. No cases of cannibalism by Whites or Chicanos have been reported — the Blacks are a race apart in this respect — but there's been a lot of killing in fights over food. And there've been some grisly atrocities where gangs of Blacks have invaded White areas and taken over White homes, especially in the wealthier districts, where the homes are more isolated from one another.

On the positive side, in some of the predominantly White middle-class and working-class neighborhoods, Whites have banded together to protect themselves from incursions by Blacks and Chicanos. This is a refreshing development, but surprising, in view of the way the morons out here have been voting in recent years. Is it possible that years of Jewish brainwashing have failed to take hold in the White masses?

Actually, I'm afraid it has taken hold in all too many cases. In the racially mixed neighborhoods, for example, the Whites have suffered terribly in the last 10 days, and they've made virtually no effort to protect themselves. Without guns, of course, self-defense is pretty much a matter of numbers — and the will to survive. Although the Whites are badly outnumbered in only a few mixed neighborhoods, they seem to have lost the feeling of identity and unity which the Blacks and Chicanos still have.

Most of all, though, many of them seem to be convinced that any effort at self-defense would be "racist," and they fear being thought of as racists — or thinking of themselves that way — more than they fear death. Even when gangs of Blacks took their children away or raped their women before their eyes, they offered no significant resistance. Really sick!

It's hard for me to feel sorry for Whites who won't even try to protect themselves, and it's even harder for me to understand why we should take chances and knock ourselves out to save such brainwashed scum from the fate they richly deserve. And yet it is in the mixed areas that we're having the most trouble and taking the most chances!

We are reluctant to fire on crowds where we may kill Whites as well as non-Whites, and the bastards apparently realize this and are taking advantage of it. In some neighborhoods we're meeting

152

so much opposition that it's nearly impossible to achieve our goal of separating the various racial groups into enclaves.

Another big problem in trying to achieve racial separation is that so many people in this area cannot easily be classified as White or non-White. The process of mongrelization has gone so far in this country and there are so many swarthy, frizzy-haired characters of all sizes and shapes running around that one doesn't know where to draw the line.

Nevertheless, we've got to draw the line somewhere, and soon! There is no way we can feed everybody in our area, and if we're to avoid mass starvation among the Whites we must separate them into clearly defined areas soon, where electricity, water, food, and other essentials are available. And we must move everyone else out of our area, one way or another. The longer we delay, the more unruly the public will become.

Actually we have done pretty well at concentrating the Blacks. About 80 per cent of them are sealed in four small enclaves now, and I understand that the first mass convoy of them is heading east tonight. But for the rest, about all we've really done is immobilize the population, so they can't move from one neighborhood to another. We certainly don't have them under control, and, so far as I'm aware, we've not even begun mass arrests or taken any other action against Jews and other hostile elements yet. Let's get on with this now!

XXII

July 19, 1993. For the past five days I've been witnessing what surely must be one of the biggest mass migrations in history: the evacuation of the Blacks and mestizos and "boat people" from southern California. We've been marching them to the east at a rate of better than a million a day, and there still seems to be no end to them.

I learned at our unit meeting this evening, however, that tomorrow is expected to be the last full day of evacuation. After that, it'll just be a matter of sending them across the lines in batches of a few thousand at a time, as we round up strays and finish separating some areas which are still racially mixed.

My men and I have had the responsibility of finding transportation for those unable to make the trek on foot. We started with flatbed trucks and large tractor-trailer rigs able to haul a couple of hundred people at a time, and we ended up using every delivery van and panel truck we could find in or near the evacuated Black and Chicano neighborhoods: nearly 6,000 trucks altogether.

At first we tried to do a careful job of making sure each truck had just enough fuel in its tank to make the one-way trip into enemy territory, but that took too long, and so we settled for trying to be reasonably sure that each vehicle had *at least* enough fuel for the trip.

Late yesterday we began running out of trucks, and so all day today we have been using passenger cars. I broke up the roughly 300 men under me into squads of 10. Each squad rounded up approximately 50 young Black volunteers — with the promise of food — who claim they are experienced at jumping the ignition on cars.

Then our squads began ferrying every parked car, from Volkswagens to Cadillacs, which can be started and whose fuel gauge indicates at least a quarter of a tank of gasoline, into the packed debarkation areas. There our Black car-thief volunteers hustle a pregnant Negress or an elderly cripple behind the wheel, pack the vehicle with as many picaninnies and miscellaneous lame, sick, and halt non-Whites as it can possibly carry — sometimes piling them on roofs and fenders — and send it on its way. Then back for more cars.

I have been surprised to see how callous our volunteer Blacks are toward their own people. Some of the older Blacks, who haven't been able to fend for themselves, are obviously near the point of death from starvation and dehydration, yet our volunteers handle them so roughly and pack them so tightly into the cars that it makes me flinch to watch them. When one overloaded Cadillac started onto the eastbound freeway with a lurch this morning, an ancient Negro lost his grip and fell off the roof, landing headfirst on the pavement and crushing his skull like an egg. The Blacks who had just loaded the car roared with laughter; it was apparently the funniest thing they've seen in a long time.

Our logistics have been terrible. We've violated every security rule in the book and taken some extraordinary risks. There were hundreds of times when the Blacks could have jumped us, because we were spread so thin and often obliged to work deep within their jam-packed enclaves without backup personnel to rescue us in the event of trouble.

I really don't have enough men to handle this job properly, and we've all been working at least 18 hours a day, often not stopping to rest until we're so tired we're stumbling. It's a good thing

154

tomorrow is the last day, because I don't think my men can last much longer — or our luck either.

What we've accomplished so far is really quite remarkable, though. We've moved out approximately half a million non-Whites who couldn't possibly have made it on foot. Each and every one of these is now the responsibility of the System — to feed and house and clothe and keep out of trouble. Together with the seven million or so able-bodied Blacks and Chicanos we're sending them, that's quite a responsibility!

This whole evacuation amounts to a new form of warfare: demographic war. Not only are we getting the non-Whites *out* of our area, but we're doing two additional things which should pay off for us later by getting them *into* the enemy's area: we're overloading the System's already strained economy, and we're making life next to intolerable for the Whites in the border areas.

Even after the evacuees have been dispersed around the country, they will constitute about a 25 per cent increase in the average non-White population density outside California. Even the most brainwashed White liberals should find this increased dose of "brotherhood" hard to swallow.

On my way to the unit meeting about an hour ago, I stopped at an overlook above the main evacuation route out of Los Angeles. It was after sunset, but still light enough to see well, and I was awed by the sight of the enormous stream of colored life moving slowly to the east. As far as I could see in either direction, the unwholesome flood crept along. Later we'll switch on the street lamps along the freeway, and the march will go on all night. Then, in the heat of the morning, the evacuation of the able-bodied ones will be reined in enough so that we will have room on the freeway for our vehicles to get through again. We found out at the beginning that when we tried keeping the marchers going during the day they dropped like flies.

The sight of that huge, flowing swarm of non-Whites left me with an overwhelming feeling of relief that it was moving away from us, out of our area. And I shuddered with revulsion at the thought of being at the other end of the evacuation route and seeing that swarm moving toward me, into my area.

If the System bosses had the option, they'd turn the niggers back at the border with machine guns. But with the border manned with mostly non-White troops, it is pretty hard to give the order to fire on that non-White flood. Since the inundation began, they haven't been able to figure any way to stop it.

They are trapped by their own propaganda line, which maintains that each of those creatures is an "equal," with

155

"human dignity" and so forth, and must be treated accordingly. Yes, sir, things are looking up here, and I'm sure they're looking Blacker and Blacker elsewhere!

The proof of that is the counterflow of White refugees into our area from the east. From a hundred or so a day 10 days ago, their numbers have grown to several thousand a day. Our border guards have processed a total of more than 25,000 Whites coming across the line, up to this afternoon.

Most of these, it seems, are simply running to get away from the Black troops and the Black and Chicano evacuees who have flooded the enemy's border areas. If it is easier for them to run west than east, they run west.

But about 10 per cent of them are not from the border areas at all. They are White volunteers who have deliberately crossed over to join our fight. Some have come from as far as the East Coast, whole families as well as young men, who made their decision as soon as it became apparent to the country that our revolution has indeed established a foothold here.

July 24. Boy! I'm really becoming a Jack of all trades. I just got back to HQ from a repair trip to the big switching station outside Santa Barbara. It's been acting up, knocking out our electrical power here every day or so, and I had to figure out what was wrong and get a repair crew to fix it. I'll certainly be glad when we get the civilian population here organized, so that the people who're supposed to keep the utilities running are back on the job again.

But we must do first things first, and that means reestablishing public order and insuring an adequate food supply. We still don't have order, but we're now bringing almost enough food into the metropolitan area to keep the people from starving. I got some insight into how we're managing that during the Santa Barbara trip.

In the countryside I passed literally hundreds of organized groups of White youngsters, some working in the orchards and fruit groves, others marching along the road singing, with fruit baskets slung across their shoulders. They all looked tanned and happy and healthy. Quite a difference from the hunger and the rioting in the cities!

I had my driver stop as we came abreast of a group of about 20 young girls, all wearing heavy work gloves and miscellaneously dressed in shorts and overalls. Their leader was a freckled 15-year-old with pigtails who happily identified her group as the 128th Los Angeles Food Brigade. They had just finished five hours of fruit-picking and were headed for lunch at their tent camp down the road.

Well, I thought to myself, this is hardly a brigade, but obviously a lot more organizing of the civilian population has been going on than I've been aware of. I knew the girl was too young to be a member of the Organization, and, it soon developed, she was totally innocent of any political understanding whatever.

All she knew was that things back in the city are frightening and unpleasant, and so when the nice lady with the armband at the emergency food-distribution center had talked to her and her parents and told them that youngsters who volunteered for farm work would be looked after and well fed, they had agreed she should go. That was a week ago, and yesterday she had been appointed the leader of her group of girls.

I asked her what she thinks about her work. She said it is hard, but she knows it is important for her and her girls to pick as much fruit as possible, so their parents and friends back in the city will be able to eat. The adults at the camp have explained to them what an important responsibility they have.

Had they also been told about the significance of the revolution? No, she doesn't know anything about that, just that the Chicano farm workers have left, and now the White people will have to do all their work. She thinks that is probably a good idea. Other than that, all that the girls have been taught is how to do their particular job — and the work songs and the hygiene lectures in the evenings, around the campfire.

Well, that's not a bad beginning for 12- to 15-year-olds. There will be time for their further education later. If only the adults were as cooperative as the kids!

The girls did have one complaint: their food. There was plenty of it, but it was all fruits and vegetables; no meat, no milk, not even any bread. Obviously, the people who're organizing the food brigades have a few logistic problems yet to work out too. We swapped the girls half a case of canned sardines and some boxes of soda crackers we had in the car in return for a basket of apples, and both sides felt they had gotten a good deal.

Coming through the mountains just north of Los Angeles we encountered a long column of marchers, heavily guarded by GI's and Organization personnel. As we drove slowly past, I observed the prisoners closely, trying to decide what they were. They didn't seem to be Blacks or Chicanos, and yet only a few of them appeared to be Whites. Many of the faces were distinctly Jewish, while others had features or hair suggesting a Negroid taint. The

157

head of the column turned off the main roadway into a little-used ranger trail which disappeared into a boulder-strewn canyon, while the tail stretched for several miles back toward the city. There may have been as many as 50,000 marchers, representing all ages and both sexes, just in the portion of the column we passed.

Back at HQ I inquired about the strange column. No one was sure, although the consensus was that they were the Jews and the mixed-breeds of too light a hue to be included with the evacuees who were sent east. I remember now something which puzzled me a few days ago: the separation of the very light Blacks — the almost Whites, the octoroons and quadroons, the unclassifiable mongrels from various Asian and southern climes — from the others during the concentration and evacuation operations.

And I think I now understand. The clearly distinguishable non-Whites are the ones we want to increase the racial pressure on the Whites outside California. The presence of more almost-White mongrels would merely confuse the issue — and there is always the danger that they will later "pass" as White. Better to deal with them now, as soon as we get our hands on them. I have a suspicion their trip into that canyon north of here will be a one-way affair!

But obviously there's still a lot of sifting-out to do. We have cleared the all-Black and all-Chicano areas and certain all-Jewish neighborhoods, but there are still areas, comprising nearly half the urban territory under our control, where utter chaos prevails. Jews in these areas, working with reactionary elements among the Whites, are becoming more brazen by the day. There is nearly continuous demonstrating and rioting going on in the worst sections, and the Jews are using leaflets and other means to maintain the general unrest in other sections. Since Friday four of our people have been killed by snipers. Something must be done soon!

July 25. A very pleasant contrast today with most of my work of late: I spent the day interviewing some of the volunteers who have crossed into our area since July 4, trying to pick a hundred or so for a special problem-solving group which will begin doing in a regular and systematic way the sort of engineering and logistic chores I and my crew have been stuck with till now.

The people I talked to had been pre-screened before they got to me, and they all have an engineering or industrial-management background. There are about 300 men, plus a hundred or so wives and children, which is an indication of the really substantial flow of new blood into our area. I don't know what the total is up to now, but I do know that the Organization has increased its strength in California several times over in the last three weeks — and we are taking as members only a small fraction of the new volunteers.

The great majority have either been organized into labor brigades, primarily for farm work, or, in the case of most of the males of military age, put into Army uniforms and given rifles we've salvaged from one of the bombed-out National Guard armories. In the latter way we are gradually increasing the overall reliability, if not the proficiency, of the military force under our control. Many of these "instant soldiers" have had little or no military training, and we haven't had a chance yet to give them any of the ideological preparation which the new Organization members are receiving, yet they are clearly more sympathetic to our cause, on the average, than the regular GI's. We are integrating them into the regular units as rapidly as we can.

I queried the people I saw today about their present living arrangements and family situations as well as about their training and work experience. Nearly all of them have been assigned to a block of recently vacated housing in a former Black area, just south of Los Angeles proper. The Organization has set up a new unit HQ in a small apartment building there, and that's where the interviews took place.

There were very few complaints from the people I talked to, although they all mentioned the extraordinarily filthy condition of the buildings into which they have moved. Some of the apartment units are so saturated with filth they are simply not habitable. Everyone, however, has pitched in cheerfully, and the disinfecting, scrubbing, and repainting effort has made a remarkable transformation in just a couple of days.

I made a brief inspection tour, and it was heartwarming to see pretty, White children playing quietly where previously hordes of screaming, young Blacks had swarmed. A group of about two dozen parents were still working on the grounds around the apartments. They have collected a small mountain of litter: beer cans, cigarette wrappers, empty TV-dinner cartons, demolished furniture, and rusted-out appliances. Two women have marked off a sizable area of barren, thoroughly trampled lawn with stakes and string and are spading up the earth for a community vegetable garden. In windows which had previously known only torn paper shades, bright curtains — improvised from bed sheets and home-dyed, I imagine — have gone up. Fresh flowers are on sills formerly occupied only by empty liquor bottles.

Most of these people arrived here with little more than the clothes on their backs, having left everything behind and risked their lives in order to be with us. It's a shame we are unable to do more for them now, but they're the type who are pretty well able to do for themselves.

One of the first volunteers I picked this morning was a man to find a suitable truck somewhere and use it regularly for hauling refuse away from the new settlement and bringing in food each day from the nearest distribution point, which is about six miles away. He will be responsible for his own mechanical maintenance and for finding gasoline wherever he can, until we have time to set up a new fuel-distribution system. He is a 60-year-old who formerly owned his own plastics factory in Indiana, but he is happy to be a garbageman here!

By the time we get the overall civilian situation whipped into shape, the average population density in our part of California will be a little less than half what it was a month ago. There'll be the greatest plenty of housing for new people coming in, and we'll probably level about half the residential and commercial areas in Los Angeles county, plant trees, and make parkland of them. That lies in the future, though, and for now our aim is simply to settle the new people temporarily in areas well separated from those we haven't pacified and weeded yet.

But even the tiny beginning we have already made fills me with joy and pride. What a miracle it is to walk streets which only a few weeks ago were filled with non-Whites lounging at every street corner and in every doorway and to see only White faces — clean, happy, enthusiastic White faces, determined and hopeful for the future! No sacrifice is too great to successfully complete our revolution and secure that future for them — and for the girls of the 128th Los Angeles Food Brigade and for millions of others like them throughout our land!

XXIII

August 1, 1993. Today has been the Day of the Rope — a grim and bloody day, but an unavoidable one. Tonight, for the first time in weeks, it is quiet and totally peaceful throughout all of southern California. But the night is filled with silent horrors; from tens of thousands of lampposts, power poles, and trees throughout this vast metropolitan area the grisly forms hang.

In the lighted areas one sees them everywhere. Even the street signs at intersections have been pressed into service, and at practically every street corner I passed this evening on my way to HQ there was a dangling corpse, four at every intersection. Hanging from a single overpass only about a mile from here is a group of about 30, each with an identical placard around its neck bearing the printed legend, "I betrayed my race." Two or three of that group had been decked out in academic robes before they were strung up, and the whole batch are apparently faculty members from the nearby UCLA campus.

In the areas to which we have not yet restored electrical power the corpses are less visible, but the feeling of horror in the air there is even worse than in the lighted areas. I had to walk through a two-block-long, unlighted residential section between HQ and my living quarters after our unit meeting tonight. In the middle of one of the unlighted blocks I saw what appeared to be a person standing on the sidewalk directly in front of me. As I approached the silent figure, whose features were hidden in the shadow of a large tree overhanging the sidewalk, it remained motionless, blocking my way.

Feeling some apprehension, I slipped my pistol out of its holster. Then, when I was within a dozen feet of the figure, which had been facing away from me, it began turning slowly toward me. There was something indescribably eerie about the movement, and I stopped in my tracks as the figure continued to turn. A slight breeze rustled the foliage overhead, and suddenly a beam of moonlight broke through the leaves and fell directly on the silently turning shape before me.

The first thing I saw in the moonlight was the placard with its legend in large, block letters: "I defiled my race." Above the placard leered the horribly bloated, purplish face of a young woman, her eyes wide open and bulging, her mouth agape Finally I could make out the thin, vertical line of rope disappearing into the branches above. Apparently the rope had slipped a bit or the branch to which it was tied had sagged, until the woman's feet were resting on the pavement, giving the uncanny appearance of a corpse standing upright of its own volition.

I shuddered and quickly went on my way. There are many thousands of hanging female corpses like that in this city tonight, all wearing identical placards around their necks. They are the White women who were married to or living with Blacks, with Jews, or with other non-White males.

There are also a number of men wearing the I-defiled-my-race placard, but the women easily outnumber them seven or eight to one. On the other hand, about ninety per cent of the corpses with

161

the I-betrayed-my-race placards are men, and overall the sexes seem to be roughly balanced.

Those wearing the latter placards are the politicians, the lawyers, the businessmen, the TV newscasters, the newspaper reporters and editors, the judges, the teachers, the school officials, the "civic leaders," the bureaucrats, the preachers, and all the others who, for reasons of career or status or votes or whatever, helped promote or implement the System's racial program. The System had already paid them their 30 pieces of silver. Today we paid them.

It started at three o'clock this morning. Yesterday was an especially bad day of rioting, with the Jews using transistorized megaphones to whip up the crowds and egg them into throwing stones and bottles at our troops. They were chanting "racism must go" and "equality forever" and other slogans the Jews had taught them. It reminded me of the mass demonstrations of the Vietnam era. The Jews have a knack for things like that.

But by three o'clock this morning the crowds had long since finished their orgy of violence and chanting and were in bed — all except a few groups of diehards who had rigged up loudspeakers and were blaring System radio broadcasts out over the surrounding neighborhoods, broadcasts which alternated between screaming rock "music" and appeals for "brotherhood."

Squads of our troops with synchronized watches suddenly appeared in a thousand blocks at once, in fifty different residential neighborhoods, and every squad leader had a long list of names and addresses. The blaring music suddenly stopped and was replaced by the sound of thousands of doors splintering, as booted feet kicked them open.

It was like the Gun Raids of four years ago, only in reverse — and the outcome was both more drastic and more permanent for those raided. One of two things happened to those the troops dragged out onto the streets. If they were non-Whites — and that included all the Jews and everyone who even looked like he had a bit of non-White ancestry — they were shoved into hastily formed columns and started on their no-return march to the canyon in the foothills north of the city. The slightest resistance, any attempt at back talk, or any lagging brought a swift bullet.

The Whites, on the other hand, were, in nearly all cases, hanged on the spot. One of the two types of pre-printed placards was hung on the victim's chest, his hands were quickly taped behind his back, a rope was thrown over a convenient limb or signpost with the other end knotted around his neck, and he was then hauled clear of the ground with no further ado and left

162

dancing on air while the soldiers went to the next name on their list.

The hangings and the formation of the death columns went on for about 10 hours without interruption. When the troops finished their grim work early this afternoon and began returning to their barracks, the Los Angeles area was utterly and completely pacified. The residents of neighborhoods in which we could venture safely only in a tank yesterday were trembling behind closed doors today, afraid even to be seen peering through the crack in drawn drapes. Throughout the morning there was no organized or large-scale opposition to our troops, and by this afternoon even the desire for opposition had evaporated.

I and my men were in the thick of things all day, mostly handling logistics. When the execution squads began running out of rope, we stripped several miles of wire from power poles to use in its place. We also rounded up hundreds of ladders.

And we were the ones who pasted up the proclamations from Revolutionary Command in each block, warning all citizens that henceforth any act of looting, rioting, or sabotage, or any failure to obey the command of a soldier, will result in the summary execution of the offender. The proclamations also carry a similar warning for anyone who knowingly harbors a Jew or other non-White or who willfully provides false information to or withholds information from our police units. Finally, they list the reporting point in each neighborhood to which every person, at a time and date depending upon the position of his name in the alphabet, is to report for registration and assignment to a work unit.

I nearly got into a shooting fight with a company commander near City Hall this morning about nine o'clock. That's where we were taking all the big shots to be hanged: the well-known politicians, a number of prominent Hollywood actors and actresses, and several TV personalities. If we had strung them up in front of their homes like everyone else, only a few people would have seen them, and we wanted their example to be instructive to a much wider audience. For the same reason many of the priests on our lists were taken to one of three large churches where we had TV crews set up to broadcast their executions.

The trouble was that many of the big shots were arriving at City Hall already more dead than alive. The troops on the transport trucks were really giving them a working over.

One famous actress, a notorious race-mixer who had starred in several large-budget, interracial "love" epics, had lost most of

163

her hair, an eye, and several teeth — not to mention all her clothes — before the rope was put around her neck. She was a bruised and bloody mess. I wouldn't have known who she was if I hadn't asked. What, I wondered, was the point in publicly hanging her if the public couldn't recognize her and draw the proper inferences between her former behavior and her punishment?

I was drawn to a commotion near one of the trucks which had just arrived. A grossly fat old man, whom I immediately recognized as the Federal judge who had handed down some of the System's most outrageous rulings in recent years — including the one confirming the power of arrest granted by the Human Relations Councils to their Black deputies — was resisting the efforts of the troops to pull off his pajamas and dress him in his judicial robe.

One of the soldiers knocked him down, and then four others began kicking him and repeatedly slamming him in the face, stomach, and groin with their rifle butts. He was unconscious, and perhaps already dead, when the rope was knotted around his neck and his limp figure was hauled about halfway up a lamppost. A TV cameraman was recording the whole scene and broadcasting it live.

I was thoroughly disgusted by this latter incident and by several others of a similar nature, and I sought out the officer in charge of the troops there to lodge my complaint. I asked him why he wasn't maintaining proper discipline among his men, and I told him in strong terms that the beatings of the prisoners were counterproductive.

We must maintain a public image of strength and uncompromising ruthlessness in dealing with the enemies of our race, but to behave like a gang of Ugandans or Puerto Ricans hardly accomplishes that. (*Note to the reader:* Uganda was a political subdivision of the continent of Africa during the Old Era, when that continent was inhabited by the Negro race. Puerto Rico was the Old Era name of the island of New Carolina. It is occupied now by the descendants of White refugees from radiocative areas of the southeastern United States, but before the race purges in the final days of the Great Revolution it was inhabited by a mongrel race of especially unsavory character.) Above all else we must show ourselves as disciplined, since we will be demanding strict discipline on the part of the civilian population. We must never give vent to our feelings of frustration or our personal hatreds but must show by our behavior at all times that what we are doing is serving a higher purpose.

The captain exploded. He shouted at me to mind my own business. When I insisted that I *was* minding my business, he became red with anger and said that he, not I, was the one who had the responsibility and that he was doing the best he could under very difficult circumstances.

He pointed out correctly that the Organization had replaced nearly half the men in his company with untrained newcomers in the last month, and so it shouldn't be surprising to me that discipline wasn't all it might be. He also told me that he knew enough about the psychology of his men to understand the value of letting them beat the prisoners as a way of justifying to themselves that the prisoners were their enemies and deserved to be hanged.

I really couldn't counter either of the captain's arguments, but I did note with some satisfaction that when he turned away from me he strode angrily over to a group of soldiers who were brutally pistol-whipping a long-haired, effeminate-looking youth in an outlandishly "mod" getup — a popular "rock" performer — and ordered them to stop.

Upon thinking about it, I have come to see things more from the captain's viewpoint. Of course, we must tighten up discipline a great deal as soon as we can, but for the moment it is better for us to have more political reliability and less discipline among the troops. We delayed our crackdown on the civilian population as long as we did just so we could weed out and disarm the questionable GI's and replace them with the new people who've been coming through the enemy lines to us.

Also, we wanted time to accustom the troops to the new order of things here and to give them at least a little ideological preparation for today's work. And we purposely let the civilians get more out of control than we might have, just so we would have a manifest excuse for taking thoroughly radical measures instead of half-measures, which could not have solved the civilian problem in the long run.

One other reason for the delay I learned today was that we needed time to finish compiling our arrest lists. For several years Organization members here, just as in other parts of the country, have been building their dossiers of System toadies, Jew-fawners, equalitarian theorists, and other White race-criminals, along with their street directories of all non-Whites residing in predominantly White areas.

We were able to use the latter, which were kept quite up to date even during the last month, without modification. But the dossiers required a huge amount of evaluation and weeding. In the first place there were far too many of them.

For example, a White family might have a dossier as race-criminals because a neighbor had once observed a Black attending a cocktail party at their home or because they displayed one of the "Equality Now" bumper stickers, which have been distributed so widely by the Human Relations Councils. In general, unless there was also other evidence in a particular dossier, these people were not put on the arrest list. Otherwise, we'd have had to hang better than 10 per cent of the White population — an entirely impractical task.

And even if we could hang that many people, there would be no good reason for it; most of that 10 per cent are really no worse than most of the other 90 per cent. They have been brainwashed; they are weak and selfish; they have no sense of racial loyalty — but the same things are true of most people these days. People are what they have become, and we have to accept that — as a starting point.

Actually, it has been true all through history that only small portions of a population are either good or evil. The great bulk are morally neutral — incapable of distinguishing absolute right from absolute wrong — and they take their cue from whoever is on top at the moment.

When good men are the rulers and the program-makers for a society, the population as a whole will reflect this, and people with no originality or moral sense of direction of their own will nevertheless fervently support the highest aims of their society. But when evil men rule, as has been the case in America for many years now, most of the population will wallow happily in degeneracy of the worst kind and will self-righteously parrot every filthy and destructive idea that they have been taught.

Most judges today, most teachers, actors, civic figures, etc., are not being consciously and deliberately evil, or even cynical, in following the lead of the Jews. They think of themselves as being "good citizens," just as they would think of themselves if they were acting in a diametrically opposite way under the influence of good leaders.

Thus, there is no point in killing them all. This moral weakness will have to be bred out of the race over hundreds of generations. For now it is sufficient for us to eliminate the consciously evil portion of the population — plus a few hundred thousand of our morally crippled "good citizens" across the country, as an example to the rest.

The hanging of a few of the worst race-criminals in every neighborhood in America will help enormously in straightening out the majority of the population and reorienting their thinking. In fact, it will not only help, but it is absolutely necessary. The people require a strong psychological shock to break old habits of thought.

I understand all this, yet I must admit that I was troubled by some of the things I witnessed today.

When the arrests first started the public didn't realize what was coming, and many citizens were cocky and abusive. I was present shortly before dawn when the soldiers dragged about a dozen young people out of a large house near one of the university campuses, and they, as well as their housemates who were not arrested, were screaming obscenities at our men and spitting on them. All but one of those arrested here were either Jews, Blacks, or mongrels of various sorts, and two of the loudest of them were immediately shot, while the others were herded into a marching column.

The last was a White girl, about 19, a bit flabby but still pretty. The shootings had calmed her down enough so that she was no longer screaming, "Racist pigs!" at the soldiers, but when the preparations for her hanging shortly thereafter awakened her to her own fate, she became hysterical. Informed that she was about to pay the price for defiling her race by living with a Black lover, the girl wailed, "But why me?"

As the rope was knotted around her neck, she blubbered out, "I was only doing what everyone else was. Why are you picking on me? It's not fair! What about Helen? She was sleeping with him too." At this last outcry before the girl's breath was cut off forever, one of the other girls (presumably Helen) in the group of now-silent spectators on the lawn shrank back in terror.

Of course, no one answered the girl's question, "Why me?" The answer is simply that her name happened to be on our list and Helen's didn't. There's nothing "fair" about that — or unfair either. The girl who was hanged deserved what she got. Helen probably deserves the same fate — and she is undoubtedly suffering the torments of the damned now, in fear that she eventually will be found out and forced to pay the price her friend did.

This little episode has taught me something about political terror. Its very arbitrariness and unpredictability are important aspects of its effectiveness. There are a great many people in Helen's situation, whose fear that lightning may strike them at any moment will keep them walking on eggs.

167

The melancholy aspect of the episode is epitomized in the girl's lament, "I was only doing what everyone else was." That is a bit of an exaggeration, but it is true enough that had others not set a bad example for her the girl probably would not have become a race-criminal. She paid as much for the sins of others as for her own. Now I realize more than ever before how essential it is that we instill in all our people a new moral basis, a new set of fundamental values, so that they will no longer be morally adrift like that unfortunate girl was — and like the great majority of Americans today are.

This total lack of any healthy or natural morality was brought home to me again just before noon. We were hanging a group of about 40 land developers and real estate brokers outside the offices of the Los Angeles County Fair Housing Association. They had all participated in a special program which made lower mortgage rates available for racially mixed families buying homes in predominantly White neighborhoods. One of the realtors was a sturdy, handsome fellow of about 35 with a blond crew cut. He was vehemently defending himself: "Hell, I never agreed with any of this race-mixing crap. It makes me sick to my stomach to see these mixed families with their mongrel brats. But a man has to earn a living. I was told by the head building inspector in the county that it would be a lot easier to avoid building-code violations for those realtors who went along with the special mortgage program."

Without realizing it, he was telling us that a bigger income came before racial loyalty in his set of values — something which is unfortunately true also of a great many who were not hanged today. Well, he made his choice freely, and he hardly deserves any sympathy.

The soldiers didn't argue with him, of course. When his turn came, he was jerked off his feet with the same impartiality they had shown toward those who had accepted their fate in silence. They were under orders not to argue with anyone or to explain anything, except a brief statement of the offense for which a person was being hanged. Not even the most convincing protestations of innocence or that "there must be some mistake" caused them to hesitate for an instant. Certainly, we must have made some mistakes today — mistaken identities, wrong addresses, false accusations — but once the executions began there was no admitting to the possibility of mistakes. We deliberately created the image of inexorability in the public mind.

And apparently we were quite convincing. Our execution squads were hardly back in their barracks this afternoon when we began receiving reports from all over the city of what appeared to be a sudden wave of murders and beatings. Corpses, most of them showing stab wounds, were being found on sidewalks, in alleys, and in apartment-building hallways. A number of injured persons — several hundred altogether — were also picked up on the streets by our patrols.

Although there were a few Blacks among these beating and stabbing victims, we quickly determined that the great majority of them were Jews. All apparently were persons whom our execution squads had missed, but the citizenry had not.

Questioning of several Jews who had been beaten soon revealed that at least some of them had been hiding with Gentile families. After our proclamations were posted, however, their protectors turned on them and drove them into the streets. Local vigilante groups armed with knives and clubs had ferreted out others who had not even been on our lists.

I am sure that, without the forceful lesson of this Day of the Rope, we would not have so quickly elicited this sort of citizen cooperation. The hangings have helped everyone get off the fence in a hurry.

Tomorrow afternoon some of my men will begin organizing civilian labor battalions to cut down the corpses and haul them to the disposal site I have already picked. It'll probably take three or four days to remove all the bodies — there are between 55 and 60 thousand of them — and in this hot weather it'll be quite unpleasant toward the end.

But what a feeling of relief it is to finally have all the negative part of our task here finished! From now on it's all uphill — in the good sense: reorganizing, re-educating, and rebuilding this whole society.

XXIV

August 8, 1993. For the last four days I've been acting head of our newly organized Department of Public Resources, Utilities, Services, and Transportation (PRUST) for southern California. It is a strictly temporary position, and within the next 10 days I will turn the post over to another engineer, one of the group of volunteers I've been working with during the last two weeks. He will have the able assistance of a number of local people who were formerly employed either by one of the state, county, or municipal agencies here or by one of the private utility

169

companies, and I have confidence he'll be able to iron the remaining bugs out of the department.

With more than half the key people back at work here now, things are beginning to run almost normally. We have restored electricity, water, sewage treatment, rubbish collection, and telephone service to all the occupied areas now — although electricity is strictly rationed. We have even put about 50 gasoline stations back in operation, and those civilians whose work assignments give them priority status can obtain fuel for their automobiles.

PRUST covers our whole enclave, all the way from Vandenberg to the Mexican border, and I've done a lot of traveling to survey the needs and resources of the various areas and to get everything roughly coordinated. I'm really very pleased with what we've been able to accomplish in such a short time. Next to the military and to the Department of Food, PRUST has the most essential function to perform and employs the most workers of all the agencies we've set up here.

One of the most interesting aspects of my work has been setting up the interfacing with the Department of Food. They produce the food; we transport it, store it, and distribute it. There were several problems to be worked out, primarily because a certain amount of the food which is produced does not go directly from the fields to the distribution points but is processed first. This means that the Department of Food needs to concern itself to a certain extent with storage and transportation from field to processing plant, before PRUST takes over the responsibility. Also DF has a specialized transportation need in moving its workers from their living quarters to the fields and back.

I have had to familiarize myself with DF's whole operation in order to decide the best way to define our respective responsibilities. I am very impressed by what I have seen. They have mobilized more than 600,000 workers — about a quarter of the entire productive segment of the population under our control — for the production of food. Between 10 and 15 per cent of these workers are those Whites who were originally in farming or ranching in this area. Nearly a third are young volunteers in the 12-to-18 age range. The rest are people from urban areas who formerly worked in non-essential occupations and have now been assigned to work crews under DF's supervision.

Many in the last group are now doing the first really productive work in their lives. This means DF is performaing an important function of social rehabilitation as well as food production, and our Department of Education is working closely with DF on this.

170

Every worker receives ten hours of lectures each week, and he is graded not only on his general attitude toward his work and on his productivity but also on his responsiveness to these lectures.

There is a continual sifting process going on, with workers being reassigned to new work groups on the basis of attitude and performance in their previous groups. In this way there are already beginning to emerge from the general mass the first leader-trainee work groups. From the latter will be selected candidates for Organization membership.

On several occasions during my tour of DF's operation I stopped to talk with workers in the fields. The morale varied considerably from the groups with a high proportion of former social parasites to the leader-trainee groups, but nowhere could it be called poor. Everyone has been made to understand that, despite the dislocations and the hardships caused by the revolution, we are now sure that there will be enough food to go around — but those who will not work will not eat either.

My most profound impression comes from the fact that every face I saw in the fields was White: no Chicanos, no Orientals, no Blacks, no mongrels. The air seems cleaner, the sun brighter, life more joyous. What a wonderful difference this single accomplishment of our revolution has made!

And the workers all feel the difference too, whether they are ideologically with us or not. There is a new feeling of solidarity among them, of kinship, of unselfish cooperation to complete a common task.

Most of the news reports from other parts of the country are very cheering to us. Although the System is still holding on, it is only doing so through increasingly open and brutal repression. The entire country is under martial law, and the government is relying heavily on hastily armed and deputized Black goon squads to keep the White civilian population intimidated. Half the System's regular military units are still confined to their barracks as "unreliable."

Conditions are deteriorating nearly everywhere. Power outages, transportation and communications breakdowns, terror bombings, food shortages, assassinations, and massive industrial sabotage are plaguing the System and helping to maintain the general unrest. The Organization's action units are doing a heroic job, but their losses are heavy. Their only aim now is to maintain the pressure on the System and the general population by striking at every available target again and again and again, without letup.

171

From the new volunteers who are slipping into our area through the enemy lines at a growing rate, we get a consistent story about the effect the chaotic conditions are having on people. The White liberals and the minorities are screaming hysterically for the government to "do something"; the conservatives are moaning, wringing their hands, and deploring the "irresponsibility" of it all; and the "average Joes" are becoming more and more exasperated with everyone concerned: us, the System, the Blacks, and the various liberal and conservative spokesmen. They just want a return to "normalcy" — and their accustomed comforts — as soon as possible.

The System propagandists are making a big thing out of our forced evacuation of non-Whites and our summary liquidation of race-criminals and other hostile and degenerate elements here. It's not having the desired effect, however, except among the liberals and the minorities. The bulk of the population is too preoccupied with its own problems at the moment to shed a tear for "the victims of racism."

The biggest fly in our ointment is northern California. Things are completely out of control there. General Harding has really botched the situation. It serves us right for having anything to do with a conservative; he, like all the rest, was standing behind the door when the brains were passed out, and so he got a double dose of pigheadedness to make up for it. (*Note to the reader:* Turner is referring to Lt. Gen. Arnold Harding, commander of Travis Air Force Base, which was located about halfway between San Francisco and Sacramento. Harding's role in the Great Revolution, though important, lasted only 11 weeks; he was finally assassinated by an Organization team on September 16, 1993, after several earlier attempts failed.)

If the situation in the San Francisco-Sacramento area doesn't improve soon, we're likely to be involved in a civil war against the troops under Harding. The System would really love that. The only thing Harding has done right so far was breaking with Washington during the first week of our July 4 offensive, as soon as it became clear that the System had lost its grip in California. On his own initiative he declared an independent military government in northern California and got nearly all the other officers in military units stationed there (except our own undercover military people, of course) to go along with him.

Revolutionary Command made the strictly practical decision to let General Harding carry the ball in his area, and our people were instructed not to oppose him. This had the effect of substantially reducing our own losses, although the military has actually suffered many more casualties in northern California than in the south. This is because Harding has failed to take sufficiently radical measures to consolidate his authority and to deal with Black military personnel.

And he has failed utterly to get the civilian population under control — again, because he seems unable to understand the necessity for radical measures. The Jews and the other Bolshevik elements in San Francisco are running circles around him, and the Chicanos in the Sacramento area have been rioting more or less continuously for a month.

When a delegation of Organization people went to Harding last month and suggested a joint Organization-military rule for northern California, with Harding's forces handling defense matters and the Organization handling civilian matters — including police functions — Harding arrested them and has refused to release them. Since then he has been issuing idiotic proclamations about "restoring the Constitution," stamping out "communism and pornography," and holding new elections to "re-establish the republican form of government intended by the Founding Fathers," whatever that means.

And he has denounced our radical measures in the south as "communism." He is appalled that we didn't hold some sort of public referendum before expelling the non-Whites and that we didn't give individual trials to the Jews and race-criminals we dealt with summarily.

Doesn't the old fool understand that the American people *voted themselves* into the mess they're in now? Doesn't he understand that the Jews have taken over the country fair and square, according to the Constitution? Doesn't he understand that the common people have already had their fling at self-government, and they blew it?

Where does he think new elections can possibly lead now, with this generation of TV-conditioned voters, except right back into the same Jewish pigsty? And how does he think we could have solved our problems down here, except by the radical measures we used?

Doesn't Harding understand that the chaos in his area will continue to grow worse until he identifies the *categories* of people responsible for that chaos and deals with them *categorically* — that it is physically impossible, considering the relative numbers involved, for him to deal with the Jews, the Blacks, the Chicanos, and the other troublesome elements on an individual basis?

Apparently not, because the idiot is still making appeals to "responsible" Black leaders and to "patriotic" Jews to help him restore order. Harding, like conservatives in general, can't bring himself to do what must be done, because it would mean punishing the "innocent" along with the "guilty," the "good" Negroes and the "loyal" Jews along with the rest — as if those terms had any meaning in the present context. And so, afraid of treating individuals "unjustly," he is floundering around helplessly while everything goes to hell and the civilians in his area die like flies from starvation. Generals should be made of sterner stuff.

The one advantage to us from the situation in the north is the flood of White refugees it has brought us. More people have been coming into our area in the last two weeks to get away from the anarchy around San Francisco than have been slipping through the System's lines from the rest of the country.

And, while they last, it is interesting to have living, breathing examples of three types of social orders simultaneously before us: in the north, a conservative regime; to the east, liberal-Jewish democracy; and here, the beginning of a whole new world rising out of the ruins of the old.

August 23. Tomorrow I leave for Washington again. I have been at Vandenberg for four days learning how nuclear warheads work. I am in charge of a group which will hand-carry four 60-kiloton warheads to Washington for concealment in key locations around the capital.

Approximately 50 other men — all members of the Order — were trained with me, and each of them has a similar mission as a group leader. That means a total of about 200 warheads to be dispersed around the country initially, with more to follow later.

All the warheads are identical; they were removed from a stockpile of 240-mm artillery projectiles our people found here. They've been slightly modified, so they can be detonated by coded radio signals. They will be our insurance, in case we lose our missile-launch facility here.

The present mission is the hairiest one I've ever been assigned. It will be a lot tougher than blowing up the FBI headquarters two years ago. Five of us must make our way through 3,500 miles of enemy territory, carrying four nuclear bombs weighing a total of just over 520 pounds, without getting caught. Then we have to sneak them into areas that will be heavily guarded and conceal them, so that there is a negligible chance of their being found.

Aside from the dangers involved, which tie my guts in knots whenever I think about them, I have mixed feelings about this mission. On the one hand, I hate to leave California. Being a participant in the birth of our new society here has been tremendously exciting and rewarding for me, and our work is just beginning. New projects are being launched every day, and I want to be a part of them. We are laying the foundations here for the new social order which will serve our race for the next thousand years.

And to be able to live and work in a sane, healthy, White man's world — that is something which is beyond valuation for me. These last few weeks have been wonderful. It is terribly depressing to think of leaving this White oasis and plunging once again into that cesspool of mongrels and Blacks and Jews and sick, twisted White liberals out there.

On the other hand, it has been more than three months since I've seen Katherine, and it seems like a year. The one thing which has limited my enthusiasm about what we've accomplished here is that she hasn't been able to share it with me. And now, with the changed situation, she and the others in Washington are living under much more difficult conditions and in greater danger than we here in California. Realizing that makes me feel guilty every day I remain.

The strongest feeling I have now, however, is one of responsibility. I am both proud and awed that I, still only a probationary member of the Order, am being entrusted with such an important and difficult task. I must try hard to put all other thoughts and feelings aside until it is successfully completed.

During the last four days I have not only learned about the structure and functioning of the warheads for which I will be responsible, but also why this mission is vital. That involved a lesson in strategy which has been very sobering.

The people in Revolutionary Command, with their eyes fixed firmly on our long-range goal of total victory over the System, have not let themselves be deluded by our gains in California and the present difficulties the System is facing elsewhere. The grim facts are these:

First, outside of California the System remains essentially intact, and the disparity in numbers between the System's forces and our own is even worse than it was before July 4. That's because we've been recklessly expending our strength everywhere else in the country to keep the System off balance long enough for us to consolidate our gains here.

Second, despite the military forces under our control here, the System — as soon as it has tidied up some of its present military morale problems — will be able to pound us into the ground by conventional means with very little trouble. The only thing that's really kept them off us this long has been our threat of nuclear reprisal against New York and Tel Aviv.

Third, our nuclear threat is in grave danger of being neutralized. The System has the capability for launching a surprise first strike against us with a high probability of knocking out all our "hardened" launch silos before we can fire our missiles. Revolutionary Command's intelligence sources indicate that such a surprise strike is exactly what is being planned. The System is holding off only until it has finished an emergency military reorganization which will give it confidence in the political reliability of the U.S. Army. It wants to follow up its destruction of our nuclear capability immediately with a massive invasion which will finish us off in a day or two.

Worse, the System has an alternative plan which calls for the nuclear annihilation of all of southern California. It will carry out that plan if it fails to regain complete confidence in the reliability of its military ground forces within the next couple of weeks.

We still don't know the System's exact timetable, but we have reports that more than 25,000 of the wealthiest and most influential Jews and their families have quietly packed up and left the New York area within the last ten days, most of them taking only a moderate amount of luggage with them — perhaps enough for a two- or three-week vacation.

Thus, our entire strategy against the System has been undermined. If we could hold the enemy off indefinitely — or even for a year or two — with our threat of nuclear retaliation, then we could pull him down. With California as a training and supply base, and with a population of more than five million Whites to recruit from, we could steadily escalate our guerrilla war throughout the rest of the country. But without California we can't do it — and the System knows that.

So what we must do — immediately — is to disperse a large number of nuclear weapons outside California. We will then detonate at least one of those weapons to convince the System that a new situation exists. If the System attacks California after that, we will be obligated to detonate all or most of our dispersed weapons, in an effort to destroy the System's capability for organized resistance.

Unfortunately, much of the White population of the country is bound to be lost if we are forced to that extremity. The country will also be open to the danger of invasion by other nations. A grim prospect, indeed.

XXV

September 4, 1993. Although I've been in Washington nearly a week now, this is the first opportunity I've had to write. After our hectic trip across the country we spent several hectic days getting two of our bombs planted. Then last night was the first uninterrupted night I've had alone with Katherine since I've been back. And tomorrow it's another bomb-planting mission. But tonight is for writing.

Our trip here from California was like something from a zany movie. Even though all the events are still fresh in my mind, I can hardly believe they really happened. Conditions in this country have changed so much in the last nine weeks that it's as if we had used a time machine to step into an entirely different era — an era in which all the old rules for coping we spent a lifetime learning have been changed. Fortunately for us, everyone else seems just as bewildered by the changes as we are.

I was surprised at the ease with which we were able to leave our enclave. The System's troops are all clumped together in just a few border areas along the major highways, with additional company-size groups stationed at roadblocks on the back roads. These back-road troops are doing practically no patrolling, and it is a simple and safe matter to bypass them — which accounts for the fact that so many White volunteers have been able to infiltrate into our area of California since July 4.

We took an Army truck north to Bakersfield and then drove northeast another 20 miles, to within half a mile of a roadblock manned by Black troops. We could see them and they could see us, but they didn't try to give us any trouble as we pulled off the main road onto a rough Forest Service trail. We were already in the foothills of the Sierra range.

After about an hour of bouncing over the steep, barely passable mountain road, we pulled back onto the highway again — safely beyond the roadblock but now deep into System-controlled territory. We weren't especially concerned about running into any opposition in the mountains; we knew the largest concentration of System troops was at China Lake, on the other side of the Sierras, and we intended to turn north along Highway 395 before then. Our plan, had we met a supply truck heading for the roadblock back near Bakersfield, was simply to blast it off the narrow mountain highway before its occupants realized we were "the enemy." All five of us kept our automatic rifles cocked and ready and we had two rocket launchers besides, but we met no other vehicles.

We knew that, despite the unnatural absence of traffic in the mountains, we would certainly encounter heavy traffic when we reached 395, the main north-south highway east of the mountains. Our reconnaissance patrols hadn't been able to give us anything but a very generalized picture of troop dispositions that far east, and we had no idea what to expect in the way of roadblocks or other controls on vehicular traffic.

We did know that fewer than 10 per cent of the System troops in the border area at that time were Whites, however. The System was gradually regaining confidence in some of its White troops, but it was still avoiding using them near the border, where they might be tempted to come over to our side. The few White military personnel in the area, even though confirmed race-mixers, were regarded with suspicion and treated with the contempt they deserved by the Blacks. Our spies had reported several instances in which these White renegades had been humiliated and abused by their Black fellow soldiers.

Considering this, we had decided that we would have a better chance as non-Whites of bluffing our way past any challengers. Accordingly, we had all applied a dark stain to our faces and hands and pinned Chicano-sounding nametags on our fatigue uniforms. We figured we could pass as *mestizos* —so long as we didn't run into any *real* Chicanos. For four days I was "Jesus Garcia."

Our driver, "Corporal Rodriguez," played his role to the hilt, giving a left-handed clenched-fist salute and flashing a toothy grin whenever we passed an idle group of Black soldiers along the highway and on the two occasions we were stopped at checkpoints. We also kept a transistor radio tuned to a Mexican station blaring soulful Chicano music whenever we were within earshot of System troops.

Once, when we needed to refuel, we were briefly tempted to pull in at a military gasoline depot, but the long line of waiting trucks and the groups of Blacks lounging about made us decide against the risk. We stopped instead at a roadside restaurant-curio shop-filling station in the shadow of Mt. Whitney. The place seemed deserted, so two of our men began filling our fuel tank at the gasoline pump, while I and the others headed for the restaurant to see if we could find any food to take along.

We found four soldiers inside, quite drunk, sitting around a table cluttered with empty bottles and glasses. Three were Blacks

178

and the fourth was White. "Anybody around here we can pay for gas and some food?" I asked.

"No, man, just take what you want. We ran the honky owners out of here three days ago," one of the Blacks responded.

"But not before we had some real fun with their daughter, eh?" the White exclaimed, grinning and nudging one of his companions.

Perhaps it was the grim stare I gave him, or perhaps he suddenly noticed "Corporal Rodriguez's" very blue eyes, or it may have been that the stain on our faces had become too streaked from perspiration; in any event, the White soldier suddenly stopped grinning and whispered something to the Blacks. At the same time he leaned back and reached for his rifle, which was resting against an adjacent table.

Before he even touched his weapon, I pivoted my M16 off my shoulder and raked the group at the table with a blast of fire which sent them all sprawling to the floor, spurting blood. The three Blacks were quite obviously dead, but their White-renegade companion, though shot through the chest, raised himself to a sitting position and asked in a plaintive voice, "Hey, man, what the shit?"

"Corporal Rodriguez" finished him off. He pulled his bayonet from his belt scabbard, seized the dying White by his hair, and hauled him off the floor, the point of the bayonet jammed under his chin. "You piece of race-mixing filth! Go join your Black 'brothers'!" And with one, savage stroke "Rodriguez" practically decapitated him.

Five miles further down the highway, at the intersection where we wanted to turn east, a Military Police jeep with two Blacks in it was blocking the side road. A third Black was directing traffic, waving all north-bound military vehicles on down the main highway. We ignored his signals and turned right, going far out on the shoulder to get around the jeep. The Black traffic controller blew his whistle furiously, and all three MP's gesticulated and waved their arms wildly at us, but our "Corporal Rodriguez" just grinned and gave his Black-power salute, shouted, "*Siesta frijole! Hasta la vista!*" and a few other Spanish words which came into his head, pointed meaningfully down the road ahead, and stepped on the accelerator. We left the Blacks in a shower of dust and gravel.

The Black with the whistle was still tooting and waving his arms as we went around the bend, and that was the last we saw of him. Apparently he and his companions did not think it worthwhile trying to follow us, but our three men hidden in the back of the truck kept their fingers on the triggers of their automatic rifles just in case.

From there until we got to the outskirts of St. Louis we didn't run into any more concentrations of System troops. But we accomplished that only by avoiding the major highways and cities and sticking to secondary roads. We rattled and bounced across the mountains and deserts of California, Nevada, Utah, and Colorado, and then the plains of Kansas and the rolling hills of Missouri, for 75 hours straight, stopping only to refuel and relieve ourselves. While two of us rode in front and a third kept watch out the back of the truck, two of us at a time tried to sleep, but without much success.

When we reached eastern Missouri we changed our tactics, for two reasons. First, we heard the radio broadcast of the bombing of Miami and Charleston and the Organization's ultimatum to the System. That made the time factor even more important than before; we couldn't afford any further delays from circuitous routes along back roads. Second, the danger of our being stopped by the authorities between St. Louis and Washington decreased sharply as all hell broke loose in the country, giving us the opportunity to adopt a new ploy.

We had been monitoring both the civilian broadcast band and the military communications bands during the trip, and we were about 80 miles west of St. Louis when a special announcer cut into the afternoon weather report. The previous day, at noon, a nuclear bomb had been detonated without warning in Miami Beach, the announcer said, killing an estimated 60,000 people and causing enormous damage. A second nuclear bomb had been detonated outside Charleston, South Carolina, just four hours ago, but casualty and damage reports were not yet available.

Both bombings were the work of the Organization, said the announcer, and he would now read the text of an Organization ultimatum. I jotted down the ultimatum almost word for word on a scrap of paper as it came over the truck radio, and this is very nearly it:

"To the President and the Congress of the United States and the commanders of all U.S. armed forces, we, the Revolutionary Command of the Organization, issue the following demands and warning:

"First, cease immediately all buildup of military forces in eastern California and adjacent areas and abandon all plans for an invasion of the liberated zone of California.

"Second, abandon all plans for a nuclear strike against the liberated zone of California or any portion of it.

"Third, make known to the people of the United States, through all the communications channels at your disposal, these demands and this warning.

"If you have failed to comply with any one of our three demands by noon tomorrow, August 27, we will detonate a second nuclear device in some population center of the United States, just as we detonated one in the Miami, Florida, area a few minutes ago. We will continue to detonate one nuclear device every 12 hours thereafter until you have complied.

"We furthermore warn you that if you make any surprise, hostile move against the liberated zone of California, we will immediately detonate more than 500 nuclear devices which have already been hidden in key target areas throughout the United States. More than 40 of these devices are now located in the New York City area. In addition, we will immediately use all the nuclear missiles still available to us to destroy the Jewish presence in Palestine.

"Finally, we warn you that, in any event, we intend to liberate, first, the entire United States and then the remainder of this planet. When we have done so we will liquidate all the enemies of our people, including in particular all White persons who have consciously aided those enemies.

"We are aware now, and we will continue to be aware, of your most confidential plans and of every order you receive from your Jewish masters. Abandon your race-treason now, or abandon all hope for yourselves when you fall into the hands of the people you have betrayed."

(*Note to the reader:* Turner's version of the Organization's ultimatum is essentially correct, except for a few minor errors in wording and his omission of one sentence from the next-to-last paragraph. The full and exact text of the ultimatum is in chapter nine of Professor Anderson's definitive *History of the Great Revolution.*)

We had pulled off the road when the special announcer came on, and it took us a few minutes to gather our thoughts and decide what to do. We had not really expected things to develop so rapidly. Those fellows who took the warheads to Miami and Charleston must have either left a day or two ahead of us or they must have really been burning up the highways to get there so soon. Despite our non-stop driving, we felt like a bunch of shirkers.

We knew the fat was really in the fire; we were in the middle of a nuclear civil war, and within the next few days the fate of the planet would be decided for all time. Now it was either the Jews or the White race, and everyone knew the game was for keeps.

I still haven't figured out all the details of our strategy leading up to the ultimatum. I don't know why, for example, Miami and Charleston were chosen as initial targets — although I've heard a rumor that the rich Jews who were evacuated from New York were being temporarily housed in the Charleston area, and Miami, of course, already had a superabundance of Jews. But why not take out the New York City area instead, with its two-and-a-half megakikes? Perhaps our bombs weren't really in place yet in New York, despite what our ultimatum said.

And I'm also not sure why our ultimatum took the particular form it did: all stick and no carrot. Perhaps it was deliberately intended to stampede the cattle — which, indeed, it has. Or perhaps there were some under-the-table communications between Revolutionary Command and the System's military leaders which determined the form of the ultimatum. In any event, it has had the effect of splitting the System right down the middle. The Jews and nearly all the politicians are in one faction, and nearly all the military leaders are in another faction.

The Jewish faction is demanding the immediate nuclear annihilation of California, regardless of the consequences. The accursed *goyim* have raised their hands against the Chosen People and must be destroyed at any cost. The military faction, on the other hand, is in favor of a temporary truce, while an effort is made to find our "500 (a forgivable exaggeration) nuclear devices" and disarm them.

After hearing that broadcast our only thought was to get our deadly cargo to Washington as soon as possible. We knew everyone would be off balance for a while as a result of what had just happened, and we decided to take advantage of the general confusion by converting our truck into an emergency vehicle and barrelling straight down the highway toward our destination. We didn't have a siren, but we did have flashing red lights front and rear, and we completed the conversion a few minutes later by stopping in a rural hardware store and buying some cans of spray paint which, with some hastily improvised stencils made from torn newspapers, we used to paint Red Cross symbols in the appropriate places on our truck.

After that, we made Washington in less than 20 hours, despite the chaotic conditions on the highways. We sped along shoulders to get past stalled traffic, drove on the wrong side of the road with horn blaring and lights flashing, bounced over culverts and open fields to get around blocked intersections, and generally ignored all traffic controllers, bluffing our way through more than a dozen checkpoints.

Our first bomb went into Fort Belvoir, the big Army base just south of Washington where I was locked up for more than a year. We had to wait two maddening days to make contact with our inside man there so we could arrange to get the bomb inside the base and hidden in the right area.

"Rodriguez" went over the fence with the bomb strapped on his back. I received a radio signal from him the next day, confirming the successful completion of his mission. Meanwhile, the rest of us planted a second bomb in the District of Columbia, where it will be able to take out a couple of hundred thousand Blacks when it goes, not to mention a few government agencies and a critical portion of the capital's transportation network.

I didn't have my final orders on the third bomb until this afternoon. That will go into the Silver Spring area north of here — the center of the Maryland-suburban Jewish community. The fourth one is intended for the Pentagon, but security is so tight there I still haven't figured a way to get it anywhere near the place.

I must confess that my mind has not been exclusively on my work since I've been back here. Katherine and I have stolen time from our Organization responsibilities to be together. Neither of us had realized how much we have come to mean to each other until we were separated again this summer, so soon after my escape from prison. In the month we were together this spring, before I was sent to Texas and then to Colorado and finally to California, we became as close as any two people can possibly be.

Things have been hard for Katherine and the others here while I was gone, especially since July 4. They have been under enormous pressure from two directions. The Organization has been pushing them without mercy to continually step up their level of activism, while the danger of being caught by the political police has grown worse every week.

The System is resorting to new methods in its fight against us: massive, house-to-house searches of multi-block areas; astronomical rewards for informers; much tighter controls on all civilian movement. In many other parts of the country these repressive measures have been more sporadic, and they have broken down entirely in those areas where the System has not been able to maintain public order — especially since the panic caused by the bombings of Miami and Charleston. But around

Washington the System still has things in a very tight grip, and it's tough.

Late this afternoon Katherine and I slipped out of the shop for a couple of hours and went for a walk. We strolled by several groups of soldiers in sandbagged machine-gun emplacements outside office buildings; on past the smoke-blackened rubble of a suburban subway station in which Katherine herself had planted a dynamite bomb just two weeks ago; through a park-like area where a loudspeaker mounted high on a lamppost was blaring out exhortations to "all right-thinking citizens" to immediately report to the political police the slightest manifestation of racism on the part of their neighbors or co-workers; and out onto one of the main highway bridges across the Potomac River from Virginia to the District of Columbia. There was no traffic on the bridge because it ended abruptly 50 yards from the Virginia shore, in a tangle of shattered concrete and twisted reinforcing rods. The Organization had blown it up in July, and no effort had yet been made to repair it.

It was fairly quiet there at the end of the bridge, with only the screaming of police sirens in the distance and the occasional clatter of a police helicopter swooping overhead. We talked, we embraced, and we silently surveyed the scene around us as the sun went down. We and our companions have certainly made an influence on the world in the last few months — both on the suburban world of ordinary White people on the Virginia side of the bridge and on the System's world of bustling government offices on the other side. And yet the System is all too evidently still alive all around us. What a contrast with the situation in California!

Katherine was full of questions about what life is like in the liberated zone, and I tried to tell her as best I could, but I am afraid that mere words are inadequate for expressing the difference between the way I felt in California and the way I feel here. It is more a spiritual thing than merely a difference in the political and social environments.

As we stood there talking above the swirling eddies at the end of the bridge, our bodies pressed together, the world growing dark around us, a group of young Negroes came out onto the other stump of the bridge, from the Washington side. They began horsing around in typical Negro fashion, a couple of them urinating into the river. Finally one of them spotted us, and they all began shouting and making obscene gestures. For me, at least, that accentuated the difference which I could not find words to express.

184

XXVI

September 18, 1993. So much has happened, so much has been lost in these last two weeks, I can hardly force myself to begin writing about it. I am alive and in good health, yet there are moments when I envy the tens of millions who have died in recent days. My soul has dried up inside me; I am like a walking dead man.

All that I have been able to think about — all that has been running through my mind, over and over again — is the single, overwhelming fact: Katherine is gone! Before today, when I was not absolutely certain of her fate, that fact tormented me and gave me no rest. Now that I know she is dead, however, the torment is gone, and I merely feel a great emptiness, an irreplaceable loss.

There is important work for me to do, and I know that I must now put the past out of my mind and get on with it. But tonight I must record my memories, my thoughts. In the chaos of these days, millions perish without leaving a ripple behind — they will be forever unremembered, forever nameless — but I can at least commit to these flimsy pages my memory of Katherine and the events which she and our other comrades have helped to shape and hope that my diary outlives me. That, at least, we owe to our dead, to our martyrs: that we do not forget them or their deeds.

It was September 7, a Wednesday, that I finished installing our third bomb. I and two other members of our bomb team picked it up Monday from the hiding place where the last warhead is still stashed, and we took it to Maryland. I had already pinpointed the location where I wanted to install it, but troop movements were so heavy that week throughout the Washington area that we had to wait in Maryland nearly three days for an opportunity to approach the target location.

Civilian vehicular traffic has long been quite encumbered in the Washington area by roadblocks, restricted sections of many roads, inspection points, and so on, but that week it had become almost impossible. On the way back to our printing shop-headquarters, the roads were congested by long streams of civilian vehicles, all going in the opposite direction and piled high with household belongings lashed to doors, hoods, and roofs. Then, about half a mile from the shop, I ran into a new military roadblock, which hadn't been there when I left. Coils of barbed wire were strung across the road, and a tank was parked behind the barbed wire.

I turned around and tried another street; it was blocked also. I shouted across the barrier to a soldier, telling him where I was headed and asking him what unblocked street I could take to get there. "You can't go there at all," he shouted back. "This is a security area. Everyone was evacuated this morning. Any civilian spotted inside the perimeter will be shot on sight."

I was stunned. What had happened to Katherine and the others?

Apparently the military authorities had suddenly extended the radius of the security area around the Pentagon from its former two miles to three miles without warning. Our shop had been a safe half-mile outside the former perimeter, and it had never occurred to us that it would be extended. But it had been, evidently to keep the Organization from planting a nuclear bumb close enough to take out the Pentagon. Actually, I considered the former perimeter adequate protection from our 60-kiloton warheads, since the Pentagon was long ago equipped with blast shutters over all windows and surrounded by reinforced-concrete blast deflectors. I'd been trying without success to figure how to get a bomb inside that perimeter since I arrived back in Washington from California.

I drove to our unit's emergency rendezvous point a few miles south of Alexandria, but there was no one there and no message for me. I had no way to contact Washington Field Command to find out where Katherine, Bill, and Carol were, because all our communications equipment was in the shop. But the fact they weren't at the rendezvous point made me almost certain that they had been arrested.

It was already past midnight, but I immediately headed north again, toward the area where the evacuees I had passed earlier were bound. I thought I might find out from someone who had lived in the vicinity of our shop what had happened to my comrades. It was a foolishly dangerous thought, born of my sense of desperation, and I was probably fortunate that a military truck convoy had the highway so thoroughly blocked that I was finally obliged to pull off the road and sleep until morning.

When I finally did reach the refugee area later that day, I soon realized that the chance of obtaining the information I sought was very slim. A sea of army tents had been erected in a huge, suburban supermarket parking lot and in an adjacent field. Around the edge of the encampment was a jam-packed mass of outdoor chemical toilets, civilian vehicles still piled high with household goods, refugees, and soldiers.

I wandered through the milling throng for nearly three hours and saw no familiar faces. I tried questioning a few people at random, but I got nowhere. People were frightened and gave me only evasive answers or none at all. They were miserable and bewildered, but they wanted no more trouble than they already had, and questions about arrests they might have witnessed spelled trouble to them.

As I passed one tent about twice as large as the others, I heard muffled screams and hysterical sobbing coming from inside, interspersed with loud, coarse, masculine laughter and banter. A dozen Black soldiers were lined up at the entrance.

I stopped to find out what was happening, just as two grinning Black soldiers forced their way through the throng in front of the tent and went inside, dragging a terrified, sobbing White girl about 14 years old between them. The raping queue moved forward another space.

I ran over to a White officer wearing a major's insignia who was standing only about 50 yards away. I began angrily protesting what was happening, but before I had finished my first sentence the officer turned shamefacedly away from me and hurried off in the opposite direction. Two White soldiers nearby cast their eyes downward and disappeared between two tents. No one wanted to be suspected of "racism." I fought down a nearly overpowering impulse to draw my pistol and begin shooting everyone in sight, and then left.

I drove to the one place I was reasonably sure was still manned by Organization personnel: the old gift shop in Georgetown. It was just outside the new Pentagon security perimeter. I arrived there as dusk was falling and pulled the pickup truck around to the rear service entrance.

I had just climbed out of the truck and stepped into the shadows at the rear of the building when the world around me suddenly lit up as bright as noon for a moment. First there was an intensely bright flash of light, then a weaker glow which cast moving shadows and changed from white to yellow to red in the course of a few seconds.

I ran to the alley, so that I could have a more nearly unobstructed view of the sky. What I saw chilled my blood and caused the hairs on the back of my neck to rise. An enormous, bulbous, glowing thing, a splotchy ruby-red in color for the most part but shot through with dark streaks and also dappled with a shifting pattern of brighter orange and yellow areas, was rising into the northern sky and casting its ominous, blood-red light over the land below. It was truly a vision from hell.

As I watched, the gigantic fireball continued to expand and rise, and a dark column, like the stem of an immense toadstool, became visible beneath it. Bright, electric-blue tongues of fire could be seen flickering and dancing over the surface of the column. They were huge lightning bolts, but at their distance no thunder could be heard from them. When the noise finally came, it was a dull, muffled sound, yet still overwhelming: the sort of sound one might expect to hear if an inconceivably powerful earthquake rocked a huge city and caused a thousand 100-story skyscrapers to crumble into ruins simultaneously.

I realized that I was witnessing the annihilation of the city of Baltimore, 35 miles away, but I could not understand the enormous magnitude of the blast. Could one of our 60-kiloton bombs have done that? It seemed more like what one would expect from a megaton bomb.

The government news reports that night and the next day claimed that the warhead which destroyed Baltimore, killing more than a million people, as well as the blasts which destroyed some two-dozen other major American cities the same day, had been set off by us. They also claimed that the government had counterattacked and destroyed the "nest of racist vipers" in California. As it turned out, both claims were false, but it was two days before I learned the full story of what had actually happened.

Meanwhile, it was with a feeling of deepest despair that I and half-a-dozen others who were gathered around the television set in the darkened basement of the gift shop late that night heard a newscaster gloatingly announce the destruction of our liberated zone in California. He was a Jew, and he really let his emotions carry him away; I have never before heard or seen anything like it.

After a solemn rundown of most of the cities which had been hit that day, with preliminary estimates of the death tolls (sample: ". . . and in Detroit, which the racist fiends struck with two of their missiles, they murdered over 1.4 million innocent American men, women, and children of all races . . ."), he came to New York. At that point tears actually appeared in his eyes and his voice broke.

Between sobs he gasped out the news that 18 separate nuclear blasts had leveled Manhattan and the surrounding boroughs and suburbs out to a radius of approximately 20 miles, with an estimated 14 million killed outright and perhaps another five million expected to die of burns or radiation sickness within the next few days. Then he lapsed into Hebrew and began a strange, wailing chant, as tears streamed down his cheeks and his clenched fists pounded his breast.

After a few seconds of this he recovered, and his demeanor changed completely. Anguish was replaced first by a burning hatred for those who had destroyed his beloved, Jewish New York City, then by an expression of grim satisfaction which gradually turned into an exultant gloating: "But we have taken our vengeance against our enemies, and they are no more. Time and again, throughout history, the nations have risen up against us and tried to expel us or kill us, but we have always triumphed in the end. No one can resist us. All those who have tried — Egypt, Persia, Rome, Spain, Russia, Germany — have themselves been destroyed, and we have always emerged triumphant from the ruins. We have always survived and prospered. And now we have utterly crushed the latest of those who have raised their hands against us. Just as Moshe smote the Egyptian, so have we smitten the Organization."

His tongue flickered wetly over his lips and his dark eyes gleamed balefully as he described the hail of nuclear annihilation which he said had been unleashed on California that very afternoon: "Their precious racial superiority did not help them a bit when we fired hundreds of nuclear missiles into the racist stronghold," the newscaster gloated. "The White vermin died like flies. We can only hope they realized in their last moments that many of the loyal soldiers who pressed the firing buttons for the missiles which killed them were Black or Chicano or Jewish. Yes, the Whites and their criminal racial pride have been wiped out in California, but now we must kill the racists everywhere else, so that racial harmony and brotherhood can be restored to America. We must kill them! Kill them! Kill! Kill! . . ."

Then he lapsed into Hebrew again, and his voice became louder and harsher. He stood up and leaned into the camera, an incarnation of pure hatred, as he shrieked and gibbered in his alien tongue, gobs of saliva flying from his mouth and dribbling down his chin.

This extraordinary performance must have been embarrassing to some of his less emotional brethren, because he was suddenly cut off in mid-shriek and replaced by a Gentile, who continued to give out revised casualty estimates into the early hours of the morning.

Gradually, during the next 48 hours, we learned the true story of that dreadful Thursday, both from later and more nearly accurate government newscasts and from our own sources. The first and most important news we received came early Friday morning, in a coded message from Revolutionary Command to all the Organization's units around the country: California had not been destroyed! Vandenberg had been annihilated, and two large missiles had struck the city of Los Angeles, causing widespread death and destruction, but at least 90 per cent of the people in the liberated zone had survived, partly because they had been given a few minutes advance warning and had been able to take shelter.

Unfortunately for the people in other parts of the country, there was no advance warning, and the total death toll — including those who have died of burns, other wounds, and radiation in the last 10 days — is approximately 60 million. The missiles which caused these deaths, however, were not ours — except in the case of New York City, which received a barrage first from Vandenberg and then from the Soviet Union. Baltimore, Detroit, and the other American cities which were hit — even Los Angeles — were all the victims of Soviet missiles. Vandenberg AFB was the only domestic target hit by the U.S. government.

The cataclysmic chain of events began with an extrordinarily painful decision by Revolutionary Command. Reports being received by RC in the first week of this month indicated a gradual but steady shift of the balance of power from the military faction in the government, which wanted to avoid a nuclear showdown with us, to the Jewish faction, which demanded the immediate annihilation of California. The Jews feared that otherwise the existing stalemate between the liberated zone and the rest of the country might become permanent, which would mean an almost certain victory for us eventually.

To prevent this they went to work behind the scenes in their customary manner, arguing, threatening, bribing, bringing pressure to bear on one of their opponents at a time. They had already succeeded in arranging the replacement of several top generals by their own creatures, and RC saw the last chance disappearing of avoiding a full-scale exchange of nuclear missiles with government forces.

So we decided to preempt. We struck first, but not at the government's forces. We fired all our missiles from Vandenberg (except for half-a-dozen targeted on New York) at two targets: Israel and the Soviet Union. As soon as our missiles had been launched, RC announced the news to the Pentagon via a direct telephone link. The Pentagon, of course, had immediate confirmation from its own radar screens, and it had no choice but to follow up our salvo with an immediate and full-scale nuclear attack of its own against the Soviet Union, in an attempt to knock out as much of the Soviet retaliatory potential as possible.

The Soviet response was horrendous, but spotty. They fired everything they had left at us, but it simply wasn't enough. Several of the largest American cities, including Washington and Chicago, were spared.

What the Organization accomplished by precipitating this fateful chain of events is fourfold: First, by hitting New York and Israel, we have completely knocked out two of world Jewry's principal nerve centers, and it should take them a while to establish a new chain of command and get their act back together.

Second, by forcing them to take a decisive action, we pushed the balance of power in the U.S. government solidly back toward the military leaders. For all practical purposes, the country is now under a military government.

Third, by provoking a Soviet counterattack, we did far more to disrupt the System in this country and break up the orderly pattern of life of the masses than we could have done by using our own weapons against domestic targets — and we still have most of our 60-kiloton warheads left! That will be of enormous advantage to us in the days ahead.

Fourth, we have eliminated a major specter which had been hanging over our plans before: the specter of Soviet intervention after we and the System had fought it out with each other.

We took an enormous chance, of course: first, that California would be devastated in the Soviet counterattack; and second, that the U.S. military would lose its cool and use its nuclear weaponry on California even though, except for Vandenberg, there was no nuclear threat there to be knocked out. In both cases the fortunes of war have been at least moderately kind to us — although the threat from the U.S. military is by no means over.

What we lost, however, is substantial: about an eighth of the Organization's members, and nearly a fifth of the White population of the country — not to mention an unknown number of millions of racial kinsmen in the Soviet Union. Fortunately, the heaviest death toll in this country has been in the largest cities, which are substantially non-White.

All in all, the strategic situation of the Organization relative to the System is enormously improved, and that is what really counts. We are willing to take as many casualties as necessary — just so the System takes proportionately more. All that matters,

191

in the long run, is that when the smoke has finally cleared the last battalion in the field is ours.

Today I finally located Bill and found out what happened back in the print shop during the evacuation. He has also suffered a grievous personal loss, and his story was brief but poignant.

The evacuation of the expanded Pentagon security area had been carried out with no warning whatever. At about eleven in the morning of September 7 tanks had suddenly appeared in the streets and soldiers had begun knocking on all doors, giving occupants only ten minutes to abandon their dwellings. They were very rough on anyone who did not move fast enough.

Bill, Carol, and Katherine were running propaganda leaflets on the press when the tanks came, and they had just enough time to hide the incriminating evidence under a tarpaulin before four Black soldiers pushed their way into the shop. Since the troops weren't taking time to search buildings, presumably everything would have gone smoothly at the shop had not one of the Blacks made a suggestive remark to Katherine as she was hastily packing some of her clothing and other personal items.

Katherine said nothing to the Black, but the icy look she gave him apparently injured his sense of "human dignity." He began the whining, "what's a matter, baby, don' you like Black people?" approach that Blacks have found works wonders with guilt-ridden, liberal White girls who are desperately afraid of being considered "racists" if they reject the unwelcome advances of rutting Black bucks. When Katherine tried to get out the shop door carrying two heavy suitcases, the amorous Black blocked her way and tried to run his hand under her dress.

She jumped back and gave the Black a well-placed kick in the groin, which immediately cooled his ardor, but it was too late: he had felt Katherine's thigh holster. He shouted the warning to his companions, and both sides began shooting at the same time. While Katherine and Carol fired their pistols, Bill blazed away at the Black soldiers with a sawed-off, autoloading shotgun.

All four Blacks were mortally wounded, but not before they had in turn wounded each of the three Whites. One of the Blacks staggered out of the shop before he collapsed, and Bill, who was least seriously hit, had only a moment to ascertain that Katherine was beyond all help before he and Carol were forced to flee out the rear of the shop.

They holed up in the attic of an adjoining building, and searchers were unable to find them. Carol soon became so weak from her wounds that she was unable to move, and Bill was not in much better condition. The night of the following day he crept painfully from their hiding place and stealthily rounded up drinking water, food, and a few medical supplies from the empty buildings in the neighborhood before returning to his wife.

Carol died on the fourth day, and it was another five days before Bill had regained sufficient strength to leave the attic again and make his way out of the security area.

I know that Bill would never lie to me, and so I have at least the consolation of knowing that Katherine did not fall into the hands of the enemy alive. What I must do now is devote whatever time I have left to the task of insuring that she has not died in vain.

XXVII

October 28, 1993. Just back from more than a month in Baltimore — what's left of it. I and four others from here hauled a batch of portable radioactivity-metering equipment up to Silver Spring, where we linked up with a Maryland unit and continued north to the vicinity of Baltimore. Since the main roads were totally impassable, we had to walk across country more than halfway, commandeering a truck for only the last dozen miles.

Although more than two weeks had passed since the bombing, the state of affairs around Baltimore was almost indescribably chaotic when we arrived. We didn't even try to go into the burned-out core of the city, but even in the suburbs and countryside 10 miles west of ground zero, half the buildings had burned. Even the secondary roads in and around the suburbs were littered with the burned hulks of vehicles, and nearly everyone we encountered was on foot.

Groups of scavengers were everywhere, poking through ruined stores, foraging in the fields with backpacks, carrying bundles of looted or salvaged goods — mostly food, but also clothing, building materials, and everything else imaginable — to and fro like an army of ants.

And the corpses! They were another good reason for staying away from the roads as much as possible. Even in the areas where relatively few people were killed by the initial blast or by subsequent radiation sickness, the corpses were strewn along the roads by the thousands. They were nearly all refugees from the blast area.

Close to the city one saw the bodies of those who had been badly burned by the fireball; most of them had not been able to walk more than a mile or so before they collapsed. Further out were those who had been less seriously burned. And far out into the countryside were the corpses of those who had succumbed to radiation days or weeks later. All had been left to rot where they fell, except in those few areas where the military had restored a semblance of order

We had at that time only about 40 Organization members among the survivors in the Baltimore area. They had been engaged in sabotage, sniping, and other guerrilla efforts against the police and military personnel there during the first week after the blast. Then they gradually discovered that the rules of the game had changed.

They found out that it was no longer necessary to operate as furtively as they had before. The System's troops returned their fire when attacked, but did not pursue them. Outside a few areas, the police no longer attempted to undertake systematic searches of persons and vehicles, and there were no house raids. The attitude almost seemed to be, "Don't bother us, and we won't bother you."

The civilian survivors also tended to take a much more nearly neutral attitude than before. There was fear of the Organization, but very little overt expression of hostility. The people did not know whether we were the ones who had fired the missile which destroyed their city, as the System broadcasts claimed, but they seemed about as disposed to blame the System for letting it happen as us for doing it.

The holocaust through which the people up there had passed had clearly convinced them quite thoroughly of one thing: the System could no longer guarantee their security. They no longer had even a trace of confidence in the old order; they merely wanted to survive now, and they would turn to anyone who could help them stay alive a while longer.

Sensing this changed attitude, our members had begun recruiting and organizing among the survivors around Baltimore in semi-public fashion and meeting with sufficient success that Revolutionary Command authorized the attempt to establish a small liberated zone west of the city.

The 11 of us who had come up from the Washington suburbs to help pitched in with enthusiasm, and within a few days we had established a reasonably defensible perimeter enclosing about 2,000 houses and other buildings with a total of nearly 12,000 occupants. My principal function was to carry out a radiological survey of the soil, the buildings, the local vegetation, and the water sources in the area, so that we could be sure of freedom from dangerous levels of nuclear radiation resulting from fallout.

194

We organized about 300 of the locals into a fairly effective militia and provided them with arms. It would be risky at this stage to try to arm a bigger militia than that, because we haven't had an opportunity to ideologically condition the local population to the extent we'd like, and they still require close observation and tight supervision. But we picked the best prospects among the able-bodied males in the enclave, and we do have quite a bit of experience in picking people. I'll not be surprised if half our new militiamen eventually graudate to membership in the Organization, and some will probably even be admitted to the Order.

Yes, I think that, by and large, we can count on our new recruits. There's still a great deal of basically sound human material left in this country, despite the widespread moral corruption. After all, that corruption has been produced largely by the instilling of an alien ideology and an alien set of values in a people disoriented by an unnatural and spiritually unhealthy life-style. The hell they're going through now is at least knocking some of the foolishness out of them and leaving them quite a bit more receptive to a correct world view than they were before.

Our first task was to weed out and eliminate the alien elements and the race criminals from the new enclave. It's astounding how many dark, kinky-haired Middle Easterners have invaded this country in the last decade. I believe they have taken over every restaurant and hot dog stand in Maryland. We must have shot at least a dozen Iranians, just in our little suburban enclave, and twice that many escaped when they realized what was happening.

Then we formed the people into labor brigades to carry out a number of necessary functions, one of which was the sanitary disposal of the hundreds of corpses of refugees. The majority of these poor creatures were White, and I overheard one of our members refer to what happened to them as "a slaughter of the innocents."

I am not sure that is a correct description of the recent holocaust. I am sorry, of course, for the millions of White people, both here and in Russia, who died — and who have yet to die before we have finished — in this war to rid ourselves of the Jewish yoke. But innocents? I think not. Certainly, that term should not be applied to the majority of the adults.

After all, is not man essentially responsible for his condition — at least, in a collective sense? If the White nations of the world had not allowed themselves to become subject to the Jew, to Jewish ideas, to the Jewish spirit, this war would not be necessary. We can hardly consider ourselves blameless. We can hardly say we had no choice, no chance to avoid the Jew's snare. We can hardly say we were not warned.

Men of wisdom, integrity, and courage have warned us over and over again of the consequences of our folly. And even after we were well down the Jewish primrose path, we had chance after chance to save ourselves — most recently 52 years ago, when the Germans and the Jews were locked in struggle for the mastery of central and eastern Europe.

We ended up on the Jewish side in that struggle, primarily because we had chosen corrupt men as our leaders. And we had chosen corrupt leaders because we valued the wrong things in life. We had chosen leaders who promised us something for nothing; who pandered to our weaknesses and vices; who had nice stage personalities and pleasant smiles, but who were without character or scruple. We ignored the really important issues in our national life and gave free rein to a criminal System to conduct the affairs of our nation as it saw fit, so long as it kept us moderately well-supplied with bread and circuses.

And are not folly, willful ignorance, laziness, greed, irresponsibility, and moral timidity as blameworthy as the most deliberate malice? Are not all our sins of omission to be counted against us as heavily as the Jew's sins of commission against him?

In the Creator's account book, that is the way things are reckoned. Nature does not accept "good" excuses in lieu of performance. No race which neglects to insure its own survival, when the means for that survival are at hand, can be judged "innocent," nor can the penalty exacted against it be considered unjust, no matter how severe.

Immediately after our success in California this summer, in my dealings with the civilian population there I had it thoroughly impressed on me why the American people do not deserve to be considered "innocents." Their reaction to the civil strife there was based almost solely on the way it affected their own private circumstances. For the first day or two — before it dawned on most people that we might actually win — the White civilians, even racially conscious ones, were generally hostile; we were messing up their life-style and making their customary pursuit of pleasure terribly inconvenient.

Then, after they learned to fear us, they were all too eager to please us. But they weren't really interested in the rights and wrongs of the struggle; they couldn't be bothered with soul-searching and long-range considerations. Their attitude was: "Just tell us what we're supposed to believe, and we'll believe it." They just wanted to be safe and comfortable again as soon as possible. And they weren't being cynical; they weren't jaded sophisticates, but ordinary people.

The fact is that the ordinary people are not really much less culpable than the not-so-ordinary people, than the pillars of the System. Take the political police, as an example. Most of them — the White ones — are not especially evil men. They serve evil masters, but they rationalize what they do; they justify it to themselves, some in patriotic terms ("protecting our free and democratic way of life") and some in religious or ideological terms ("upholding Christian ideals of equality and justice").

One can call them hypocrites — one can point out that they deliberately avoid thinking about anything which might call into question the validity of the shallow catch-phrases with which they justify themselves — but is not everyone who has *tolerated* the System also a hypocrite, whether he actively supported it or not? Is not everyone who mindlessly parrots the same catch-phrases, refusing to examine their implications and contradictions, whether he uses them as justifications for his deeds or not, also to be blamed?

I cannot think of any segment of White society, from the Maryland red-necks and their families whose radioactive bodies we bulldozed into a huge pit a few days ago to the university professors we strung up in Los Angeles last July, which can truly claim that it did not deserve what happened to it. It was not so many months ago that nearly all those who are wandering homeless and bemoaning their fate today were talking from the other side of their mouths.

Not a few of our people have been badly roughed up in the past — and two that I know of were killed — when they fell into the hands of red-necks — "good ol' boys" who, although not liberals or *shabbos goyim* in any way, had no use for "radicals" who wanted to "overthrow the gummint." In their case it was sheer ignorance.

But ignorance of that sort is no more excusable than the bleating, sheeplike liberalism of the the pseudo-intellectuals who have smugly promoted Jewish ideology for so many years; or than the selfishness and cowardice of the great American middle class who went along for the ride, complaining only when their pocketbooks suffered.

No, talk of "innocents" has no meaning. We must look at our situation collectively, in a race-wide sense. We must understand that our race is like a cancer patient undergoing drastic surgery in order to save his life. There is no sense in asking whether the tissue being cut out now is "innocent" or not. That is no more reasonable than trying to distinguish the "good" Jews from the bad ones — or, as some of our thicker-skulled "good ol' boys" still insist on trying, separating the "good niggers" from the rest of their race.

The fact is that we are all responsible, as individuals, for the morals and the behavior of our race as a whole. There is no evading that responsibility, in the long run, any more for the members of our own race than for those of other races, and each of us individually must be prepared to be called to account for that responsibility at any time. In these days many are being called.

But the enemy is also paying a price. He's still got a grip on things here, more or less, but he's just about finished outside North America. Although the government is blocking most of the foreign news from the networks here, we have been receiving clandestine reports from our overseas units and also monitoring the European news broadcasts.

Within 24 hours after we hit Tel Aviv and half-a-dozen other Israeli targets last month, hundreds of thousands of Arabs were swarming across the borders of occupied Palestine. Most of them were civilians, armed only with knives or clubs, and Jewish border guards mowed down thousands of them, until their ammunition was exhausted. The Arabs' hatred, pent up for 45 years, drove them on — across mine fields, through Jewish machine-gun fire, and into the radioactive chaos of burning cities, their single thought being to slay the people who had stolen their land, killed their fathers, and humiliated them for two generations. Within a week the throat of the last Jewish survivor in the last *kibbutz* and in the last, smoking ruin in Tel Aviv had been cut.

News from the Soviet Union is very scanty, but the reports are that the Russian survivors have dealt with the Jews there in much the same way. In the ruins of Moscow and Leningrad during the first few days the people rounded up all the Jews they could get their hands on and hurled them into burning buildings or onto burning heaps of debris.

And anti-Jewish riots have broken out in London, Paris, Brussels, Rotterdam, Bucharest, Buenos Aires, Johannesburg, and Sydney. The governments of France and the Netherlands, both rotten to the core with Jewish corruption, have fallen, and the people are settling scores in the towns and villages throughout those countries.

It's the sort of thing which happened time after time during the Middle Ages, of course — every time the people had finally had

198

their fill of the Jews and their tricks. Unfortunately, they never finished the job, and they won't this time either. I'm sure the Jews are already making their plans for a comeback, as soon as the people have calmed down and forgotten. The people have such short memories!

But *we* won't forget! That alone is enough to insure that history will not repeat itself. No matter how long it takes us and no matter to what lengths we must go, we'll demand a final settlement of the account between our two races. If the Organization survives this contest, no Jew will — anywhere. We'll go to the uttermost ends of the earth to hunt down the last of Satan's spawn.

The organizational principles we are using in Maryland are a bit different from those used in California, because the situations are different. Here, unlike southern California, there are neither natural, geographical barriers nor a ring of government troops to separate our enclave from its surroundings.

Of course, we did what we could to make up for this lack. We chose a perimeter, in the first place, which follows natural gaps in the pattern of man-made structures — although, for nearly half a mile the gap is only the 100-yard width of a highway right-of-way, with the System's troops controlling the other side. We plugged some open areas with barbed wire and mines, and we torched buildings and brush outside the enclave which might provide concealment or cover for snipers or hostile troop concentrations.

But if the people in our enclave want to leave, there is really no way our militia can stop more than a few of them. We are depending on three things, much more than the fear of being shot, to hold them. First, we have given the people order, and we are doing a substantially better job of maintaining the order inside our enclave than the government is doing outside it. After the dose of chaos these people have swallowed, all but the most brainwashed "do your own thing" types are hungry for authority and discipline.

Second, we are well on the way to establishing a subsistence economy in the enclave. We have a large water storage tank, which we should be able to keep full just by pumping groundwater from already-existing wells; there are two substantially intact food warehouses and a nearly full grain silo; and there are four working farms — including one dairy farm — with almost enough production capacity to feed half our people. We are making up our present food deficit by raiding outside the enclave, but by the time we've put everyone to work converting

199

every arable patch of ground to vegetable gardens, that shouldn't be necessary.

Last, and perhaps not least, everyone in the enclave is indisputably White — we dealt summarily with every questionable case — while outside it is the usual godawful assortment of Whites, mostly Whites, half-Whites, Gypsies, Chicanos, Puerto Ricans, Jews, Blacks, Orientals, Arabs, Persians, and everything else under the sun: the typical, cosmopolitan racial goulash one finds in every American metropolitan area these days. Anyone who feels a need for a little "brotherhood," Jewish style, can leave our enclave. I doubt that many will feel the need.

November 2. We had a long meeting this afternoon at which we were briefed on the latest national developments and given new priorities for our local action program.

There has been remarkably little change in the national situation during the past six weeks: the government has been able to do very little to restore order in the devastated areas or to compensate for the damage done to the nation's transportation network, its power generating and distribution facilities, and the other essential components of the national economy. The people are being left on their own to a very large extent, while the System grapples with its own problems, not the least of which is its renewed uncertainty over the reliability of its military forces.

That lack of change is, in itself, very encouraging, because it means that the System is not recovering the degree of control over the country which it exercised prior to September 8. The government has simply not been able to cope with the chaotic conditions which now prevail throughout wide areas.

Our units have been doing everything they can in the way of sabotage, of course, just for the purpose of keeping things destabilized. But Revolutionary Command has apparently been waiting to see what sort of intermediate-term situation would gel before deciding the next phase of the Organization's strategy.

The decision has now been made, and it is for us to begin doing in many other places the sort of thing we did in Maryland last month. We will be shifting a large part of the emphasis of our struggle from guerrilla actions to public and semi-public organizing. That is exciting news: it means a new escalation of our offensive — an escalation which is only being undertaken because of our confidence that the tide of battle is now running in our favor!

But the old phase of the fight is by no means over, and one of the most worrisome dangers we are facing is a large-scale military assault on California. Government forces are now undergoing a rapid buildup in the southern California area, and an invasion of the liberated zone seems imminent. If the System succeeds in California, then it will certainly move similarly against Baltimore and any other enclaves we may establish in the future, despite our threats of nuclear retaliation.

The problem seems to be a clique of conservative generals in the Pentagon who see us more as a threat to their own authority than to the System itself. They have no love for the Jews and are not particularly unhappy with the present state of affairs, in which they are the *de facto* rulers of the country. What they would like is to permanently institutionalize the present state of martial law and then gradually restore order, bringing about a new *status quo* based on their rather reactionary and shortsighted ideas.

We, of course, are the fly in their ointment, and they are moving to squash us. What makes them especially dangerous to us is that they are not as afraid of our nuclear-reprisal capability as their predecessors were. They know we can destroy more cities and kill a lot more civilians, but they don't think we can kill them.

I conferred privately with Major Williams of Washington Field Command for more than an hour on the problem of attacking the Pentagon. The military's other major command centers were either knocked out on September 8 or subsequently consolidated with the Pentagon, which the top brass apparently regard as impregnable.

And it damned near is. We went over every possibility we could think of, and we came up with no really convincing plan — except, perhaps, one. That is to make an air delivery of a bomb.

In the massive ring of defenses around the Pentagon there is a great deal of anti-aircraft firepower, but we decided that a small plane, flying just above the ground, might be able to get through the three-mile gauntlet with one of our 60-kiloton warheads. One factor in favor of such an attempt is that we have never before used aircraft in such a way, and we might hope to catch the anti-aircraft crews off their guard.

Although the military is guarding all civil airfields, it just happens that we have an old crop duster stashed in a barn only a few miles from here. My immediate assignment is to prepare a detailed plan for an aerial attack on the Pentagon by next Monday. We must make a final decision at that time and then act without further delay.

201

XXVIII

November 9, 1993. It's still three hours until first light, and all systems are "go." I'll use the time to write a few pages — my last diary entry. Then it's a one-way trip to the Pentagon for me. The warhead is strapped into the front seat of the old Stearman and rigged to detonate either on impact or when I flip a switch in the back seat. Hopefully, I'll be able to manage a low-level air burst directly over the center of the Pentagon. Failing that, I'll at least try to fly as close as I can before I'm shot down.

It's been more than four years since I've flown, but I've thoroughly familiarized myself with the Stearman cockpit and been briefed on the plane's peculiarities: I don't anticipate any piloting problems. The barn-hangar here is only eight miles from the Pentagon. We'll thoroughly warm up the engine in the barn, and when the door is opened I'll go like a bat out of hell, straight for the Pentagon, at an altitude of about 50 feet.

By the time I hit the defensive perimeter I should be making about 150 miles an hour, and it'll take me just under another 70 seconds to reach the target. Two-thirds of the troops around the Pentagon are niggers, which should greatly boost my chances of getting through.

The sky should still be heavily overcast, and there'll be just enough light for me to make out my landmarks. We've painted the plane to be as nearly invisible as possible under the anticipated flying conditions, and I'll be too low for radar-controlled fire. Considering everything, I believe my chances are excellent.

I regret that I won't be around to participate in the final success of our revolution, but I am happy that I have been allowed to do as much as I have. It is a comforting thought in these last hours of my physical existence that, of all the billions of men and women of my race who have ever lived, I will have been able to play a more vital role than all but a handful of them in determining the ultimate destiny of mankind. What I will do today will be of more weight in the annals of the race than all the conquests of Caesar and Napoleon — if I succeed!

And succeed I must, or the entire revolution will be in the gravest danger. Revolutionary Command estimates that the System will launch its invasion against California within the next 48 hours. Once the order is issued from the Pentagon, we will be unable to halt the invasion. And if my mission today fails, there'll not be enough time for us to try something else.

Monday night, after we had made the final decision on this mission, I underwent the rite of Union. Actually, I have been undergoing the rite for the past 30 hours, and it will not be complete for another three; only in the moment of my death will I achieve full membership in the Order.

To many that may seem a gloomy prospect, I suppose, but not to me. I have known what was ahead of me since my trial last March, and I am grateful that my probationary period has been cut short by five months, partly because of the present crisis and partly because my performance since March has been considered exemplary.

The ceremony Monday was more moving and beautiful than I could have imagined it would be. More than 200 of us assembled in the cellar of the Georgetown gift shop, from which the partitions and stacked crates had been removed to make room for us. Thirty new probationary members were sworn into the Order, and 18 others, including me, participated in the rite of Union. I alone, however, was singled out, because of my unique status.

When Major Williams summoned me, I stepped forward and then turned to face the silent sea of robed figures. What a contrast with the tiny gathering only two years earlier, when seven of us met upstairs for my initiation! The Order, even with its extraordinary standards, is growing with astonishing rapidity.

Knowing fully what was demanded in character and commitment of each man who stood before me, my chest swelled with pride. These were no soft-bellied, conservative businessmen assembled for some Masonic mumbo-jumbo; no loudmouthed, beery red-necks letting off a little ritualized steam about "the goddam niggers"; no pious, frightened churchgoers whining for the guidance or protection of an anthropomorphic deity. These were *real men, White* men, men who were now *one* with me in spirit and consciousness as well as in blood.

As the torchlight flickered over the coarse, gray robes of the motionless throng, I thought to myself: These men are the best my race has produced in this generation — and they are as good as have been produced in any generation. In them are combined fiery passion and icy discipline, deep intelligence and instant readiness for action, a strong sense of self-worth and a total commitment to our common cause. On them hang the hopes of everything that will ever be. They are the vanguard of the coming New Era, the pioneers who will lead our race out of its present depths and toward the unexplored heights above. And I am *one* with them!

Then I made my brief declaration: "Brothers! Two years ago, when I entered your ranks for the first time, I consecrated my life to our Order and to the purpose for which it exists. But then I faltered in the fulfillment of my obligation to you. Now I am ready to meet my obligation fully. I offer you my life. Do you accept it?"

In a rumbling unison their reply came back: "Brother! We accept your life. In return we offer you everlasting life in us. Your deed shall not be in vain, nor shall it be forgotten, until the end of time. To this commitment we pledge our lives."

I know, as certainly as it is possible for a man to know anything, that the Order will not fail me if I do not fail it. The Order has a life which is more than the sum of the lives of its members. When it speaks collectively, as it did Monday, something deeper and older and wiser than any of us speaks — something which cannot die. Of that deeper life I am now about to partake.

Of course, I would have liked to have children by Katherine, so that I could also have immortality of another sort, but that is not to be. I am satisfied.

They've been warming up the engine for about 10 minutes now, and Bill is signalling to me that it's time to go. The rest of the crew has already taken cover in the blast shelter we dug under the barn floor. I will now entrust my diary to Bill, and he will later put it in the hiding place with the other volumes.

Epilog

Thus end Earl Turner's diaries, as unpretentiously as they began.

His final mission was successful, of course, as we all are reminded each year on November 9 — our traditional Day of the Martyrs.

With the System's principal military nerve center destroyed, the System's forces poised outside the Organization's California enclave continued to wait for orders which never came. Declining morale, soaring desertions, growing Black indiscipline, and finally, the inability of the System to maintain the integrity of its supply line to its California troops resulted in the gradual erosion of the threat of invasion. Eventually the System began regrouping its forces elsewhere, to meet new challenges in other parts of the country.

And then, just as the Jews had feared, the flow of Organization activists turned exactly 180 degrees from what it had been in the weeks and months immediately prior to July 4, 1993. From scores of training camps in the liberated zone, first hundreds, then thousands of highly motivated guerrilla fighters began slipping through the System's diminishing ring of troops and moving eastward. With these guerrilla forces the Organization followed the example of its Baltimore members and rapidly established dozens of new enclaves, primarily in the nuclear-devastated areas, where System authority was weakest.

The Detroit enclave was initially the most important of these. Bloody anarchy had reigned among the survivors in the Detroit area for several weeks after the nuclear blasts of September 8. Eventually, a semblance of order had been restored, with System troops loosely sharing power with the leaders of a number of Black gangs in the area. Although there were a few isolated White strongholds which kept the roving mobs of Black plunderers and rapists at bay, most of the disorganized and demoralized White survivors in and around Detroit offered no effective resistance to the Blacks, and, just as in other heavily Black areas of the country, they suffered terribly.

Then, in mid-December, the Organization seized the initiative. A number of synchronized lightning raids on the System's military strongpoints in the Detroit area resulted in an easy victory.

205

The Organization then established certain patterns in Detroit which were soon followed elsewhere. All captured White troops, as soon as they had laid down their weapons, were offered a chance to fight with the Organization against the System. Those who immediately volunteered were taken aside for preliminary screening and then sent to camps for indoctrination and special training. The others were machine-gunned on the spot, without further ado.

The same degree of ruthlessness was used in dealing with the White civilian population. When the Organization's cadres moved into the White strongholds in the Detroit suburbs, the first thing they found it necessary to do was to liquidate most of the local White leaders, in order to establish the unquestioned authority of the Organization. There was no time or patience for trying to reason with shortsighted Whites who insisted that they weren't "racists" or "revolutionaries" and didn't need the help of any "outside agitators" in dealing with their problems, or who had some other conservative or parochial fixation.

The Whites of Detroit and the other new enclaves were organized more along the lines described by Earl Turner for Baltimore than for California, but even more rapidly and roughly. In most areas of the country there was no opportunity for an orderly, large-scale separation of non-Whites, as in California, and consequently a bloody race war raged for months, taking a terrible toll of those Whites who were not in one of the Organization's tightly controlled, all-White enclaves.

Food became critically scarce everywhere during the winter of 1993-1994. The Blacks lapsed into cannibalism, just as they had in California, while hundreds of thousands of starving Whites, who earlier had ignored the Organization's call for a rising against the System, began appearing at the borders of the various liberated zones begging for food. The Organization was only able to feed the White populations already under its control by imposing the severest rationing, and it was necessary to turn many of the latecomers away.

Those who were admitted — and that meant only children, women of childbearing age, and able-bodied men willing to fight in the Organization's ranks — were subjected to much more severe racial screening than had been used to separate Whites from non-Whites in California. It was no longer sufficient to be merely White; in order to eat one had to be judged the bearer of especially valuable genes.

In Detroit the practice was first established (and it was later adopted elsewhere) of providing any able-bodied White male who

206

sought admittance to the Organization's enclave with one hot meal and a bayonet or other edged weapon. His forehead was then marked with an indelible dye, and he was turned out and could be readmitted permanently only by bringing back the head of a freshly killed Black or other non-White. This practice assured that precious food would not be wasted on those who would not or could not add to the Organization's fighting strength, but it took a terrible toll of the weaker and more decadent White elements.

Tens of millions perished during the first half of 1994, and the total White population of the country reached a low point of approximately 50 million by August of that year. By then, however, nearly half the remaining Whites were in Organization enclaves, and food production and distribution in the enclaves had grown until it was barely sufficient to prevent further losses from starvation.

Although a central government of sorts still existed, the System's military and police forces were, for all practical purposes, reduced to a number of essentially autonomous local commands, whose principal activity became looting for food, liquor, gasoline, and women. Both the Organization and the System avoided large-scale encounters with each other, the Organization confining itself to short, intense raids on System troop concentrations and other facilities, and the System's forces confining themselves to guarding their sources of supply and, in some areas, to attempting to limit the further expansion of the Organization's enclaves.

But the Organization's enclaves continued to expand, nevertheless, both in size and number, all through the five Dark Years preceding the New Era. At one time there were nearly 2,000 separate Organization enclaves in North America. Outside these zones of order and security, the anarchy and savagery grew steadily worse, with the only real authority wielded by marauding bands which preyed on each other and on the unorganized and defenseless masses.

Many of these bands were composed of Blacks, Puerto Ricans, Chicanos, and half-White mongrels. In growing numbers, however, Whites also formed bands along racial lines, even without Organization guidance. As the war of extermination wore on, millions of soft, city-bred, brainwashed Whites gradually began regaining their manhood. The rest died.

The Organization's growing success was not without its setbacks, of course. One of the most notable of these was the terrible Pittsburgh Massacre, of June 1994. The Organization had established an enclave there in May of that year, forcing the retreat of local System forces, but it did not act swiftly enough in identifying and liquidating the local Jewish element.

A number of Jews, in collaboration with White conservatives and liberals, had time to work out a plan of subversion. The consequence was that System troops, aided by their fifth column inside the enclave, recaptured Pittsburgh. The Jews and Blacks then went on a wild rampage of mass murder, reminiscent of the worst excesses of the Jew-instigated Bolshevik Revolution in Russia, 75 years earlier. By the time the blood-orgy ended, virtually every White in the area had either been butchered or forced to flee. The surviving staff members of the Organization's Pittsburgh Field Command, whose hesitation in dealing with the Jews had brought on the catastrophe, were rounded up and shot by a special disciplinary squad acting on orders from Revolutionary Command.

The only time, after November 9, 1993, the Organization was forced to detonate a nuclear weapon on the North American continent was a year later, in Toronto. Hundreds of thousands of Jews had fled the United States to that Canadian city during 1993 and 1994, making almost a second New York of it and using it as their command center for the war raging to the south. So far as both the Jews and the Organization were concerned, the U.S.-Canadian border had no real significance during the later stages of the Great Revolution, and by mid-1994 conditions were only slightly less chaotic north of the border than south of it.

Throughout the Dark Years neither the Organization nor the System could hope for a completely decisive advantage over the other, so long as they both retained the capability for nuclear warfare. During the first part of this period, when the System's conventional military strength greatly exceeded the Organization's, only the Organization's threat of retaliation with its more than 100 nuclear warheads hidden inside the major population centers still under System control kept the System, in most cases, from moving against the Organization's liberated zones.

Later, when Organizational gains, together with growing attrition of the System's forces through desertions, tilted the balance of conventional strength toward the Organization, the System retained control over a number of military units armed with nuclear weapons and, by threatening to use these, forced the Organization to leave certain System strongholds inviolate.

Even the System's elite, pampered nuclear troops were not immune to the processes of attrition which sapped the System's conventional strength, however, and they could postpone the

208

inevitable only temporarily. On January 30, 1999, in the momentous Truce of Omaha, the last group of System generals surrendered their commands to the Organization, in return for a pledge that they and their immediate families would be allowed to live out the remainders of their lives unmolested. The Organization kept its pledge, and a special reservation on an island off the California coast was set aside for the generals.

Then, of course, came the mopping-up period, when the last of the non-White bands were hunted down and exterminated, followed by the final purge of undesirable racial elements among the remaining White population.

From the liberation of North America until the beginning of the New Era for our whole planet, there elapsed the remarkably short time of just under 11 months. Professor Anderson has recorded and analyzed the events of this climactic period in detail in his *History of the Great Revolution*. Here it is sufficient to note that, with the principal centers of world Jewish power annihilated and the nuclear threat of the Soviet Union neutralized, the most important obstacles to the Organization's worldwide victory were out of the way.

From as early as 1993 the Organization had had active cells in Western Europe, and they grew with extraordinary rapidity in the six years preceding the victory in North America. Liberalism had taken its toll in Europe, just as in America, and the old order in most places was a rotted-out shell with only a surface semblance of strength. The disastrous economic collapse in Europe in the spring of 1999, following the demise of the System in North America, greatly helped in preparing the European masses morally for the Organization's final takeover.

That takeover came in a great, Europe-wide rush in the summer and fall of 1999, as a cleansing hurricane of change swept over the continent, clearing away in a few months the refuse of a millennium or more of alien ideology and a century or more of profound moral and material decadence. The blood flowed ankle-deep in the streets of many of Europe's great cities momentarily, as the race traitors, the offspring of generations of dysgenic breeding, and hordes of *Gastarbeiter* met a common fate. Then the great dawn of the New Era broke over the Western world.

The single remaining power center on earth not under Organizational control by early December 1999 was China. The Organization was willing to postpone the solution of the Chinese problem for several years, but the Chinese themselves forced the Organization to take immediate and drastic action. The Chinese,

209

of course, had invaded the Asiatic regions of the Soviet Union immediately after the nuclear strike of September 8, 1993, but until the fall of 1999 they had remained east of the Urals, consolidating the vast, new, conquered territory.

When, during the summer and early fall of 1999, one European nation after another was liberated by the Organization, the Chinese decided to make a grab for European Russia. The Organization countered this move massively, using nuclear missiles to knock out the still-primitive Chinese missile and strategic-bomber capabilities, as well as hitting a number of new Chinese troop concentrations west of the Urals. Unfortunately, this action did not stem the Yellow tide flowing north and west from China.

The Organization still required time to reorganize and reorient the European populations newly under its control before it could hope to deal in a conventional manner with the enormous numbers of Chinese infantry pouring across the Urals into Europe; all its dependable troops at that time were hardly sufficient even for garrison duty in the newly liberated and still not entirely pacified areas of eastern and southern Europe.

Therefore, the Organization resorted to a combination of chemical, biological, and radiological means, on an enormous scale, to deal with the problem. Over a period of four years some 16 million square miles of the earth's surface, from the Ural Mountains to the Pacific and from the Arctic Ocean to the Indian Ocean, were effectively sterilized. Thus was the Great Eastern Waste created.

Only in the last decade have certain areas of the Waste been declared safe for colonization. Even so, they are "safe" only in the sense that the poisons sowed there a century ago have abated to the point that they are no longer a hazard to life. As everyone is aware, the bands of mutants which roam the Waste remain a real threat, and it may be another century before the last of them has been eliminated and White colonization has once again established a human presence throughout this vast area.

But it was in the year 1999, according to the chronology of the Old Era — just 110 years after the birth of the Great One — that the dream of a White world finally became a certainty. And it was the sacrifice of the lives of uncounted thousands of brave men and women of the Organization during the preceding years which had kept that dream alive until its realization could no longer be denied.

Among those uncounted thousands Earl Turner played no small part. He gained immortality for himself on that dark

November day 106 years ago when he faithfully fulfilled his obligation to his race, to the Organization, and to the holy Order which had accepted him into its ranks. And in so doing he helped greatly to assure that his race would survive and prosper, that the Organization would achieve its worldwide political and military goals, and that the Order would spread its wise and benevolent rule over the earth for all time to come.